TYNESSA PRESENTS

A YOUNG RICH BOSS CAPTURED My Heart

Allie Marie

Text TYNESSA PRESENTS
to 22828 to join out mailing list

To submit a manuscript for our review
email us at
Tynessapublications@gmail.com

Tynessa Presents

Tynessa Presents Is Currently
Accepting Submissions
From Urban Fiction Authors...

Please send in the first four chapters of your
COMPLETED manuscript
along with the synopsis & contact
info to
Tynessapublications@gmail.com.
Once submitted, please allow 24 hours
for a response.

Serious Inquiries Only!

SYNOPSIS

Synopsis

Camille had always been a devoted wife and mother, sacrificing her own dreams to build her husband's career. After fifteen years of marriage, Kameron is demanding a divorce on the night of their anniversary, leaving Camille shattered and confused. Needing a relief from the pain and anger that seems to now live where her heart once lived, Camille finds herself in the bed of a handsome stranger. Despite her one night of unforgettable relief, Camille runs for the hill the next morning, making sure not to awaken the man that she only knows by the name of, DJ. Even after things between Camille and Kameron comes to an end, Kameron continues to shake her world with his lies and betrayals.

Dion 'DJ' Roberts is a twenty-five-year-old NFL quarterback, who had made up in his mind that he is done with love and relationships. After learning the woman that he once loved, loved the money and fame more than him, DJ vowed to never be weakened by the four letter word again. To DJ, the only woman that was worth loving is his sister, until a one-night stand left him wondering…

On a night out in the town, DJ and Camille finds themselves in the same club, and neither had not forgotten one detail of the night of passion they shared together. This time, DJ refused to let the lovely Camille disappear without a trace. Even though Camille is finally now divorced, her life is still far from drama free. Will DJ be able to put the broken pieces of Camille's heart back together, or will his own trust issues alone with obstacles in the form of people make them both walk away, sticking to their vows to never love again?

1

IT'S OUR ANNIVERSARY

Tony Toni Tone: *Won't be no secret at the end of the day. It's our*
anniversary!

"$\mathcal{I}$ want a divorce," Kameron said to his wife of fifteen years. They were currently sitting at Ruth Chris Steak House, celebrating their 15th wedding anniversary.

"What?" Camille muttered. It was like the walls of the restaurant were closing in on her. Those four words had just knocked the wind from her body. "You want a divorce?" She repeated.

Camille knew she had to have heard her husband wrong. This was the man she'd loved since she was sixteen years old. The man she gave up everything for to make sure he succeeded in his life goals, they shared two beautiful children together.

"Listen, Millie, you know our marriage have run its course." Kameron said, barely able to look his wife in the eyes. He had been putting off asking her for a divorce for quite some time now. Truth is, he had fallen in love with another woman. A doctor that worked at his Practice. The same practice that his wife helped him build from the ground up. Kameron was a pediatrician with his own practice in downtown Philadelphia.

For years he would never look in another woman's direction. That's how strong the love he shared for his wife was. However, last year during the annual Christmas party, he started an affair with Olive Walters. The two of them would flirt on and off in the office, but it never turned to anything serious until the night of the party.

Last year's Christmas party was the first party that Camille didn't attend, because their five year old daughter had came down with the flu. After too many drinks, Kameron found himself in a hotel room with Olive. Her legs were behind her head as he pounded her middle. After that night, they would meet three days out the week and now it was to the point where Kameron didn't even care enough to come home at all.

"Are you seriously doing this on our wedding anniversary?" She shouted, causing some of the people around them to stare in their direction. She knew their marriage wasn't perfect. In the past year her husband barely touched her and when he did, it felt like he was forcing himself to make love to her. Camille saw plenty of times the love he held for her diminishing in his eyes. She was just hoping with their anniversary, it would be a start for new beginnings. "You brought me out to enjoy dinner, to celebrate our wedding anniversary by asking me for a fucking divorce?"

"Camille, lowered your damn voice." Kameron hissed looking around the restaurant because he could feel people eyes piercing through them. He thought taking her out to a public restaurant was the best way to break the news to his wife. He knew at home she probably would have tried to kill him. But he knew Camille was a woman that cared about her appearance and what people thought about her. So he knew she wouldn't get too crazy.

"Who is the bitch?" She asked in a lower tone. She didn't want these strangers in their business. She was already embarrassed as she looked at the sympathetic looks other women were giving her. Damn near everybody in the restaurant heard what she had said, and just like she was getting sympathetic looks, Kameron was getting death stares by the women. One of the ladies was even bold enough to call him an asshole as she walked pass their table, heading to the restroom.

"There's no other person," Kameron lied straight through his teeth. "I'm just not in love with you anymore. There's not another person influencing my decision. We've been together since high school, and you know we moved fast getting married. If we want to be honest. We only got married because you were pregnant with Kyron."

"Kameron, you know me better than that, to think I would accept the bullshit that just came out of your mouth." She said fighting the tears that was threatening to fall from her eyes. "I'm not stupid or blind. I know you are having an affair. The evidence has been right in my face. You don't think I notice lipstick on the collar of your shirt, the smell of perfume on your clothes. If that's not enough to convince me, then the fact that you barely come home at night and you make it a point to return early in the morning before the kids wake up for school is convincing enough."

Camille had Kameron stuck. He knew she would rake him over the coals if he admitted to the affair that he was having with Olive. He wanted this divorce to be as amiable as possible. So, he knew his best bet was to deny any and every accusation she had just brought to light.

"All I want is for this divorce to go over as smooth as possible. We don't have to make it ugly. We both leave with what we came with in this marriage."

"Leave with what we came with?" Camille muttered in disbelief. "Kameron, I'm the reason you are the man you are today. It was me who worked two, sometimes three jobs to put you through medical school and keep a roof over our head and food on the table. I was the one who help you save half of the startup money to start your own practice. Now you want me to walk away like I was not a part of your success? Like I didn't put my dreams and aspiration on the back burner to make sure you were good. I have a fucking master's degree in business management. How many times I told you that I wanted to open up my own catering business? How many times you told me no we need all the money for your practice?"

"Don't go there with throwing the past in my face. I know what you did for me. And if you walk into the walk-in closet in our bedroom, it's filled with nothing but designer clothes, shoes and pocketbooks. I'll say I've paid you tenfold. If you want ya money back, sell all of the materialistic things you accumulated over the years. Now, I'm willing to be more than fair. You know my kids will be well taken care of. I would love to have joint custody. You can keep the house and your car. As for me taking care of you, those days are over. So, I suggest you get a job. Better yet, you can start that catering business you always dreamed of." Kameron said, snidely.

That was the one thing he hated about his wife. He hated the fact that Camille had such a helping hand in his career. Some men would be grateful that they had a woman to stand by them in their time of need and help them reach their goals. But, not Kameron. He knew everything she said about helping him be the man he was today was true. In some odd way it made him feel less than a man. Those years while he was in medical school, he watched his wife bend over backwards to keep up with his tuition, the rent and childcare. Many people in his and her family turn their backs and look down on them. They couldn't respect

Kameron because he never worked while he was in college or medical school.

They survived because Camille was able to get section eight housing and food stamps. He didn't even try to get a job to help. Even during the summer months, he stayed at home and did nothing. But, Camille always saw the bigger picture. She knew Kameron would give them the life they both deserved. In her eyes, marriage was 50/50 and other people opinions didn't matter to her. Plus, the opinions that she was getting were from people who never been married a day in their lives.

When Kameron graduated and landed a job, he moved his family out the projects and eventually his goals became bigger. He wanted to own his own practice. Once again Camille supported her husband one hundred percent. Kameron was so grateful at the time when his dreams came through, he made sure to reward and gift his wife with everything her heart desired. But as the years went by his feelings changed. Even though he was the major roadblock in her life, dreams and aspiration, Kameron hated that his wife greatest achievement was being a good mother.

Camille went back to school and received her master's degree and in his opinion, her going to school was a waste of time. She never put the degree to use. As much as Camille wanted to blame him for holding her back, she never made the first step to start making her dreams come true.

The first thing that attracted Kameron to Olive was that

she was a go-getter. Nothing stopped her from reaching her goals. In his eyes, Olive was more on his level than Camille. Kameron was tired of Camille living high off the hog because of him. He wanted to share his success to someone who could contribute to it. Knowing his wife would be nothing more than a housewife, he refused to spend another year in misery. The idea of a divorce had been on his mind for quite some time. The only thing that stopped him was his kids. He knew that his kids would be affected. But divorcing Camille was the best thing for him to do.

"You know what, fuck you! I'm not going to beg you to be with me. It's clear you don't love or respect me. The family we share doesn't mean anything to you. I gave you some of the best years of my life and for you to think you're going to walk away and take everything from me is beyond a slap in my face."

"Camille, I love you and I love you enough to let you go. Why do you want to continue to live in misery? We're in a loveless marriage. This is what you want to teach our kids, to settle? I'm sorry I will no longer be with you. I will have someone come for my things in the morning. I will not come back to the house unless I'm picking up or dropping off my children. Camille, make this as easy as possible there's no reason to drag this out. In the morning you will be receiving the divorce papers. Do us a favor and just sign them. Save yourself the heartache and the financial debt of taking this to court."

"Oh, baby, if you think I'm going to walk away with my

head down and tail in between my legs. You have another thing coming. You will be hearing from my lawyer." Camille said before throwing her glass of wine in his face and walking out the restaurant, taking the car, not caring how Kameron made it to his next destination. All Camille knew was hell has no fury like a woman's scorned.

Kameron was going to regret breaking her heart and throwing her away like yesterday's trash. The saying it's cheaper to keep her will ring true by the time she finished taking what she deserved, plus more.

2

THE WEEKEND

*Sza: I'll be at your door, ready to take her place. Ready to give you,
what you've been missing' on weekdays.*

"Thanks for picking me up," Kameron said to his brother, Kyler, as soon as he got inside his car.

"No problem. I thought it was you and Camille's anniversary tonight."

"It is," Kameron muttered, not really wanting to go into details of his night. All he needed was to get home and get out of the wet clothes he was in. The Davidson family loved the ground Camille walked on. So to find out that he asked his wife, for over a decade, for a divorce will not sit well with them.

"So, where is sis? Wait, don't tell me she realized her

worth and left you." Kyler joked. Kyler always joked to his brother about how Camille was too perfect for him.

"She was there. She's the reason why I'm cover in wine. Not only did she create a scene, she left me stranded. Hence, the reason why you're here picking me up."

Kyler looked over at his brother with questioning eyes before shaking his head. At this day and age, Camille causing a scene was out of character. So, he knew his brother had to have done something to push her over the edge.

"What did you do?"

Kyler also knew his brother was the farthest thing from innocent. As low key as Kameron thought his extra marital affairs were kept, Kyler personally knew his brother was a dog and womanizer. That's why he made it a point to let Kameron know Camille deserved better than him.

"I asked for a divorce."

"Wait... You did what? Tell me you're joking?" Kyler asked in disbelief.

"No. I'm not joking. It's over between me and Camille. I'm not in love with my wife anymore, and I refuse to stay in an unhappy marriage."

"I didn't even know you and Camille were having problems." Kyler muttered. But then again, he wouldn't have known. When Kameron became successful, he began to drift away from his family. When the success came, Kameron had a sense of entitlement and sad to say, his family truly didn't fit in his lifestyle with him. The only reason why he was still in contact with them was because of Camille. She was all about family and refused to allow Kameron to distance her kids from their family.

"Yeah, that's the problem. Camille loves to put on a front instead of accepting the truth. I'm at a point in my life that I'm finally putting myself first and Camille can't move forward with me on this journey."

"Maybe divorce is not the answer." Kyler started as Kameron shook his head. He knew his family would never understand. "Did you even think about marriage counseling? You just can't throw years of love and marriage away because you guys are going through a rough patch. Or better yet, how about you stop fucking around on her. That will solve half of your problems."

"Kyler, don't sit here and preach to me. You don't think I thought this through?" Kameron snapped, tired of his brother judgmental tone. He had enough people judging him at the restaurant after Camille's dramatic outburst.

"You couldn't have obviously thought this through to ask your wife for a divorce on your wedding anniversary. That's some cold-hearted shit. What are you trying to do, break the woman?"

"It is what it is…. Camille's a big girl and will learn to deal with the hurt. Shit, I don't even know why this is even coming as a shock. I've barely touched her in a whole year. I'm hardly home. I'm not going to keep living in hell to satisfy her. Camille is a bum. She has no drive or goals in life. She's content with being a housewife living off my hard work."

"You and I both know that's a lie. The sacrifices she made are proof of your success, and even if that is true, you don't think your wife deserve to be a housewife? She carried the whole family and help put you through medical school."

"Just because Camille helped me out in the beginning doesn't mean I have to be trapped in a loveless marriage. Yeah, she helped me start my career. She was my biggest supporter, but over the years things changed." Kameron said, looking out the window as his brother drove.

"Listen, Kameron. I'm telling you as your brother, and from somebody who had to learn the hard way. You going to regret this in the long run. They don't make women like her anymore. Camille has been down with you before you had a pot to piss in or a window to throw it out. Women now of days always want the finish product of a successful man. There are a few who are willing to go through the process of helping their man reach his goal, but many that aren't. Let along put their dreams on hold to be a wife and mother. You have a real one on your team. Best believe she won't be on the market long."

"You talking like you want her," Kameron hissed. As much as he wanted to hate his reaction, he couldn't shake off the thought of Camille being with someone else. And it really bothered him.

"Naw. That's my little sister. I don't look at her that way."

"Yeah, that's because she let herself go." Kameron said in disgust.

"Where am I taking you?" Kyler asked, ready for Kameron to get out of his car. He hated the person his little brother was turning into. Kyler was proud of Kameron's success, but in his eyes, his success was making him want to erase his past and kick people out his life that helped him get where he was today. And listening to him talk down about Camille, after all she had done for him, had Kyler looking at Kameron sideways.

"You can take me to my townhouse out in Lower Marian," Kameron said before rattling off the address to his brother.

The rest of the ride to his new place was quiet. The only thing that kept running through his mind were Camille's last words. He knew his wife and knew she wasn't going down without a fight. All he wanted was a clean, speedy divorce.

In Kameron's eyes, he worked hard for the life he lived, and he wanted to share it with the woman who deserved it most. The woman he loved. He hated that he'd been placing Olive on the backburner. She had been patient, but he knew that wouldn't last long. Olive was a woman who knew what she wanted. She wanted to get married and create a family of her own. So, when she gave Kameron an ultimatum, either her or his wife, Kameron knew he had to ask Camille for a divorce, or miss out on his one true love.

Pulling up inside the gated community, Kyler shook his head. Kameron was seriously living a double life, and for the simple fact that a woman was waiting in her car that was parked in the driveway, it had him lost for words.

"Thanks," Kameron said. "Listen, if you can do me a favor and not mention my divorce to anyone, I would truly appreciate it. I don't need mama calling me with her nonsense."

"You do know that mama and Camille speak every day on the phone? So don't be surprise if she calls you tomorrow cussing you out."

"Whatever," Kameron muttered, not ready for the headache he will have to deal with after trying to explain his decision to his mother.

"So, she's the reason?" Kyler asked as he watched Olive get out of her car. She had been parked outside his house ever since he text her saying that he asked Camille for the divorce.

"Nobody is pushing me to make this decision. I'm doing this for myself, and I wish ya'll would support me."

"This your life bro. You the one that have to live with your choices. But you already know mama and pops not going to accept anybody, but Camille. That girl been with you from rags to riches, and now you leaving her for a white girl."

"Everything is not about race. Olive is very successful, and honestly, she's a better look on my arm. Olive is on my level and we want the same things in life. We just have more in common with her being a doctor. She actually works at my practice."

"That shit makes it even worse. Plus, you know mama all about black love. Man, this shit going to break her heart."

"Mama will be fine. She needs to get with the time. Interracial couples are what's in, and she needs to understand that me and Camille is over. She will get over it when I give her another grandbaby."

"You ain't got to explain shit to me," Kyler said, deading the conversation. In Kyler's eyes, Kameron was a damn fool and will learn the hard way that he is about to lose the best thing that ever happened to him. Instead of being grateful for Camille, he started thinking she was below him.

"Alright, man. I'm out," Kameron said, getting out of the car

"Hey, babe!" Olive smiled, damn near jumping into his arms. She could barely hold her excitement in.

"Hey." Kameron pulled her into him, kissing Olive passionately. It felt good to have her in his arms. Reluctantly pulling away, he led her to the front door of the house.

"How did it go?" Olive asked, knowing it was a stupid question, especially since she could see his suit was ruined by the red wine. It was just, she just wanted the details of how he told Camille. There were so many questions she needed answers to.

Did Camille know about her and the affair? Could they finally go public? When could she officially meet the kids as his girlfriend and not his co-worker?

Those were the questions running through her mind.

"Being that I'm still alive…. I guess better than I expected."

"You're so silly. But babe…."

"After that disaster dinner, I don't want to think or talk about Camille, my marriage or my soon to be divorce. Olive. I love you. The hard part is out of the way. Now I just want to celebrate our new beginning." Kameron said, cutting her off.

"I love you too, babe." Olive let it go for now. Kameron was right, and tonight, he'd finally man up and came through on his promise. He left his wife and she wanted to relieve him of any stress that may have caused. "Let's get you cleaned up."

Pulling Kameron up by his hand, she led him up the stairs to the bathroom and started to run a shower for him. This was one of the reasons why Kameron fell so hard for Olive. She was completely different from his wife. Not only was she in the same profession as him, but she still made time to cater to him like a woman was supposed to do for her man.

Watching him undress, she decided to join him for a night of passion. Olive used to feel guilty for sleeping with a married man, and she never thought she would unexpectedly fall in love with her boss, but the heart wants what the heart wants.

Life was too short to care about the people standing in the way of her true happiness.

3

COGNAC & CONVERSATION

Teedra Moses: *Glad you're here tonight. Wanna take my time and show you what's been on my mind.*

Camille couldn't even go home to the empty house that was about to become her reality. Heartbroken was an understatement of what she was currently feeling. She knew she had to pick up her kids in the morning from her best friend, Kelly, and she honestly didn't know how she was going to break the news to them. Being a family was all they knew. Now Camille felt like a failure being as though her marriage would soon end in divorce.

She headed to the closest hotel and got a room. Her misery did not like company so she quickly called Kelly to see if the kids could stay for the weekend and she picked them up on Sunday morning.

"Hello," Kelly answered after the fourth ring.

"Hey girl."

"Why are you calling me and not enjoying your anniversary? Girl, the kids are fine. Kyron is playing the PlayStation and me and Kasie is baking cookies," Kelly explained.

"I... I ... I was calling to see if the kids could stay the weekend with you. I can pick them up early Sunday morning," Camille said, trying not to break down on the phone.

"Oh, okay. That's not a problem. I see Kameron finally got the stick out of his ass to see how much of a great woman you are. What ya'll plan on doing?" Kelly asked but Camille couldn't lie to her best friend. She needed to release some of the emotions that was building up. She couldn't help but allow the tears and her sorrowful cries to be release.

"What the fuck is wrong, Camille?" Kelly asked nervously, walking out of the kitchen to her bedroom.

"Girl, this nigga took me out on our anniversary to ask me for a divorce."

"What!" Kelly then yelled into the phone. She couldn't believe what her best friend had just revealed to her.

"Girl, yes. Like, what the fuck did I do wrong as a wife? I gave this man my life and I built him up while damn near tearing myself down." So many emotions were going through her body. Beside heartache, the other dominant emotion was regret.

Camille regretted the day she decided to put her dreams and aspiration on hold to help Kameron with his. She always thought once Kameron got to where he needed to be she could go back to school for culinary. She wanted to be a chef and own her own catering business, and eventually own a restaurant. Cooking had always been her passion. Now here she was with nothing to fall back on.

"No, Camille. I will not allow you to internalize this shit. Any man would have been lucky to have you as a wife. There is nothing wrong with you. Honestly, you are too good for Kameron. Kameron is just a bitch ass nigga who needs a yes woman. He done forgot his struggle and how you helped him become the man he is today. I remember watching my god kids so you could work multiple jobs so he could study. Fuck him! It's cool. God don't like ugly." Kelly was so mad that you would have thought Kameron asked her for a divorce. It was just that Kelly knew her best friend was hurting and there was nothing she could do to help her.

"Damn, what the hell am I supposed to tell my kids? I need a drink," Camille said, looking around her hotel room.

"Where are you?"

"I'm at the Jameson Hotel. I got a room for the night."

"Go to the bar, get a drink and go back to ya room. In the morning, I can drop the kids off at my mom and we can go waiting to exhale on his shit." Kelly was ready to ride for anything.

"I'm going to get me a drink. I'll call you tomorrow to see if I want to take you up on ya offer." Camille chuckled, sadly. She could always count on Kelly's crazy ass to make her laugh.

"You're laughing but I'm dead ass serious," Kelly stated, happy she'd at least made her friend smile.

"I know ya crazy ass is. Just take care of my babies," Camille told her before they said their goodbyes and ended the call.

❦

DJ HAD BEEN SITTING AT THE BAR IN THE JAMESON HOTEL and Casino ordering drinks after drinks. You would think a man of his stature would be happy and not trying to drink the crazy thoughts out of his head. The saying, more money, more problems, rang true. He was the first draft round pick in the 2014 NFL draft. It was then that DJ quickly learned that everybody around him was not truly happy for him and money certainly had a way of changing people.

This past season, he tore his ACL and for some professional athletes, that could be a career ending injury. Everybody was saying that he was surely done for, and for a minute, he was allowing doubts to creep in. Not only did he have to deal with the world doubting his comeback, but he also had to learn the hard way that the people close to him would be the first to betray him.

DJ had been with his college sweetheart, Yazmine, since his freshman year of college. Was he the best boyfriend back in college? The answer would be, no. He was Penn State University's golden boy. The number of women throwing

26

themselves at him was unbelievable. So, he dibbled and dabbled into temptation on more than a few occasions. But after his first two semesters of sleeping with random women, it started getting old, and he wanted to be with someone who truly wanted to be with him, and not because of the promising future that was ahead of him.

Yazmine Kane was strong and independent in his eyes. While he was a freshman, she was a junior in the same college, and she had her whole life planned ahead of her. When she caught DJ's eyes, he thought she would be one of the normal groupies willing to drop her panties at the snap of his fingers. But, he soon found out that Yazmine was a woman who wasn't easily impressed by someone's popularity. If anything, him being Dion 'DJ' Roberts aka Bullet was a turn off.

Yazmine Kane became DJ's challenge. Seeing that his normal approach was not working with her, DJ faked like he needed tutoring in Chemistry. Being as though Yazmine's major was chemistry and she was a tutor, he signed up for tutoring session every Thursday with Yazmine. Once Yazmine realized he didn't need tutoring in chemistry, she was flattered that he went through the trouble of getting her attention. Eventually, they started to date and had been inseparable ever since. The year he got drafted Yazmine graduated from Penn State with a bachelor's degree in chemistry.

Throughout the years, Yazmine slowly started to change, especially when DJ's big checks started coming in. She was no longer the independent woman with the natural beauty who could carry herself. She was now this materialistic plastic girl who wouldn't even put her college degree to use. Everything about Yazmine turned out to be fake.

When he had his injury, Yazmine was the first to disappear out of his life, scared that DJ would not be able to afford the lifestyle she had become accustomed too. She dropped him like a bad habit and ended up dating some NBA Player from the Boston Celtics.

DJ learned the hard way that when you're up, everybody wanted to be around you. Mainly because you could benefit them in some shape, way or form. But when shit got real, only the real stayed around. And, the real was his family. Not only did Yazmine embarrass him and make him look like a fool, she was now in the tabloids because she was pregnant. He was being tagged in every post from the shaderoom, the gossip blogs to social media, asking was he the father. To be honest, he didn't know. That's what led him to the bar at the Jameson hotel, taking shots of Patrón to the head.

"Hi, can I get a double shot of Cognac, and keep them coming."

"Rough night?" DJ asked the woman who'd came to sit next to him. Turning to face her, he could tell she was older than him, but her age didn't take away from her beauty.

"I can say the same about you?" Camille said, eyeing the five empty shot glasses that was sitting in front of him.

"I guess you can say that. I'm DJ," DJ said, holding out his hand for her to shake.

"Camille," She replied back, shaking his hand then immediately taking her shot, followed by waving the bartender back over to pour her another one. "Why you down here drinking ya troubles away?"

"I just learned the hard way that people ain't always who they pretend to be." He answered, vaguely.

The way Camille was throwing back those shots, he knew she was probably having men problems. She looked like she was about to flip any second, and the last thing she needed to hear was that he was drinking because of his nerves.

DJ couldn't handle the possibility of Yazmine carrying his child. He remembered Yazmine claiming she never wanted to have kids when they were dating, and he was okay with that. So, for her to pop up in the tabloids and pregnant, he knew this baby was her meal ticket. She tried to call him on multiple occasion, but he ignored every called until she popped up on him.

DJ's lawyer advised her to keep his name out of the press and don't mention him being the father until a DNA test could prove he was.

"What have you down here ready to get faded?" DJ had to ask, especially since she had just downed two shots and it didn't look like she was stopping any time soon.

"I'm getting a divorce. Fifteen years of marriage and my

husband thought it would be a great idea to ask me for a divorce, on our wedding anniversary?"

"Damn," he muttered. Even he had to admit that was some cold-hearted shit.

"Yup. I need another round, and get my friend here another round of whatever he is drinking," Camille demanded the bartender.

For the next two hours, DJ and Camille talked, drink and joked around. For the first time in years, Camille heard words of encouragement to start her catering business and go to culinary school like she always wanted.

DJ on the other hand, he didn't really go into details as to who he was or his job description. He liked the fact that Camille had no clue who he was and that she was genuinely enjoying his company without any ulterior motives. They were having such a good time that they forgot why they were drinking in the first place.

"Alright, lady and gentleman. I have to shut the bar down," The bartender said, handing both of them their bills. DJ took both bills and gave the bartender his black card.

"It's too bad that our night is about to end," Camille sadly said. It was like sadness had rushed through her body once again as reality hit her that she was about to be alone on her anniversary.

"It don't have to end," DJ said, smoothly. He was attracted to Camille, and there was no denying that he wanted her in the worst way.

"Okay." She smiled as he led the way to the penthouse that he was staying in for the night. Once inside the room, DJ noticed how quiet Camille had became. She looked to be a little nervous as she looked at her surroundings.

"We don't have to do anything if your uncomfortable," DJ said, and she relaxed a little. "I just enjoyed your company, too, and didn't want the night to end, either."

Being around Camille totally took his mind off of the craziness that was surrounding him. Finally, he was able to just relax and be himself and not think about the upcoming season where he would have to prove that he was still the same player that was drafted, and that his injury was not a career ending injury. Plus, the pressure on him was heavy for the simple fact that he was up for a new contract.

"No. I want to have sex," she blurted out. *Shit, I need some dick.* Camille then thought to herself. She was in a one-sided marriage and had damn near become celibate because Kameron was so busy having an affair. "It's just been a minute, and the only man I've been with was my husband."

DJ's dick hardened at the thought of Camille's tightness. Being that she was in her thirties and had only been with one man, it made the experience even more interesting. In DJ's eyes, Camille was damn near pure.

Making his way over to her, he grabbed her hand and walked her to the master bedroom. Once inside the bedroom, you could cut the sexual tension with a knife. DJ invaded her personal space, pulling down the zipper to her dress, letting it drop to the floor. DJ's eyes roamed her body as she currently stood in front of him in nothing but a thong and stilettos.

This nigga dumb as hell. He thought.

Camille was 5'5. Skin the color of brown sugar. Her eyes were a shade of cognac. And her body was perfect with her 36C breast, flat stomach and her ass was just enough to grab a hand full of. Camille had the perfect hourglass shape to say the least.

Camille wanted to cower out under his intense stare. Unable to take it any longer, she reached down to unbuckle her heels.

"Leave them on," DJ demanded before picking her up. She instantly wrapped her legs around his waist. Walking toward the bed, he placed her on her back. DJ wanted to take his time with Camille, not exactly knowing why he wanted this to be more than a fuck.

After Yazmine dipped, any female he entertained, he fucked and duck, not caring about her feelings. Honestly, he only used them for his pleasure. But with Camille, he already had it in his mind that he was about to be the best she'd ever had. For at least one night, she wouldn't have to deal with the storm her husband had heading her way. As soon as her body hit the soft sheets, DJ started to kiss her, starting on her lips, leading a trail down her body.

"Mmmm," a moan escaped Camille's lips as DJ tongue swirled around her nipples. The sensation DJ was giving her had her on the verge of having an orgasm.

Continuing his mission to take her body to ecstasy, he moved down her body, pulling her soak and wet thong off.

"Damn you wet." DJ muttered and Camille instantly became embarrassed, covering her face. The way her pussy was dripping, you would've thought she was a running faucet. DJ reached up to remove her hands, he felt it was nothing sexier than seeing the passion express on a woman's face while she climaxed.

Without warning, he dived face first, kissing, licking, and sucking the soul out of her pussy. Throughout the room, you could hear the soft, but, loud moans of Camille.

"Oh... my...god!" She screamed as she tried to scoot away from his monstrous tongue. Never in her life had she received head that had her ready to climb the walls. She couldn't handle the pressure from her orgasm building up.

"Stop running," DJ demanded without missing a beat. He lifted her legs up and placed them by her ears as he continued to feast on her love juices.

"Wait... a damn minute...." Camille shouted in shock. She could not believe this young nigga damn near had her folded into a pretzel, and she couldn't move if she wanted too. The way his tongue was snaking all around her clit had her ready to risk it all. "Mmmm... I'm about to cum," she muttered in labor breaths.

That was all DJ needed to hear to go on overdrive as his tongue caressed her sensitive pearl while he slid two fingers inside, quickly finding her g-spot and massaged it until her body started to shutter. It wasn't long before Camille was screaming, calling his name and cumming all at the same time.

"Shit…." she mumbled, trying to get her breathing back under control. She had never cum that hard in her life before, and all DJ was doing was giving her head.

What the hell was Kameron doing all of these years? She thought. To be honest, Camille would barely cum when her and Kameron had sex. She thought it was normal that she didn't have an orgasm during every sex session. Sex had gotten so bad between her and Kameron that she just stopped initiating it because it was a waste of time.

"You good?" DJ asked with a cocky smirk as he removed his clothes. Camille eyes were fixated on his cut body.

"Yeah." *This damn boy is going to turn my ass out. Bitch this is a one-time thing.* She coached herself. Having a one-night stand and being interested with a man younger than her was way out of her character. "Damn…" she muttered as soon as he dropped his boxer briefs. DJ chuckled because that was the reaction he always seemed to get. He reached into his wallet to obtain his magnum condom and placed it on.

Climbing on the bed, he climb right between her legs. She gasped as she felt the head of his penis at her opening. Taking her right leg, he gently placed it on his shoulder while her left leg was in the crook of his arm.

"Fuck," DJ groaned as he pushed his way through her tight opening. Camille's pussy was so tight that he felt like a vice grip on him.

"Ahhhh," Camille whimpered as he finally pushed all of himself inside of her. He was stretching her to her limit.

Once DJ was fully inside, he had to stop for a brief moment to get his head together. The way Camille's pussy muscles were gripping his dick had him thinking of everything under the sun to keep from embarrassing himself. The last thing he wanted to do was cum prematurely like he was a virgin and this was his first time sliding into some pussy.

"Oh, DJ," Camille moaned as he started to give her long deep strokes. The only thing that could be heard throughout the room was the sound of her pussy making macaroni noise.

"Damn… Baby, ya pussy good as shit," DJ admitted as he started to pound her middle, causing her to become wetter and wetter.

"Harder, baby, please," Camille demanded, rotating her hips harder to meet his every stroke. She never knew pain could feel so good. In honesty, she felt like he was rearranging her insides. But she couldn't find it in herself to stop him because she could feel the gut-wrenching orgasm that was about to succumb her body.

"What you waiting for? Let that shit go, ma," DJ muttered in her ear, continuously hitting her g-spot until he felt her juices pouring all over him.

"What are you doing to me?" Camille asked, looking at him.

"Fucking the pain away," he answered, not allowing her

to recover from her orgasm as he flipped her onto all four, ready to take her to another height of pure ecstasy.

The next morning, Camille woke up in DJ's arms. This was the first time in a year that she'd awakened in a man's arms. She almost didn't want to get up and leave.

They went at it for hours. DJ had her all out of her element. Missionary was the only sex position Kameron used with her. DJ had her in so many positions she could barely keep up. Not to mention, she stopped counting her orgasms after six.

Camille carefully got out of bed without waking him and quickly got dress. Looking back, she smiled as he snored. Last night brought her heartbreak and pleasure. But the pleasure her body received from him would always be embedded in her mind.

4

DESTROYED

TXS: If I didn't cry these tears. I don't deserve the things you put me through. I could be adored by someone new, but I rather be destroyed by you.

"Get it together," Olive coached herself to stop the tears from falling from her eyes. Her first appointment of the day was in a few minutes and she couldn't even will herself out of the car to step foot into her job. If she didn't have a full schedule ahead of her, she would have called out. But being a doctor was her passion, and she wouldn't let her patient suffer because her personal life was a wreck.

For the past three months, Kameron had been lying and sneaking out of bed early in the mornings to return back to the house he shared with his wife and kids.

"Just ignore him." Olive said to herself.

Getting out the car, Olive quickly made her way into her office to get her day started.

He think he is so smooth. She thought as she saw a coffee from Starbucks along with a banana muffin sitting on her desk, there was a bouquet of roses as well. Kameron knew Olive would be upset with him and he was trying to get back in her good gracious. Shaking her head, she never thought this was how their new life together would turn out after he asked his wife for a divorce.

"Dr. Walters." Olive heard her name being called. It was one of the fellow doctors at the practice named, Dr. Paul Delipizzi. Paul had been interested in Olive for quite some time and he finally wanted to ask her out on a date.

"Hey Paul," Olive said, stopping at the front counter. She was about to tell one of the nurses to call her first patient to the back.

"Hey, I just wanted to make sure you were okay this morning. I saw you in the parking lot. I didn't want to intrude, but I just notice you haven't been yourself lately."

"Oh my god, I'm so embarrassed," Olive said as her skin started to turn beet red. "I just been going through a lot and I guess you can say I'm finally at my breaking point."

As soon as the words left off of Olive's lips, Kameron walked out one of the rooms he had just seen a patient in. Seeing Olive speaking with Paul had him kind of uptight, especially since Paul mentioned to him on multiple occasions that he liked Olive.

"No need to be embarrassed. I'm just checking on you. Also, I wanted to know if you wanted to catch a movie or go out to dinner?" Paul asked, patiently waiting for her response. Olive could feel Kameron's eyes burning through her as he too waited for her response. They were still not public, so no one knew about their relationship. Olive knew she shouldn't lead Paul on, but she couldn't miss the opportunity to get under Kameron's skin. Kameron needed to realize that she was a wanted woman and he wasn't the only man that wanted her.

"Yeah, sure. Call me so we can set up a date and time."

"Cool…" Paul started but was cut off by Kameron.

"Don't ya'll have patients waiting for you?" Kameron asked with irritation dripping from his voice. He couldn't believe Olive would disrespect him like that.

"Paul, I'll speak to you later," Olive said before letting the nurse know she was ready for her patient. The whole morning, Olive ignored Kameron as much as possible, but she really wanted to confront him on how he acted with her and Paul. She was tired of the back and forth and quite frankly, if Kameron wasn't ready to be the man she needed him to be, he needed to step aside.

Knock, Knock

"Come in," Kameron said, looking up to see Olive at his door. He had been trying to focus on work instead of her and her childish games. The last thing he needed was to cause unnecessary problems with another doctor because of her.

"So, are you going to explain your actions?" asked Olive, with her hands on her hips.

"Olive, what you call yourself doing? Huh?" Kameron asked, looking up from the menu of the restaurant he was about to order his lunch from.

"I woke up again to an empty bed, Kameron. So, the question is, what are we doing? Do you not want to get a divorce from your wife? Why do I still feel like the other woman?"

"You're not the other woman," he said, trying to convince her. Truth was, after speaking to his lawyer, he knew his divorce with Camille could get ugly. Not wanting Camille to go for jugular, he felt like he needed to make this divorce process as easy as possible. Even if that meant giving Camille a false sense of hope that their marriage could work.

"That's how I feel. When you asked her for a divorce, we were supposed to be free and open with our relationship. I'm tired of being your secret. Not only am I your secret, but you sneaking off to be with your wife. Are you cheating on me?" Olive asked, looking Kameron in the eyes, daring him to lie to her.

"No, I'm not cheating on you. We haven't gotten around to telling the kids yet."

"What are you waiting for? The longer you wait, the harder it's going to be for them, especially if you and Camille are still playing house." She knew Kameron was using the kids as an excuse.

"Listen, Olive. You know I love you, and I know I'm asking for a lot when I ask you to be patient while I go through this process, but I'm telling you, it will be worth it. Our life together will be nothing short of extraordinary. However, I have to play this divorce carefully. As of now, Camille knows I want the divorce because I'm not happy and I need to find myself. If she knows I'm having an affair, she will drag me through the dirt and take me for everything I have."

"You didn't sign a prenuptial agreement?" Olive questioned, knowing he couldn't have been that stupid. Kameron was a very successful man, and she couldn't imagine him not protecting his assets.

"I didn't need to sign a prenup when I married Camille. I didn't have any of this," he said, motioning around his office as he referred to his business.

"Okay."

"Olive, I love you and I know things haven't been what you imagined, but just give me the time to do what I need to do. You are the number one lady in my life," Kameron said, getting out of his office chair and walking into Olive's personal space. He needed her to understand where he was coming from.

"Kameron, you have to put yourself in my shoes. How can you expect me to put my life on hold? Now, I understand why we cannot be public. I don't want Camille to gain the benefits of your hard work, either. That wouldn't be fair. However, why do you expect me to put my life on hold to cater to your wife? If the divorce is what you want, you need to let the kids know as soon as possible. Stop using them as an excuse. The kids can visit you at the townhouse. I don't want your ex having any false hope that ya'll will work."

"You're right. I'll let Camille know we need to tell the kids this weekend. I completely understand. Other than speaking about Kyron and Kasie, I will cut off all communication with Camille."

"That's all I ask. You have to meet me halfway," Olive said, looking down at her watch. She had another patient scheduled within the next ten minutes. "I have to get ready for my patient."

"Okay. You want me to order you lunch...." Kameron asked before he was cut off by his office door opening and in waltzed Camille with a bag from Panera Bread.

"Hey," Camille smiled at Olive.

"Camille, what are you doing here?" Kameron asked with irritation in his voice. He had no idea as to why Camille thought popping up on him was such a great idea.

"Oh, I was in the neighborhood and decided to bring you lunch," Camille said in a low tone, slightly embarrassed that he was speaking to her like that in front of Olive.

"You shouldn't have wasted your time or you're money. I'm busy. You can let yourself out," Kameron dismissed her without hesitation.

"Okay, I didn't mean to interrupt you. I was just trying to be nice."

"I'm going to head out. I have a patient waiting for me,"

Olive said, ready to get out of the line of fire. She could feel Camille's eyes on her. When Camille first walked into the office, she didn't think anything was going on between Kameron and Olive. It wasn't unusual for the other doctors to be in his office.

"Olive, wait. I want to finish talking to you about this patient."

Catching the hint, Camille sat the Panera Bread on his desk and started making her way towards the door of his office.

"Camille, we need to have a talk soon about how we're going to tell the kids." Kameron said. Camille didn't even response as she walked out of his office, slamming his door behind her.

"See? I'm taking the steps in the right direction. Now go out there and tell Paul you can't go out on a date with him, and tell him not to call your phone." Kameron demanded Olive. All she could do was smile. The way he'd handled Camille showed her that she had nothing to worry about.

&

"HE DID WHAT!" CADDIE, CAMILLE'S LITTLE SISTER, ASKED in disbelief. Tonight, Camille was having a little girl's night at her place with her sisters. She needed to vent and get some opinion on how she should handle the situation in her life.

"Yes. He dismissed me like I was a bum on the streets,"

she said, thinking about how Kameron spoke to her earlier today. The past couple of months Camille had been trying to save her marriage in every way possible.

"My question is, who is the bitch that was in his office?" Cassie, Camille's other little sister asked with questioning eyes. Cassie hated that Kameron was doing this to her sister. Never in life had she seen Camille so broken. Camille had always been the stronger one out of the four.

"Her name is Dr. Walters. It's not unusual for Kameron to have another doctor in his office. Before I popped up, they were speaking about a patient," Camille said. She didn't want to turn into the crazy lady who thought every woman within five feet of her husband was having an affair with him.

"You think he's having an affair?" Cassie asked before Camille walked away to answer her ringing phone. Camille had mentioned she felt like Kameron was having an affair to her before, and the way Kameron dismissed Camille in front of Dr. Walter seemed like he had something to prove. Otherwise he would have asked Dr. Walters to leave his office.

"Who was that?" Candace asked as soon as Camille returned back to the living room.

"Oh, that was Kelly. She's not going to be able to make girls night. She got held up at work."

"Why would you have me here, knowing you invited that bitch?" Candace hissed, rolling her eyes.

"Candy, Kelly is Camille's best friend. Everyone just wants to be with her during this tough time. This is not about you," Caddie said, shaking her head.

"Candace, don't disrespect Kelly. She doesn't speak badly about you, and you seriously need to grow up and move on because Kelly is definitely not worried about you."Camille said.

"For real. If anybody should have the problem it should be Kelly." Cassie added.

"Whatever," Candace muttered.

"Anyway. Why do you think he's having an affair?" Caddie asked, bringing the question back up.

"I know he's having an affair. Kameron doesn't touch me. When we do have sex it's forced and honestly a waste of time. And before he asked me for a divorce, he stayed out late and returned early in the mornings. I just don't know who the woman is."

"You trying to find out who the chick is?" Cassie asked, ready for anything. She was already on her phone looking up private investigators.

"A part of me does so I can confront the bitch." Camille hissed, pissed. She couldn't understand why a woman would want to stoop that low and mess with a married man. Why destroy a family? Better yet, why destroy another woman in the process?

"Why you want to confront this woman? The unknown woman does not owe you any loyalty. She didn't marry you!" Candace snapped, looking at her sister like she was dumb.

"She may not owe Millie any loyalty, and she may not even know Kameron is married, but if Camille make her presence known the bitch can either fall back or get her ass beat," Cassie shot back.

"Sis, do you truly want to know who the woman is? Can you handle that truth? Right now, you are making speculations, and even though they might be true, I have to agree with Candy. That lady doesn't owe you anything, Kameron does," Caddie said.

"Exactly! Don't go out there and search for the woman to embarrass yourself. What happened after you make your presence known and she still continue to fuck your husband that asked you for a divorce? What you going to do?" Candace said, happy that someone finally seen it her way.

"I don't know. What I do know is that I want my marriage to work. Fifteen years of my life would be wasted. I'm not trying to start over with someone new. I love my husband. I'm not saying I was the perfect wife, because I know I have placed our children before Kameron. Also, when mama and daddy were sick, they were my first priority, making sure their last days were comfortable. I know in my heart we can make this work if he let me in and let me know what I did wrong so I can fix it."

"Naw, Millie. I'm not going to let you sit here and make up excuses for Kameron being a hoe. He shouldn't fault or disrespect your marriage because you are good mother and daughter to your parents. Kameron is not the only person in your life, and he should not be jealous of his own kids, or find a problem with you helping your dying parents. He needs to learn to step aside for once. He's been your priority for the longest. It's okay for your attention to go elsewhere." Cassie said.

Candace rolled her eyes. Camille sounded weak. "Millie, you can't make a man love you nor force him to stay married to you. Just face the facts, your perfect little marriage is over," Candace said in a taunting tone.

"Candy!" Caddie called her name in disbelief. If she didn't know any better, she would've thought her older sister liked the misery and pain Camille was going through.

"What? Ya'll not making it any better, coddling her, giving her false hope. Kameron does not want her anymore. You need to accept that, Camille," Candace stated, shaking her head.

"Bitch, get the fuck out!" Camille hissed. She didn't want her sisters to be a whole bunch of yes men; but Candace could have handled her better.

"Are you serious?" Candace asked in surprise.

"She dead serious, with your negative Nancy ass. You just want people to be just as miserable as you," Cassie said. This was nothing new. Candace had always been a hater.

"Fuck ya'll! Wack ass girls night!" Candace snapped, grabbing her purse before storming out of Camille's house.

Cassie, Caddie and Camille ganging up on Candace was nothing new. Candace was what you would call the black sheep of the family.

"I swear she gets on my nerves," Camille said, pouring her another drink. It was bad enough she had to deal with so much negativity in her life because of Kameron, and she damn sure didn't need her sister to add on to it with her judgmental attitude.

"Fuck her!" Cassie stated, meaning every word. Sad to say, she couldn't stand her older sister.

"Millie, nobody in this room has ever been married, and nobody can tell you how to feel. You been with that man for twenty years and ya'll been married for fifteen of them. Like you said, you may not have been the perfect wife, but you dedicated your life to Kameron, and on the outside looking in, Kameron damn sure wasn't the perfect husband. You both have flaws. I believe you guys can find the love that was lost. So there's no judgment this way if you want to fight for your marriage."

"Yeah, sis. Fight for your marriage. So at the end of the day if it don't work, all you can say is you tried your best to make it work. However, keep in mind there is a chance that this will end in divorce. You have to protect yourself. If things turn left, you're going to need proof of him having an affair. So I will seriously look into the private investigator or do it old school style and go through his personal thing, like his phone to get the proof. Kameron is only going to look out for himself, and you need to make sure you and the kids are protected," Cassie explained.

Camille listened to her sisters advice and knew her next step was fighting for her marriage. She wasn't accepting that divorce was in her near future. Kameron was the love of her life, and she knew he still had love in his heart for her.

5

SOMETHING IN MY HEART

Michel'le: Baby if we try. Things will get better. No one can tell me different. We should be together.

Camille's nerves were on overdrive as she walked to the front door to let Kameron inside. He had come over directly after work because today was the day they were supposed to tell the kids about the divorce. However, the kids were currently at Caddie's house. Camille was making this her time and opportunity to fight for her marriage. During the past couple of months, Kameron was still coming by the house trying to play like he didn't ask her for a divorce. Him prolonging telling the children made Camille feel like he was probably having second thoughts about moving forward with it.

"Hey," Camille spoke as she opened the door for Kameron to let him in.

Camille had set up a romantic dinner. She had cooked all of Kameron's favorite food, and his drink was already made. The lights were dimmed and candles outlined the living room and dining room. To set the mood, slow jams was playing in the background.

"Camille..." Kameron started looking around the room, realizing they were alone. "Where are the kids?"

"They aren't here," Camille answered. Shaking his head, Kameron turned around to head back out the door. He was highly annoyed because Olive had been on his back about telling the kids and getting the divorce papers sign, and now Camille wanted to pull this.

"Kam, wait," Camille said, calling out to him. "Can you please stay and hear me out? Can we please have a conversation over dinner?"

"I didn't come over here for this Millie. You know where I stand on this topic. I don't know why you keep making this difficult. You told me you agreed on letting the kids know. Now you're telling me that the kids are not here. What are we supposed to do, spend a romantic dinner together?"

"Fifteen years of marriage and you just want to end it? You couldn't even respect me enough to not do it on our wedding anniversary. You can't respect me enough to fight for what we had?"

"Camille...." Kameron started. He honestly didn't know what else to say to get her to understand that it was over.

"Fifteen years of marriage and you can't even have dinner with me." Camille chuckled, angrily. She knew fighting for Kameron's heart would be hard, and she was starting to get discourage.

For the first time in a long time, Kameron took in his wife presence, and he had to admit, Camille was still beautiful in her own way. She was dressed in a nice black fitted dress with a plunging neckline, and she topped it off with a pair of black red bottoms. He tried to find where they went wrong, but all he knew was that another woman had his heart.

"It smells good in here," Kameron smiled, thinking one dinner is something he could give his wife.

"I made all of your favorites. Roast beef, potatoes and spinach, and banana pudding for dessert."

"You always knew the way to my heart," Kameron said, ready to dig in. Camille was one of the best cooks that he had ever known. And if he did help her pursue her dreams like she had helped him, she would be very successful with a catering business. But Kameron wasn't willing to put in the risk or money towards a project that had a fifty percent chance of failing, because Camille may not have follow through on the commitment. In Kameron eyes Camille was too use to being a house wife to run a buiness. Even if Camille started her business, Kameron's practice would always be his priority. Also, Camille would still have to keep up with her motherly duties.

After Camille fixed the plates, she and Kameron digged

in and started small talk. Nothing about their marriage. Actually it seemed like they were honestly making it a point to stay away from the topic. This was the first time they were actually able to spend time and enjoy each other's company in a long time.

"Camille, I want to apologize for speaking to you the way I did at the office, especially in front of Dr. Walters. That was inappropriate and uncalled for." Kameron apologized. Regardless of what he wanted with the divorce, he could respect her more.

"Thank you. I didn't mean to interrupt. I was genuinely being nice. I just don't know where we went wrong. I know things weren't the best this past year or so, but I do love you Kameron."

"I know Millie, but the place I'm in in my life, I'm not good for you. I feel trapped inside of this marriage."

"Why? What did I do? Is there someone else?" She asked instead of assuming.

"No, there's no one else, baby. I just truly feel like we have outgrown one another. Camille, I will always love you, and as much as you think I don't appreciate you, I do. You've been there for me when others counted me out. I know the sacrifices you made, and trust me, it don't go unnoticed."

"Then let's try, again." Camille said with so much hope, walking towards her husband. "Let's give it our all before we throw in the towel."

Standing in front of her husband, Camille looked at

him, silently praying that he could see the love she had so deeply embedded in her body. She needed her marriage to work. Being without Kameron was not an option. It was like fate as Michel'le song, *Something in my heart,* started to play. That song basically said everything she wanted to say to her husband.

Standing up, Kameron knew he couldn't give Camille what she wanted, but oddly, he didn't want the night to end.

"I love you," Camille said, making the first move by placing her lips on her husband's. Kameron did not stop her. Instead, he just deepened the kissed, knowing it would only end in heartbreak for his wife.

Pulling away, Camille quickly blew out the candles. For the first time in months, the sexual attraction towards his wife was in full fledge and he couldn't wait to have her. No words needed to be said as they soon reached their bedroom, they wasted no time stripping each other out of their clothes.

"Climb on top," Kameron demanded as he laid flat on his back.

No four play? Camille silently thought, frowning, and also fighting the urge of rolling her eyes as memories of DJ instantly started flooding her mind.

"Let's try something new, and take our time. There's no rush," Camille said, climbing on the bed. Grabbing Kameron's manhood, she started to massage it, causing it to harden. Kameron was so turned on with anticipation that precum started to ease out of the tip of his dick.

DJ is definitely bigger and thicker. Camille thought. She couldn't understand why DJ kept plaguing her mind at a time like this, nor could she understand why she was comparing Kameron to DJ, a man she would never see again. Maybe it was because the night she spent with him, he took control, making her body feel things she had never felt before. Now here she was, trying to imitate that experience with her husband.

Get it together. She told herself. Tonight was the night that she needed to remind her husband that they were compatible and was still attracted to one another. Clearing any and all thoughts of DJ from her mind, she took her husband into her mouth.

"Damn, Camille," Kameron moaned as he felt the tip of his dick hitting the back of his wife's throat.

"Mmmm," Camille moaned as well. She was in her own little zone. Sucking, licking and spitting, all the while, massaging his shaft and balls. Camille had watched a few pornos before tonight, so she had learned a lot. She didn't know what made Kameron lose interest in her, sexually, but all she did know was that she needed to brush up on some skills.

"Fuck… I'm about to bust," Kameron said, trying to forewarn his wife, but Camille continued to take him on his way to ecstasy, making sure she drained him of every drop of cum.

Kameron was surprised and turned on at the same time that his wife had swallowed. In all of the years they'd been together, she had never did that, and it was one of the main reasons why he had stepped out on her. In his opinion, Camille was not opening enough to experience different things, mainly things that would satisfy him more.

"What has gotten in to you?" Kameron muttered in lust as he flipped his wife on her back and climbed on top of her. Camille was definitely in rare form. Not bothering to return the favor, he hungrily kissed his wife on her lips, and not the bottom ones. Kameron wanted their last time together to be rememberable. He wanted and needed Camille to know she would have no one better than him.

Finally releasing his wife's lips, Kameron slid into Camille's inviting flesh. Savoring the moment, Camille fit him like a glove.

"Kam..." A moan escaped Camille's mouth as she started to rock her hips forward to meet his every thrust.

"You missed this dick, didn't you?" Kameron boosted as he helped her get wetter and wetter.

"Yes! Baby!" Camille screamed as her pussy muscle gripped his dick as the wave of her orgasm hit her at once.

"Damn," Kameron muttered, watching the aftermath of his wife's orgasm. Camille's legs were still shaking as he laid down on his back and pulled her on top. Looking at his wife's body, for the first time in a long time, he wasn't disgusted by the light colored stretch marks that cascaded her hips and ass. The stretch marks that was received from carrying and birthing his children.

Planting both feet firmly on the bed and her hands on

Kameron's rock hard abs, Camille slid down his pole and didn't stop until it felt like he was hitting her cervix.

"Fuck Millie...." Kameron moaned through gritted teeth. Camille was riding him, making sure he tapped her g-spot with each stroke. Gripping her hips, Kameron tried to gain some control over Camille movements. "Slow down."

Camille ignored him and continued to ride his dick as she was reaching a total bliss. Seeing that she was already on the verge of cumming, Kameron started to massage her sensitive throbbing pearl, causing her to surrender to a gut wrenching orgasm.

"Oh… my... god, Kameron!" She collapsed on his chest, trying to regain her breathing.

"I told you to slow down." He slapped her on her ass before flipping her over on her stomach. Without hesitation, Camille got on all fours and arched her back, giving Kameron the perfect view. "You think you're in control?"

"Hmmmm." Camille was dripping wet with anticipation, ready for her husband to take her on a natural high. Tonight was the first night in the entire relationship that Camille had multiple orgasms. In the past, she used to pray to at least cum at least once. But tonight, it seemed like Kameron had something to prove.

Filling his wife up for the third time, he almost had a change of heart. If only Camille had showed him this side of her before now, divorce may not have been on the table. His life with her was boring. Even though it took two to make a marriage work, Kameron believed Camille allowed the marriage to go down the drain. But life with Olive was spontaneous.

"Oh, baby, I'm about to cum!" Camille screamed as she started to throw her ass back to intensify her orgasm.

"Come on, babe..." Kameron said as he felt himself reaching his own peak of bliss. Giving Camille three more long rough strokes, she and him both let go and experienced the most intensifying orgasm they'd ever had as a couple.

"Damn, Mille... I love you," Kameron foolishly admitted, knowing he had just made a huge mistake. Kameron didn't even know what lead him to say that, but it was definitely too late to take it back.

"I love you, too," Camille responded as butterflies filled her heart and stomach. It had been a full year since her husband muttered those three little words to her, and sounded like he meant them. Climbing back on top of him, Camille knew tonight was a great start for their new beginning.

It seemed like the Davidson's were staying together after all!

6

THE STORM IS OVER NOW

Kirk Franklin: *No more crying at night. The storm is over now.*

Camille woke up to the sun invading her room through the blinds. A smile spread across her face as she remembered the night of passion that she and Kameron had shared. Last night was the perfect way to start the new chapter in their life and marriage. Camille knew sex couldn't fix everything, and they definitely needed outside help, like marriage counseling, but nothing could take away the joy she was feeling this morning.

She hadn't slept in this late on a Sunday in a long time. It was going on 9am. Sitting up in bed, she realized that she was all alone. Panic started to set in, thinking Kameron had left, but the panic cease as soon as she saw Kameron walk through the bedroom door fully dress. He was holding a silver plate that had breakfast that he'd cooked, ready to be served.

"Breakfast in bed?" Camille asked with a smile.

"Yeah. You deserve it," Kameron said, placing the tray on her lap then he quickly walked back out of the bedroom only to return back with a vase of yellow roses and some papers that he gently placed on the nightstand.

"Thanks for the flowers and the food," Camille said as she started to dig into her food. She couldn't remember that last time Kameron cooked for her.

"No problem. Are we picking up the kids or is Caddie bringing them back home?" Kameron asked, looking everywhere but at Camille.

"I was going to pick them up."

"Cool. Listen, last night was amazing, and I think it was the best way to end this chapter in our lives." Kameron said, causing Camille to stop eating and look at him through eyes filled with hurt and confusion. This was not what she expected Kameron to say.

"What…"

"Millie, baby, I still want a divorce," Kameron said, now looking at her. He knew sleeping with Camille was wrong, especially since he knew his feelings didn't mirror hers. "Next to your flowers are the divorce papers. My signature is already signed. You can have your lawyer look over it so you can sign."

"About last night…"

"Last night didn't change anything for me. I love you,

but I'm no longer in love with you, and nothing you say or do will change that. I just want us to leave each other on good terms, and I believe last night did that."

Camille was seriously loss for words. She never thought her heart could break more than it did the night he asked her for a divorce. The way he made love to her last night wasn't the way you make love to a woman you wanted to divorce. As much as she wanted to stop the tears from falling, she couldn't. This man had finally broken her.

"Why did you sleep with me? Why lead me on?" Camille asked in just above a whisper.

"Trust me, that wasn't my attentions. Camille, the reason why I came over here last night was to tell the kids about the divorce, together. You caught me off guard with the romantic dinner. Things happened that shouldn't have ever happen. I'm sorry, but I don't regret sharing one more night with you.

"Get out!" Camille screamed, tossing the tray of food at him, causing him to quickly jump out of the way.

"Camille…."

"Fuck you, Kam!" She yelled, this time grabbing the vase he had place on the nightstand, throwing it at him, barely missing his head before it crashed into the wall, shattering on impact.

"Chill the fuck out!" Kameron barked as Camille came full force and started swing on him. All Kameron could do was try to block her punches the best way he that could. Hurt was an understatement as to explain the feeling she was currently feeling. Camille had never felt so foolish a day in her life.

"I hate you!" She expressed, trying to hurt him as much as he'd hurt her. Eventually, she could no longer swing on the man that she called, husband. The man who held her heart and held the power to break her.

In Camille opinion, Kameron couldn't have possibly cared, loved or respected her. If he did, he would have cared more about her sanity instead of playing with her emotions.

Last night, she clearly mentioned her intentions with him. She made it clear that she wanted their marriage to work. When she poured her heart out to him, he should have shut down any false hope she still had. Instead, he kissed her and gave her the one thing she'd been craving from him.

"Millie…." Kameron started before thinking about his next words. He honestly felt like shit as he watched his wife of fifteen years ball her eyes out on the floor, asking God why he was doing this to them. "I going to get the kids from your sister. I will explain to them that we're getting a divorce. I don't think you're able to handle this conversation. The kids don't need to see you like this. Pull it together. They will spend the night with me tonight and I'll take them to school tomorrow."

With that being said, Kameron quickly made his exit. He wasted no time heading to Kyron's room first to gather his uniform, then to Kasie's room to get her some clothes.

Once he had collected everything he needed, Kameron made his way out of the front door.

Hearing the front door shut, Camille let out a gut-wrenching scream.

Pull it together! She thought, trying to get her cries under control. Looking at herself in the mirror, she hated the woman that stared back at her. The woman who was staring back at her was weak. She allowed herself to get lost in a man who obviously didn't feel the same way she felt. Camille hated that she loved Kameron more than she loved herself, because it made her heartbreak seemed unbearable.

"God, Please," Camille muttered, wanting God to take the pain away from her. Wiping her tears, she walked into the bathroom and ran her a nice hot shower. While in the shower, she knew she needed to get out of the house because she was surely going to go crazy if she didn't.

❧

"KAMERON, WHAT ARE YOU DOING HERE?" CADDIE ASKED, wondering why her brother-in-law was standing at her front door.

"Hey, Caddie. I came to pick up the kids for your sister," he answered, not trying to go into details as to what happened last night. Even though Caddie was the most calm and sweeter sister out of Camille and her other sisters, Caddie also had another side that he was not trying to see.

Camille had given him enough craziness that he could handle in one day.

"Oh, okay. Is everything okay with Millie?" In all of the years that Kameron had been a father, he'd never did any pick-ups or drop off. Camille was the one who ran her kids around to where they needed to be.

"She's fine. I'm sorry for not calling, but if you can get the kids, that will be great."

"Sure," Caddie said, shutting the door right in his face, not even bothering to invite him in. Kameron was definitely on her shit list. She just wanted to be supportive of Camille because she truly wanted to make their marriage work.

"Kyron and Kasie, pack your things up. Your dad is waiting for you outside," Caddie said to the kids. They didn't ask any question and just did what they aunt told them to do. Caddie picked up her phone to call Camille, but of course she didn't get an answer.

After standing in Caddie's doorstep for about five minutes, Kameron ring her doorbell again, pissed. His nerves were already on edge for the simple fact that he had to tell the kids about the divorce, and the anticipation was killing him.

"Daddy!" Kasie screamed, jumping into his arms as soon as her aunt opened the door.

"Hey, sweet pea. Look how much you grew just in one night," Kameron said, kissing his daughter on the cheek. Kasie was totally a daddy girl, and in her eyes, her father could do no wrong.

"Hey dad. I thought mommy was going to pick us up," Kyron said, giving his dad their special handshake. Kameron and Kyron had a good relationship, too. However, Kyron was a mama's boy, and worshiped the ground Camille walked on. Mainly, because, over the years, Camille was the more present parent.

"I'm giving mommy some much needed, *me time.* So, it's just us three today. Tell Aunt Caddie, bye, so we can go to IHOP then Dave and Busters," Kameron said as he watched the excitement fill his kids eyes. He couldn't lie, he and Camille had made some beautiful children, and there was no doubt in his mind that they were made out of love. Yet, looking at them, he knew they weren't a strong enough reason to stay in his marriage.

"Yay!" Kasie jumped for joy.

"Bye Aunt Caddie. Love you," Kyron said before giving her a hug, followed bye his sister.

"Thanks, Caddie," Kameron said, only for Caddie to roll her eyes before walking back into her house. The whole ride to IHOP, Kameron was quiet and allowed his kids to fill him in on what was happening with school and how much fun they had spending the night with their aunt.

"So, guys," Kameron started and saw the frown on his daughter's face. Kasie hated when he said guys. She always wanted to her dad to call her by one of his many pet names he had given her. "Kyron and Sweet Pea."

"Better," Kasie said and Kameron and Kyron chuckled at her silliness. Kameron knew his four-year-old daughter was just as sassy as her mother. That thought brought a smile on his face.

"So, I wanted to spend some time with you today because I have to tell you something. Things are going to start changing around the house."

"Changing like how?" Kyron asked.

"Me and your mother are going to get a divorce." Kameron gave it to them straight.

"What's a divorce?" Kasie asked. He knew she wouldn't understand what was going on, and that was okay. He would explain it to her the best way he could. Camille was the one who could talk to their children in the way to make them understand and not worry.

"Me and mommy will no longer be married. We still love you and we will always be there for you. It's just, we can't be husband and wife anymore."

"So, you cheated?" Kyron asked, catching Kameron off guard. Unbeknownst to Kyron's parents, he was very intoned with the vibes in the household. He had known things weren't right with his parent for quite some time now, but he knew to stay in a child's place, and asking his parent about their marriage was not the way to go.

"No! Why you say that?" Kameron asked, nervously. He didn't want to lose his bond with his children for divorcing his mother, and he knew Kyron would take this the hardest. He was a teenager, and honestly, out of all his friends, his parent was the only one that was still married.

"I mean, you and mom been different lately, and when

my friends told me when their parents got divorced, it was because someone cheated," Kyron answered his father, honestly.

"No. Listen, I love your mother, and nothing will ever change that. Your mother and I are just better off as friends. Sometimes people just grow apart." Kameron tried to explain the best he could.

"Okay, daddy," Kasie said, not really understanding what he was truly saying, but that could be expected.

"How's mom? Is she okay?" Kyron asked.

"Yeah. Your mom is one hundred percent down with this. Now enough about that. I don't want you to worry about our divorce. This has nothing to do with you or your sister." Kameron made clear to Kyron.

"Okay." Kyron nodded his head and continued to eat.

"As soon as we finish here, we're going straight to Dave and Busters."

"You know I'm going to dust you in the basketball game," Kyron said, causing Kameron to jerk his head back and laugh. His son was so competitive.

"We'll see. Eat up." Kameron said, happy that the talk went well. Now he was just going to enjoy the much needed bonding time with his children because only God knows how crazy the divorce could turn out.

❦

CAMILLE LOOKED AT THE TEXT MESSAGE THAT KAMERON

had just sent her. It was of the kids playing at Dave & Busters. He wanted to let her know that they'd taken the talk very well and now they were having the time of their lives. Camille could only imagine the lies Kameron had come up with for the talk to go so smoothly, but that was the least of her concern right now.

Walking up to the big wooden door with stained glass window, church would have been the last place she thought she would find herself, but it was where her heart led her.

It was going on 10:45am and service had already started at Glory to God Baptist Church. But as Camille mother always stated, *it's better to go late than not at all.* Quietly, she sat on the last pew and listened to the choir's beautiful melody.

"Thanks, choir, for that lovely selection." Pastor Gabriel said as he walked up to the pulpit. "This Sunday morning, I want to talk to you about storms. I'm talking about personal storms. Things may be happening in your life that you don't understand at this moment, but you know God gives his toughest battle to his strongest soldiers." Pastor Gabriel said, and the church started to shout, *Amen.* Camille looked up at the pulpit and it was like fate that God lead her there today in church. The pastor's words were truly resonating with her.

"God place you in certain situations so you can receive your blessings. Maybe the storm you are going through is a hard lesson. Sometimes you have to let go and let god!"

"Yes pastor!" A woman yelled while standing up and clapping her hands.

"According to Psalms 34:17-18. The righteous cry out, and the Lord hears them. He delivers them from all their troubles. The Lord is close to the brokenhearted and saves those who are crushed in spirit."

The tears came to Camille's eyes. She needed to let go and let God. This storm that she was going through was because she had lost herself. Camille had buried her, hope, and dreams in order to build up Kameron. He had been the roadblock in her life, one of the main reasons she was at a standstill. He put a stop to any and everything that was supposed to help her grow as an individual.

"I don't know, but I feel like someone really need to hear this. The battle is almost over. God is with you every step of the way. I want to let you know the storm is almost over now!"

"It's almost over," Camille mumbled to herself.

"Yes sister. It's almost over now." An older lady declared sitting next to her, placing her hand on Camille's shoulder. At that moment, Camille knew she had to let go of the past, the history and even the love she shared with Kameron. She decided she was no longer going to be the weak minded woman Kameron painted her to be. She knew she was strong and could weather this storm. On cue the choir started to sing The Storm *Is Over Now*, by Kirk Franklin. Standing up next to the lady Camille leaned into her embrace and they swayed side to side and sing alone to the song.

"Sister you will get through this. God is right by your

side." Sister Cora didn't know this young lady from a can of paint. Nor did she know her story but she prayed that God would lead this beautiful woman out of the storm and to bring her to his glory light.

"I feel like I can make it. The storm is over now," Camille sang with so much conviction.

"Amen. Put your trust in him sweetheart." Ms. Cora said, pulling Camille into another hug. "He will pull you through."

Camille truly believed Ms. Cora. By the end of service Camille knew the storm would clear soon. She just had to let things take its course but in the end, she knew she would be standing strong.

7

HOT GIRL SUMMER

Megan Thee Stallion: *Hot Girl Summer so you know she got*
it lit

O ***ne dreadful year later...***
"Are you ready to turn the fuck up!" Camille
little sister Cassie screamed as she poured everybody a shot.

Tonight, Camille twin little sisters Cassie and Caddie
along with her best friend Kelly was going out to celebrate
her divorce. The past year Camille experienced every
emotion that a human being could experience. As much as
it hurt to divorce her husband, she realized it was for the
best. Not only was Kameron cheating on her and fell in love
with another woman, throughout the years he had
purchases multiple rental properties, storefronts, and everything was in his name. Kameron made sure he had multiple

sources of income that his wife never knew about. He even had a vacation house in Mexico and Jamaica.

Camille was beyond hurt after finding out about Kameron sneakiness. She came into the marriage with an open heart and with the willingness to make things work by any means necessary. She would never in a million years go on a business adventure and not include him. What hurt her the most were the rental properties he selfishly purchased without her. She always told him that they should get other sources of income, like rental properties but he always said his practice provided for them just fine. Sad to say for Kameron, since they never signed a prenup, Camille was granted alimony and child support. She also now owns fifty percent of his medical practice, along with gaining ownership of five of his properties and the vacation house in Jamaica.

"Yes, it's time to celebrate you're finally free from that bitch ass nigga." Caddie, Cassie's twin made known right before everybody took their shot to the head.

"Yall ready!" Camille screamed like a mad woman, already feeling the shot. She was just happy the whole thing was over, and she can now start on her new life.

"Hell yeah. You know one of the Philadelphia Eagles players is celebrating their birthday at Club Royal. Shit, we might get all of us a baller tonight." Cassie said checking her make up in her compact mirror.

"So, Candace not coming?" Kelly asked looking at her

best friend only for Camille to roll her eyes upward. Candace was Camille twin sister.

Camille parents had two sets of twin girls. Cassie and Caddie were the younger set of the two twins, born ten years after Camille and Candace. Cassie and Caddie, were best friends and sisters. They didn't need other friends because they had each other. They were so close and in sync with one another that they would finish each other sentences. If Cassie got a beating Caddie legs will welp up, that's how close they were, but you couldn't say the same about Camille and Candace. In all honesty, Candace barely spoke to Camille. Growing up everything was a competition, and it seemed that Candace was always on the losing end.

She hated that Camille lived in the suburbs, in a big house with a pool in the back yard, while she still lived in the same house that her parents left them after they passed away. She was even jealous of the fact that Camille was married to a doctor, forgetting the fact that Camille helped her husband at the time to reach his goals. Candace was the main one talking trash when Camille was working two and sometimes three jobs to secure her family future.

Candace jealousy for Camille allowed her to find joy in the news that Camille's perfect life was shattering when her husband left her for another woman, a more accomplished woman. Candace was around for the misery and the dark times Camille experienced last year, but as soon as things started to look up, Candace went away. When Caddie called

Candace to let her know Camille had won the divorce settlement and they were going out to celebrate, of course, Candace wanted nothing to do with her sister's victory. Instead she called Camille immature and a fucked-up individual to celebrate something that was probably tearing her kids up inside.

The truth was, she just hated that Camille came out on top once again. Candace just thought she knew Camille would suffer and would've been knocked off her high horse because of this divorce. So to find out she made it out better than anybody thought, was a disappointment that she couldn't stomach. She didn't feel like Camille deserved the money, houses or the business. Therefore, she wouldn't dare celebrate with her.

"No, you know her hating ass not coming." Cassie said with the roll of her eyes.

"Cassie, she's not a hater, you know she couldn't find a babysitter to watch the kids." Caddie lied. She hated that she had to make up a story to cover for her sister selfishness. She hated that Candace was so distant from them. Cassie didn't particular care for Candace. She noticed a long time ago the hate Candace held for Camille. It was a shame because Camille had always been a good sister to every one of them. When Candace was about to lose their parents' house for not paying the property taxes, who came to saved her and her children from being homeless? You guessed right, it was Camille, and she did it without a second thought.

"Caddie I know you're not going to sit up here and lie.

You know the kids are with their daddy. Leon comes to get those kids every weekend, faithfully."

"I just don't understand why she act the way she does. If mommy and daddy was here, she wouldn't be acting this way." Caddie let out a deep sigh, not understanding her sister ways.

"Listen, I don't care about Candace not coming out to celebrate with us. Shit, she had a problem with me since we shared mama'd womb. Tonight, is about me and I will not let her negativity kill my vibe. Bitches, I'm divorce!" Camille was too happy to allow her bitter sister to mess up her night. She took the bottle of Crown to the head. She wanted to have fun with the close genuine people in her life.

"Yasss, bitch!" Kelly's hyped her girlfriend up. After taken another shot, they all left the house and hopped into Kelly Range Rover to head to club Royal.

"Do you see that long ass line that I'm not about to be standing in.? Camille couldn't believe her eyes. She was drunk and had on six-inch heels. Standing in line for however long would definitely sober her ass up and make her want to go home.

"We don't have to stand in line. Matthew is working the door. Caddie smile. Matthew was her longtime boyfriend.

"That nigga working security now." Cassie joked, instantly rubbing Caddie the wrong way.. Matthew had just gotten out of jail after doing a five-year stint for carrying an unregistered, illegal, firearm.

"Fuck you mean, this nigga working security? Caddie

mocked her sister's voice. "Yes, he is working an honest paying job. He just got out of jail and instead of going back to selling drugs or doing anything that could put him back behind bars like most convicted felons. He bossed the fuck up and got him a job that suits him." Caddie snapped, not at all feeling her sister's comment about.

"Damn twin, I was just joking. I just never thought I'll see the day Matthew get a real job. You know all that nigga knows is hustling and making easy money." Cassie cleared up, reaching over, giving her sister a hug before telling her that she was sorry.

"Well, he loves me. At first he did think he was going to get out and pick up where he left off. You know he's G.M.M for life and it's really no getting out of that gang alive. Once you in your in. But he loves me more and I straight up told him I wasn't holding him down again if he goes back to jail. So, he spoke to Angelo and them. They pulled some strings to get him a job here. Sometimes he does other jobs like being security for their families."

When Matthew went to jail, it didn't affect just him. Even though he was the one who had lost his freedom for five years, Caddie felt like she was in prison as she held him down. Therefore she refused to go through that again. No matter how much she loved him, she would never put her life on hold to satisfy another person again.

"Well I for one is proud of my little brother." Camille stated matter-of-factly.

Kelly parked and they walked into the front of the line. They could hear people complaining but they didn't care.

"Hey, babe." Caddie smiled, kissing Matthew.

"Wassup, babe? I see you trying to have a nigga catch a case tonight." Matthew eyes scanned over Caddie's outfit before he looked over her sisters and Kelly's outfit as well. "Aww hell naw. Ya'll all showing the fuck out."

"Brother, you have to admit, we look fly," Cassie said, doing a little spin.

"Camille you out here looking like you are looking for trouble." Matthew joked.

"Shit I'm trying to live my best life." Camille let him know as he let them through the entrance.

"Millie you know my offer still stands." Matthew was referring to beating the dog breaks off Kameron. Matthew never fucked with Kameron because Kameron always felt a sense of entitlement when he literally came from the same slums in Philadelphia as Matthew. Then Matthew hated the way he tried to dog Camille in the divorce. Camille had always been the strong one in the family, so to see her almost broke had him ready to put a bullet in Kameron head. Honestly the only thing that stopped him from doing just that was the kids who he considered his nephew and niece.

"The way I came out on top in the divorce, he will always feel my wrath every time he signs a check knowing half of it is coming to me."

* * *

79

Club Royal was pack, anybody and everybody was there to celebrate Dion DJ Roberts twenty-six birthday. This had been a great year for the young quarterback of the Philadelphia Eagles. So many people had counted him out after his injury but that only motivated him to go into beast mode. Now he was one of the highest paid quarterbacks in the league.

"Happy Birthday, Bro," Pharaoh said, walking into DJ's VIP section. Looking around, he couldn't stop the smile that was gracing his face. DJ had a great turn out. Not only were the celebrities pouring in, but the exposure from the press was great, especially since Pharaoh was making plans to open a club in Los Angeles.

"Thanks, bro." Looking around, DJ noticed that a lot of the people showing him love were some of the same people that had counted him out. The only people in the building that he really rocked with were his family. His sister, Reign, and the Black family. Angelo, Cream and Ira were there, too, with their ladies and GMM.

"DJ.... DJ... I know him! I'm not some damn groupie." He heard his name being called and a commotion being made at the entrance of VIP. Looking up, he saw no one other than Yazmine.

"You still dealing with this hoe." Reign wanted to know as she walked up to her brother.

"Fuck no, she just won't let me the fuck be," DJ muttered fully annoyed. Yazmine was a hard lesson learned. Money changed people and it changed her for the worst.

Last year she had left him high and dry when she thought his career was over. She had found a new baller to leech off,, but everything changed when she became pregnant and didn't know who the father of her baby was.

"Bone, turn her away," Reign ordered the head of security before he walked off to do what he was told only for Yazmine to start to making a scene.

"This bitch!" Reign said

"Babe," Pharaoh grabbed Reign's arm, stopping her from walking over to Yazmine. The last thing he wanted was for his wife to put hands on the girl. "You don't need to be trying to square up with that bitch."

"Pharaoh, I'm not about to beat her ass, even though she deserves the ass whooping everybody keep saving her from. She put my brother through hell and tried to drag his name through the mud because she's a hoe. The last thing I'm going to do is let her ruin his birthday. So, I'll let her stay at the party, but shorty needs to keep her distance." Reign gently pulled away from her husband and made her way towards a very loud and over dramatic Yazmine. "Yazmine, what do you call yourself doing?"

"I want to speak with DJ! Not you." Yazmine yelled, rolling her eyes. She hated Reign and best believe the feeling was mutual. Yazmine couldn't stand the closeness of DJ and Reign's relationship. In all honesty it made her uncomfortable. Yazmine being a spoil and only child couldn't understand that Reign and DJ struggle and childhood brought them closer. They were all each other had in the end, but she would have known that if she were genuinely all about DJ.

"Now listen and listen good. I will allow you to stay at the party because you paid your money, but stay away from DJ the whole night."

"Or what?" Yazmine challenge. Deep down she believed she still had a chance to fix her broken relationship with DJ.

"Or I'm going to give the gossip sites something to talk about and I will give you that ass whooping that everybody keeps trying to save you from. Bitch, you're foul as shit. You and my brother don't fuck with one another. There is no reason why you are trying to be in the same space as him, trying to make yourself relevant."

"He's my baby's father." Yazmine spat thinking that had any pull. She had brought so much drama into DJ's life this last year that she knew she should've just backed away, but her heart wouldn't allow her to do that. She now realized she made a mistake, allowing the fame to go to her head. When she found out she was pregnant it was a nightmare and a blessing. There were so many tabloids about her and its sad to say most of them was the truth and not gossip. Yazmine was pregnant with twins. She didn't know who the father was. It could only have been between DJ and Jo Jo the point guard on the Boston Celtics basketball team.

Yazmine had started an affair with JoJo that lasted a full year. She met him at his house party that she went to with some new friends that she could now see were full time groupies. They were the type of girls that went to every sporting event and parties. They were out looking for the next baller while Yazmine was too dumb to appreciate the one she had. The night of his house party she slept with JoJo and promise to take that secret to the grave with her. But with DJ continuously being on the road barely making time for her during football season, she slowly but surely started creeping around almost on a weekly basis with JoJo.

To JoJo, dealing with Yazmine was all a game. He knew she had a man and honestly that's why he preferred her. With Yazmine having a man he knew she wouldn't catch feelings, but he was wrong. She did, and when DJ tore his ACL, and everyone counted him out, it made it much easier to make her decision to leave him. She was thinking that she was going to be accepted with open arms but she learned quickly that she had made a mistake by leaving DJ. When she found out that she was pregnant, she thought she might've had just the thing to get back with DJ. She knew DJ was big on family, especially since the only family he had was his sister Reign and her husband family. But with the tabloid and her being in the blogs, he immediately denied being the father. He even went as far as having his lawyer draft up some paper so Yazmine couldn't mention him or the baby until they got a DNA test done.

Yazmine endured a long and lonely pregnancy. JoJo allowed her to live with him, but he was barely there to enjoy her pregnancy. He knew there was a possibility that he could be the father. That was the reason why he gave her shelter, but he also knew DJ could be the father. Being that she was carrying twins, she went into labor at 29 weeks pregnant. Sad to say one of the babies came out stillborn. When DJ and JoJo finally decided to show their faces at the hospital they both took DNA test.

If things couldn't get any worst the results came back that they were both the father. DJ was the father of baby A. The baby who came out stillborn and JoJo was the father of baby B. As oddly as it was, it was the truth. The doctor explained that it was superfecundation. That was the fertilization of two or more ova from the same cycle by sperm from separate acts of sexual intercourse, which can lead to twin babies from two separate biological fathers. DJ was sad because he lost a child, but he couldn't help but think it was a blessing in disguise. Yazmine was the last person he wanted to be tied to for the last 18 years.

"Unfortunately, my nephew died at birth. Ya'll didn't have a relationship while you were pregnant and you damn sure don't have one now since you lost the baby. Worry about your other son," Reign knew what she said was harsh, but she wasn't going to allow Yazmine to use their dead child as bate to lure DJ back into her scandalous life. Yazmine made her choice and showed her true colors. It was now time for her to accept her reality.

"I know you don't like me…" Yazmine tried to take another approach.

"Girl, take ya ass downstairs and enjoy the party and stop embarrassing yourself. Whatever you and DJ had is dead. Accept that shit and move the fuck on!" Reign preached, wanting Yazmine to get it through her head. Yazmine decided to turn around and do what she was told because she obviously wasn't going to get pass his bulldog of a sister.

Real hot girl shit
Real, real ass bitch, give a fuck 'bout a nigga
Hot Barbie summer
(What Juicy say? He be like, "Shut the fuck up")
Real, real, real ass bitch, give a fuck 'bout a nigga
(Don't run from me, friend, ha-ha)
Real ass nigga, give a fuck 'bout a bitch
It is what it is, this some five-star dick
She a big ol' freak, it's a must that I hit
It's a Hot Girl Summer, so you know she got it lit

Megan Thee Stallion's *Hot Girl Summer* was blasting through the club speakers. All of the ladies were dancing to the summer anthem. Camille and her girls were in the middle of the dance floor. This was the first time in years that she had so much fun with her sisters and best friend.

"Yasss, Millie fuck it up." Cassie hyped her sister up loving the new Camille. Ever since Camille dated and married Kameron, clubbing days was a no for her. Camille was the type of mother and wife that put her husband and kids needs and wants before her own. That meant she rarely did anything for herself.

"Let's get another drink," Caddie told them as she made her way through the crowd to get to the bar. As they were walking, Camille felt a pair of eyes on her, but when she looked around she noticed there was a couple men staring in the group direction.

"Your name is Camille, right?" The bartender asked.

"Ummm, yeah." Camille confirmed, puzzled that he knew that information.

"Here, this was ordered for you and your girls. Also all of the other drink ya want is on the house." The bartender handed her a bottle of D'Usse. "These are some VIP bands to get into the section."

"Omg! Bitch, who you know up in here?" Kelly side eyed her best friend.

"Girl, nobody. I'm just confused as you are."

"Damn, I never thought I'll see you again." A deep smooth voice said from behind Camille. Turning around she came face to face with a man who was responsible for all her wet dreams.

"DJ..."

8

LATE NIGHTS EARLY MORNINGS

__Marsha Ambrosius__: When I think about the freaky things I got in mind.

"How have you been?" DJ asked, pulling her into a hug. Camille swore the smell of his cologne had her ready to cum as memories of their one night of passion flooded back to her mind.

"I'm great. Are you the person I need to thank for my bottle and VIP bands?"

"Yeah. I had to make sure you had your cognac. What's the celebration?"

"Her divorce!" Kelly, Cassie and Caddie all yelled over the music and started to dance. If Camille didn't know how much her sisters and Kelly hated Kameron, she knew then, because they was celebrating harder than she was.

"Congrats." DJ could remember the last time he seen her, her husband had asked her for a divorce on their anniversary.

"How ya'll know each other?" Cassie didn't care that she was being nosey. The man who had her sister dreamy eyed look to be her age.

"Me and DJ met last year." Camille kept it short and simple.

"Then why we're just hearing about his fine ass, I see you're holding out on us." Kelly asked.

"I did tell you about him," Camille whispered back.

"Oh, shit this not the big dick DJ that had my girl busting back to back.." Kelly tried to whisper but the cocky smile that was spread across his face said he heard everything.

"Bitch, you getting water from here on out." Camille said, shaking her head. Kelly didn't have any type of filter when she was drunk.

"Come on." DJ grabbed Camille's hand, guiding her to his VIP section.

"What are you doing here?" Camille asked as he and her sat at a table in the cut. Cassie, Caddie and Kelly went to enjoy themselves in VIP.

"It's my birthday."

"Happy birthday. I'm scared to ask you how old you are." All she knew was that he was legal, but she knew he was definitely younger than her.

"Twenty-six."

"Damn, you got me out here on some cougar shit. I'm a whole decade older than you." Camille shook her head, causing him to laugh.

"Naw, ten years not as bad as you think, especially when I make ya body feel the way it does." He whispered in her ear causing her to shutter. Camille had been a lovely memory that he had replayed over and over in his head. He chuckled at the thought of how she got ghost on him before he woke up. When he spotted her on the dance floor, he knew he couldn't let her slip through his fingers again. "Why you dip on me that morning?"

"I left because honestly, I was embarrassed. I never had a one-night stand in my life. Then you were obviously younger than me. Plus, I was about to go through hell and back in this divorce, there was no reason to drag you along through the craziness."

"True. I feel you. I had a lot of drama in my life last year too. So, let's toast to new beginnings." He poured them both a shot of D'Usse.

"New beginnings." Camille clinked her glass against his.

After downing the shot, DJ pulled Camille up out of her seat. Chris Brown *No Guidance* was blasting through the speakers. He turned her body around so her ass was up against his man hood. They started dancing and was so into one another one would have thought they was about to fuck right there in the VIP section.

"Yo, bro, let me talk to you for a minute," one of DJ's teammates said, walking up to him giving him dap.

"Where are you going?" DJ asked when he noticed Camille was about to walk away.

"It's okay it's ya birthday. I can't hold you to myself." Camille gave him a shy smile.

"I'll be right back, don't leave without seeing me first." DJ was about to walk away but retraced back. "Naw, put ya number in my phone. You like to get ghost on a nigga. I ain't trying to let another year pass before I see you again," Camille chuckled.

"I'll be around. I'm about to find my sisters and best friend," she told him before walking away. As she searched for her girls, she couldn't ignore the nasty looks she was getting from other females. One was even bold enough to bump her as they crossed paths but she could care less. She was too old to beat some young's girl ass because she was in her feelings about DJ. If things go her way, she would be leaving with DJ for another night of mind-blowing sex.

The whole night DJ was partying, but he had kept his eyes on Camille, making sure she didn't go too far or have another nigga in her face.

"DJ!" Yazmine called his name as she saw him making his way out of the bathroom. She had been lurking all night, trying to get his attention. What made her mad was the fact that it seemed like he had moved on with someone else.

"Yo, what the fuck do you want?" DJ spoke, pissed off. He turned around, knowing it was going to be only a matter of time before Yazmine cornered him.

"Really? That's how we talk to one another now? You

can't show me no respect because ya old bitch here?" Yazmine snapped.

"Stop fucking hating, Shorty's not that older than us, and she look way better than you. Did you really stop me to talk shit?" DJ was over the conversation already.

"No. DJ, I miss you. I miss us." Yazmine reached for him only for him to pull out her grasped.

"There will never be another us, Yaz. I don't know what else to say in order for you to get it through ya head."

"That's it. You really going to throw everything we had out the window? I know I made a mistake, but you cheated on me too, Dion. I forgave you but you can't forgive me?"

"Bitch, you been fucking a nigga during the same time you was fucking me. I took care of you. You didn't have to want for nothing. Maybe that was my fault, because once I drafted and you got a taste of money and fame, you changed as a person. Then when you thought a nigga career was over you left me high and dry. That's when you should have been there for me, helping me get back. Many mutha-fuckas doubted me but I should've been able to count on my girl to have my back. But naw, I came home to a fucking Dear John letter." DJ snapped, ,hating how Yazmine kept trying to play the victim.

"DJ...." Yazmine, started but he cut her off with the quickness.

"Then I saw you on Instagram with that nigga JoJo the next fucking day. So, fuck no we can't be what we use to be. You had a whole baby on a nigga. Then you had my name dragged through the tabloid and blogs because ya hoe ass didn't know who ya kids' father was. And you bringing up some shit from back in college when we weren't official is nutty as hell."

"I'm sorry, I made a mistake by leaving you." Yazmine admitted looking into his eyes. She saw nothing but pure disgust. It wasn't an ounce of love left for her.

"And I made a mistake of not dropping you when I realized my money made you change for the worst." Allowing them to be his final words, DJ left Yazmine where she stood. He just hoped that would be the last time he would have to have that talk with her.

DJ walked back up to VIP only to find Camille and her girls about to make their exit.

"Yo, so you just going to dip on a nigga, again?" He asked, causing Camille to stop in her tracks.

"I texted you." She had noticed the little dispute he was having with the girl near the bathroom, and her goal for this new beginning in life was to have absolutely no drama.

"I don't want you to leave, yet."

"They're my ride and as you can see Cassie is done." She pointed towards her sister who was barely standing.

"I'm about to be out with ya'll then. I have the penthouse in the Jameson Hotel again. I knew I wasn't going to want to drive home after this party." DJ informed her.

"Is that an invitation?"

"Yeah."

"Let me get them home and I will meet you back at the hotel. Plus, I'll have my car. It's the same room number?"

"Yeah, I'll let them know you coming to visit me so they'll let you up." DJ said before pulling Camille in for a hug while placing a kiss on her neck.

"Okay, I'll see you in a bit." Camille reluctantly pulled away. She wanted to get back to her house and freshen up before heading over to the Jameson Hotel. Her body was hot with anticipation of what the night was to bring. By the time Kelly dropped everybody off at Camille's house, Cassie was knocked out.

"Just let Cassie stay at my house for the night. Caddie, are you okay driving or should I called Matthew to come pick you up?" Camille asked her sister.

"You already know he's coming to pick me up from your house. What are you about to do?"

"Yes, best friend. Let me find out you like them young." Kelly joked.

"Girl, hell yeah, if he is swinging dick like DJ." Camille high fiving Kelly caused Caddie to bust out laughing. "Sike. Naw, DJ is nothing serious. Shit, this is only my second time seeing him. I just want to end my divorce celebration with some bomb ass dick. God knows I deserve it."

"I feel you. Don't hurt the boy now." Kelly joked, side eyeing her friend.

"Girl, his ass better not hurt me. Last time there was no limits to how far he pushed my body." Camille body shuttered just from the memories. "Girl, last time his ass had me folded up like a damn pretzel."

"That's my type of nigga." Caddie said, twerking.

"You so nasty." Kelly threw a pillow at Caddie. "But best friend, do you. Girl, you're free to do whatever you want, no restrictions, no judgement." Kelly said as her phone chimed. "And that will be my booty call. I'll see ya'll hoes later." With that, Kelly picked up her purse before giving her best friend a hug and heading out of the house.

Camille took this opportunity to take a shower. When she got out, she moisturized her body. Going to her dresser, she knew there was no doubt in her or DJ's mind what was about to happen. She pulled out her three-piece red lace body language lingerie set that she had bought from Fashion Nova. Once she put it on there was nothing left to do but freshen up and apply her makeup. She pulled a light black trench coat out of her closet because she couldn't just walk around with lingerie. Once she checked herself out in the mirror and she was satisfied, she headed to the front door and made it to the Jameson Hotel in record time

Knock, Knock

Camille stood in front of the door patiently waiting with her trench coat wide open, giving him the perfect view of her body.

"I thought you was going to stand a nigga up," DJ said opening the door to get the shock of the lifetime.

"Damn." He pulled her into the room and was on her like white on rice. Camille had one of the best bodies he had ever seen on a woman. You couldn't even tell she had two kids beside some of the light stretchmarks on the side of her stomach and hip, but that still didn't take away from her sex appeal.

"Happy Birthday, DJ," Camille moaned as he picked her up and started to walk into the bedroom. She knew it was about to be a late night and early morning of mind-blowing orgasms.

9

ON CHILL

Wale: We've been on that tragedy for months
Why can't you agree with me for once?

Kameron woke up to the smell of waffles, eggs and bacon. Yesterday was the end of his divorce from his wife of fifteen years. He never thought Camille would make out the way she did, and he was bitter because of it. He had learned the hard way that it was cheaper to keep her. However, he knew the divorce was always the end game. There were plenty of times during the divorce he thought about calling it off, but when he found out Olive was pregnant with his child, he knew there was no point in doing so. There was no way Camille would have stayed, and honestly, she shouldn't have because he didn't love her anymore. It was his choice to have an affair so he just had to deal with the cost.

They set up visitation agreement as part of the divorce settlement. On the weekends Kameron got Kyron and Kasie, which was going to be a huge adjustment for Kameron. Over the years he had slacked on his fatherly duties. He hardly had a bond with his sixteen-year-old son and the divorce didn't make it better. However, his baby girl Kasie who was five years old loved the ground he walked on. But that love was mainly because he brought her a lot of toys to make up for his absence.

Getting up out of bed, Kameron slid on his slippers to make sure his son was not trying to burn down his house. Kyron had picked up on cooking because he spent a lot of time in the kitchen with his mother. Reaching the kitchen, Kameron got the surprise of his life when he saw a very pregnant Olive standing at his stove.

"What the hell are you doing here?" Kameron snapped scaring Olive half to death to the point that she dropped the spatula that she held in her hand.

"Kam, you scared me." Olive said, turning around with her hand on her chest as she rubbed her three-month belly. "What do you mean what the hell I'm doing here?"

Olive going to Kameron's house had never been a problem. As a matter of fact, she had a key and passcodes to the alarm system. Olive had been at home yesterday missing her man terribly. She knew yesterday was the big day and she could now finally have Kameron Davidson to herself. They could be the power couple that she always dreamed of them being. She could admit that the past few months had been rocky, but she put that on the divorce. She felt that Camille was being greedy, trying to take everything that Kameron worked hard for. She couldn't stand Camille, but she was happy that she got the last laugh.

"Olive, I told you I have my children on the weekends. You can't be here."

"Why not, Kameron? For God sakes, we are engaged to be married. Your divorce is over. Why are you hiding us from your children? I'm pregnant with their little brother. Like it or not, we are about to be one happy blended family. You might as well rip the band-aid off. The faster they know, the faster they can adjust to the changes in the family."

Olive refuse to be a secret any longer. She had to deal with hiding her love for Kameron when he was married, now she would be damn if she came second to his children. In her opinion, they needed to get with the program, or they could be replaced just like their mother.

"I know. Everything you said is right, but…" Kameron started but stop when his children made their entrance into the kitchen.

"Good morning, daddy." Kasie greeted sweetly, running up to him, giving him a big hug.

"Good morning sweet pea. Son."

"Dad." Kyron tone was dry as he looked at Olive. "Doctor Walters what are you doing here?" He didn't really care for the formalities, he needed answers because what was in front of him had just confirmed that his father was a liar.

"Kyron, boy you better act like you have some manners." Kameron chastise his son. He was pissed because this was not the way he wanted his kids to find out about Olive. Little did Olive know; she was doing more harm than good.

"Good Morning Kyron and Kasie. I made breakfast, how about we all take a seat. Me and your father can answer any questions you may have." Olive quickly said as she began to start making everyone plates. Silently praying that the kids take the news well. "Shoot your question off. I hope you guys enjoy your breakfast."

"You didn't even put salt and pepper in the eggs." Kyron mumbled, causing his father to kick him under the table. Kyron was being beyond rude. Even though he had to admit to himself that Olive wasn't the best cook. She was nothing like Camille in the kitchen, but that was why she was a doctor and not a stay at home wife.

"So, you're having a baby." Kasie asked the obvious.

"Yes Kasie…." Olive started but was cut off by Kyron.

"Why are you here? You come to all of your co-worker's house and make breakfast for them and their kids?" Kyron was not pulling any punches.

When Camille and Kameron sat down and explain to the kids that they were getting a divorce. As parents, they explain that they were no longer happy with one another and it was time for them to go their separate ways. Kyron being a teenager asked his parents if it was because someone had cheated. A lot of his friends' parents were divorce and from his understanding most divorces happened because of someone having an affair. Deep down Kyron always knew his father was the one who wanted the divorce. Some night when his mother thought he and his sister was sleep, he heard her crying and praying for God to save her marriage. Unbeknownst to Camille, after hearing her cries Kyron dislike grew for his father. In Kyron eyes, his mother was the best and he hate to hear her cry even though she always tried to put on a façade that said she was happy. Kyron knew deep down his father was trying to break her.

"Ummm…No." Olive stammered over her words trying to get her thoughts together. This was not how she pictured things going in her head.

"Kyron this is your last warning," Kameron said sternly. "I asked Olive over her because we have some news to share with you. We are engaged to be married and the baby she is now pregnant with is your little brother," Kameron said, giving it to them straight.

"I'm going to be a big sister!" Kasie said excitedly. The news of being a big sister was a dream come true.

"You lied. Dad, you and mom just got a divorce yesterday and now you ready to marry someone else. So, you did cheat on my mom? Dr. Walters is your reason why we're not a family anymore. Is this new baby is something to replace us?"

"Listen, Kyron, this is the reality of our family now. I

will be your step-mother and you should show me a little more respect." Olive snapped, tired of his attitude and his assumption of her being a homewrecker. The truth stung, but she didn't want to be known as the homewrecker who got lucky because she believe what she and Kameron shared was true love.

"You will never be anything to me! I want to go home." Kyron let her know while standing up from the table.

"Sit down and let's talk about this, Ky. When me and your mother decided to end things, you had to know that we would move on with our lives. I'm in love with Olive and she is carrying your little brother. I expect you to love and accept the changes that's happening."

"Yeah, I expected ya'll to move on, eventually, but not the next day. You didn't even allow us to get use to the idea that our parents were no longer married. Now here she is pregnant and you want me to respect her? She doesn't even respect herself, sleeping with a married man." Kyron walked away and immediately called his mom to come pick him up, no longer wanting to stay at his father house.

"Kasie, sweetheart, are you okay with the idea of dad getting married again?" He asked his daughter. Kasie didn't even realize the reality of what was going on? All Kasie knew was that this was her chance to be a flower girl.

"I'm okay, only if I could be the flower girl!"

"Anything you want, baby."

"Excuse me," Olive said, getting up from the kitchen table. Kyron words cut deep, and she now wished she had listened to Kameron and followed his lead. "I'm going to head out."

"Kasie, go upstairs and play with ya toys, I'll be up soon." Kameron instructed his daughter. "Olive."

"Kameron, you need to get control over your son. How dare he speak to me like that?" She tried her best to hold back her tears.

"Olive, how did you think he was going to react? You need to listen to me. You popping up was for your own selfish needs. You didn't think about anyone but yourself. You didn't care how my divorce with Camille affected them. All you wanted was to make yourself known. Now you're upset because of his rejection and him calling you out on your shit. How did you think he would look at you?" Kameron watched as Olive's tears fell. "Now you probably did more damage than good. Now I have to be the one who have to hear Camille's mouth!"

"I didn't mean any harm," Olive said, now realizing her actions was inconsiderate.

"I know." Kameron sighed. "Its best you get out of here. I don't need Camille coming over here acting crazy. She didn't take the divorce well and this was the last way I wanted her to find out about our engagement and the baby."

"Why do you care about her feelings? You guys are over. Honestly, if it doesn't have anything to do with Kyron or Kasie she is irrelevant." Olive was getting frus-trated. She waited for it to be just her, and to hear

Kameron considering Camille feelings caused a rush of jealousy.

"She's very relevant. Camille is my kids' mother. I'm just tired of the drama and fighting with her. I wanted to start this co-parent thing on a clean slate, but thanks to you, that's going to be impossible. Just go home and give me some time to straighten everything out." Kameron said opening the door.

"Things between us have been so rocky. Do you regret choosing me? Do regret our baby?" Olive was now feeling insecure. She didn't know how much longer she could take his cold shoulder. Deep down, she felt like he blames her for the divorce and the outcome.

"No, baby. I don't regret you or our child, but you need to be understanding and mindful of your actions. I'll come by when the kids leave, and we can work on us. This is what we wanted and its finally happening. But I don't want to lose my kids in the process." Olive completely understood. Kameron loved his kids and if they stop being in his life, he would be miserable. She gave him a peck on the cheek before walking out of the house.

"Kyron." Kameron called out to his son, knocking on his bedroom door before opening it. "What are you doing?"

"What it looks like?" Kyron said getting smart. He was packing his clothes. He had already called his mom and asked her to come get him and she was on the way.

"I'm losing patience with you Kyron. I don't know what gotten into you, but you better act like you know.

"Dad, I just don't respect you. You always told me to be a man about my word, but you lied. Then how do you think my mom will feel about this news?" Kyron question Kameron?

"Ya mom understand what we had is over, and eventually we'll both move on."

Ding Dong

"Did you really call your mother over here?" Kameron asked, shaking his head.

"Yeah, how else was I supposed to get home?" Kyron yelled at his father's back as Kameron walk down the steps to open the door to a very piss Camille.

"Camille…."

"Engage to be fucking married Kameron? Are you fucking serious!" Camille snapped, making her way into his house.

"Don't come in here acting crazy."

"I swear, you a dirty ass dog. You left me and the kids for Olive! The bitch that I told you to hire. You really left me for a white bitch!" Camille was really in disbelief. Olive always smiled in her face when she stopped by the office. Camille was the one who had told Kameron to hire her. Before Olive, Kameron practice only had him and another male doctor working there. She convinced them they would get more business if they had a woman doctor there also.

"First, I didn't leave my kids. I divorced you! And please, don't bring race in this." Kameron said to make it clear. He didn't want Kyron or Kasie to think he was abandoning them, even though he believed the damage was already done by the way Kyron had been acting. "Millie, I don't need you poisoning my kids with the lies of me leaving them."

"I'm not poisoning them with anything. I kept my kids out of the divorce. I never even spoken badly about you to them." Camille said, trying to calm down. "If you notice a difference in your children, that's probably because this is the first-time you spent time with them in months."

Kameron sighed, hating that Camille had just called him out on his shit. "Then when they finally get to spend time with you, you decided to have your little homewrecking girlfriend over to announce that you are engaged, a day after our divorce is final. The ink on our divorce papers is not even dry yet." Hearing Camille go off, he knew he seemed like the biggest jerk in the world.

"Listen, I didn't want you nor the kids to find out like this. But yes, I'm engaged to Olive and she is three months pregnant with our son." By the look on Camille's face, Kameron knew he had just broken her heart again.

10

NOT GON CRY

Mary J Blige: No, I'm not gon cry, it's not the time, cause you're not worth my tears

Kameron words shot through Camille's heart like daggers. She hated the fact that she still held some love for the man that was standing in front of her, but how could she not. They had been married for fifteen years and had dated five years before that. Twenty years of her life spent loving a man who obviously never saw her self-worth.

When Kyron called her, all he told her was that his dad made an announcement about getting married to Dr. Walters and he wanted to leave, and Camille had no problem with picking him up. She never wanted her kids to feel uncomfortable anywhere they stayed, even if it was at their father's new house.

"Mom, I'm ready," Kyron announced, walking down the steps. But he noticed his parents facial expression and asked, "What's wrong?"

"Kyron, you have to spend time with me on the weekends. That's part of me and your mother's custody agreement." Kameron's voice was filled with annoyance.

"Why? So we can pretend to be a happy family with you and Dr. Walters?" Kyron snapped at his father. In his eyes, his father was a fraud. Kameron always preached to him about how a man was only as good as his word. At this moment, Kameron's word didn't mean anything.

"Mommy! Mommy! I'm going to be a flower girl!" Kasie yelled, running down the steps, not knowing she had just hurt her mother's feelings by announcing that. Camille couldn't believe Kameron would stoop so low.

"Let's go," Camille said as the tears immediately started burning her eyes.

"I don't want to leave, mommy!" Kasie started to cry.

"You can stay, baby." Instantly, Kasie stopped crying. Camille wasn't trying to be petty. She just wanted to get her son since he was pissed and didn't want to be there

"Kyron is staying, too. He doesn't have a choice whether he can to stay or not." Kameron said, trying to put his foot down.

"I didn't come over here for nothing," Camille snapped back.

"Then you should have called first to save yourself the damn trip!"

"Kameron, he doesn't feel comfortable being here. So you're not going to force him."

"Camille, he a fucking teenager! Kyron can't even tell you why he feels uncomfortable. Nobody did anything to him. If he want to be mad, let him, but his black ass going to be mad in his fucking room, here, until Sunday night when I drop him back off at your house."

"Mom, I ain't staying here!" Kyron spoke up, making his way to the door as Camille turned on her heels to leave, too. She wanted to get out of Kameron's presence before she had to beat his ass.

"Camille, if you drive off with that boy, I will call the police. We have a court order custody agreement for a reason. This is not the time to become a bitter baby mama, and please don't try to call my bluff. The last thing your kids need to see is the police escorting you off of my property. And I will drag you back to court since this arrangement don't seem to work," Kameron said.

"You going to call the cops on me? Seriously?" Camille was lost for words. Never in her life did she think she and Kameron would ever be in such predicament.

"Yes. I'm trying to co-parent the best way we can, but that's not going to happen if you're overstepping your boundaries. Now, Kyron, apologize to your mother for the nonsense you just caused."

"Mom...." Kyron said, feeling like crap. "I'm sorry." His

head hung low and Camille reached out to give him a hug. Kyron had been taking the divorce really hard, and if Kameron spent more time with his kids instead of trying to avoid Camille, he would've known.

"It's okay, baby, I'll see you tomorrow. If you need me, call me." After saying that to her son, she walked over to give Kasie a hug and kiss..

"Bye, mommy," Kasie said, waving.

"And we cannot allow the kids to dictate how we move. This whole situation could have been avoided with a phone call. I don't want to call the police on you, or drag you back to court, but I know my rights as a father, and I will not allow you to take advantage because the kids seems to like you more at the moment."

"You want to sit here and preach about being a united front when you thought it was a great idea to introduce your children to your fiancée the day after you divorced their mother. How considerate was that. Kameron, I don't know if you haven't noticed, but Kyron does not like you. You're losing your son, and pulling moves like this is not making the situation better. Yes, we are divorce, and yes, common sense let me know you will move on. Shit, I knew you had moved on being the reason why you wanted the divorce in the first place, but it's a respect thing. I'm not trying to control your life or anything, but why would you not talk to me about introducing the kids to your *fiancée*, so we both can be on the same page. We could have talked to them together."

"Was I really supposed to bring my pregnant fiancée

around you? The woman you blame for our divorce." Kameron said, arrogantly. He knew his ex-wife's temper, and Olive didn't stand a chance.

"Is she not the blame?" Camille asked, daring him to lie.

Camille wasn't placing the whole blame on Olive, because at the end of the day, Olive was not her friend and she wasn't her husband. Kameron was the one who had broken his vowels. However, Olive knew for a fact that Kameron was married and because of that, she should have respected their marriage.

"If you weren't so busy fucking and caring for that bitch like she was your wife, we probably wouldn't be here, but that's not the point. There's no need to worry about me, I'm not going to beat that girl's ass. I refuse to go to jail over a no-good nigga, like you. The saying, how you get them is how you lose them, always seem to ring true. That poor girl don't even know the real you, but she will soon learn. Anyway, I'm not that sixteen-year-old girl who was ready to fight any girl who looked in your direction. I'm thirty-six years old. If Olive is going to be a part of my kids' lives and be around them, I know how to keep it cordial. The last thing I want is for her to mistreat my children because she's trying to get back at me. Then I'll have to go to jail for killing the both of you."

Kameron shook his head. He knew one thing about Camille, and that was, she would gladly smile in a mugshot picture behind her kids.

"Camille, I don't know how many times I have to tell

you, I'm sorry. I know I hurt you deeply, but I just want us to be civil with one another."

"That's not a problem. I don't want my kids to see us arguing every time we're in each other's presence. So like I said, I can be cordial, but that's it. We will never be cool or friends. The only communication we will have is if it's about Kyron and Kasie."

With that being said, Camille hopped in her car and headed home. She would be lying if she didn't say the news of Kameron and Olive being engaged didn't break her heart. It was too soon. Kameron was already trying to start a new family, and here she was, trying to mend a broken heart. Camille wanted to cry, but she didn't want to give Kameron the satisfaction of knowing she was shedding another tear over him. It was time to pull up her big girl pants and accept her reality, no matter how hard it was.

Camille was pulled out of her depressing thoughts by the ringing of her phone.

"Hello?" she dryly answered.

"Hey, twin. What are you doing?" Candace asked, loudly, through the car speaker.

"Driving. Wassup, Candy? "Camille got straight to the point. Camille's relationship with her twin, Candace, was basically nonexistent, and the only reason Candace would reach out to Camille was for money.

"Damn, I can't call and check on you and my niece and nephew."

"You never do. So what make today any different?"

"I see you're in a funky ass mood. I was calling to see if you wanted to go out to eat for lunch at Bahama Breeze since I missed your little divorce party," Candace said, ready to hang up on Camille. Here she was, trying to be a nice sister and Camille always wanted to show her ass.

"I'm sorry, Candace. Yeah, we can go. I'm already near King of Prussia. Where are you?"

"I'm in the King of Prussia Mall doing a little shopping for the kids."

"Cool. I'll meet you there in thirty minutes," Camille said, and Candace agreed before hanging up. A thirty-minute drive turned into twenty minutes.

Camille was ready for a good meal and a drink after the day she had.

"Millie!" Candace called out while waving so she could see her. Candace was already seated, sipping on a glass of water.

"Hey," Camille spoke as she walked over to the table by the window. Candace got up and gave her a hug.

"I've already order the crab cake appetizers for us. So, how have you been?"

"I need a drink." Camille muttered, causing Candace to smile.

"Damn, that bad? Girl, its only twelve noon. You already drinking?" Candace said in a judgmental tone.

"It's happy hour somewhere, right?" Camille answered, ready to pick up her purse and leave. Camille could only deal with Candace in small doses. Plus, Caddie wasn't there to play referee.

"I'm just saying…."

"Did you invite me to lunch to annoy the fuck out of me, or did you really want to chill and spend time with me?"

"Millie, I didn't call you here to argue or fight. I know were not the closest, and honestly, I feel like none of my sisters like me, ya'll just tolerate me. And I want to change that. Caddie told me how fucked up I was for missing the divorce celebration. You know I don't do clubs, but I should have still gone out with you."

"Candy, you're the one that exclude yourself from every-thing we do. How many trips did me, Cassie, Caddie and Kelly takes to Jamaica, Cancun and other countries and islands? We always extend the invitation, but you never want to come."

"Why would I want to come? Ya'll always inviting Kelly, and you know I don't like her," Candace stated, causing Camille to shake her head. Candace couldn't stand Kelly and she hated the fact that Camille kept her friendship with her after all of these years.

"Candace, when are you going to get over this little dislike? If anyone shouldn't like someone, it's Kelly. You're the one who had an affair with *her* fiancée that resulted in my niece and nephew. That was ten years ago, and Kelly is not worried about you or Leon. Plus, you and Leon was never together so why all the hostility against Kelly."

"She knew I liked him, and she still got with him."

"Candace, are you serious right now? Kameron introduced Kelly and Leon way before you met Leon. By the time you laid eyes on him, Kelly and him was basically in a full-blown relationship. But thanks for lunch, I'm going to head out," Camille said, standing up from the table.

"Camille, really? I'm just answering your question. But you're right, that's old news and I will be around more often. If Kelly's over it, I'm over it. I just feel like it's going to be awkward."

"Girl, Kelly got over the awkwardness when she attended her god kids birthday party and had to look at the kids you and Leon created with ya'll secret affair." Camille was getting pissed just thinking about it. She loved her niece and nephew, but the way they were conceived was fucked up and she hated the pain that it brought her best friend.

"Leaving already?" The waitress asked, and Camille looked at Candace.

"No, she's staying, It's my treat," Candace said and Camille sat back down. The waitress took their orders and told them she'll be right out with the drinks. "So, tell me how you've really been?"

"This is an adjustment for me and the kids, as you can imagine. Especially since Kameron dropped the news on the kids that he was now engaged and expecting a baby with Olive, one of the doctors at his practice."

"What!"

"Girl, yes. Kyron called me and told me. I was so pissed"

"But you can't be mad. Ya'll are divorced now."

Candace said. She felt like once Kameron came out and asked for the divorced, it was fair game.

"I have every right to be mad, Candy. He's been having an affair with her for the longest. Twenty years of my life have been wasted and all I have to show for this marriage is Kyron and Kasie. Then the day after we divorce, you announce this shit to the kids, not even caring that this divorce been bothering them from the start."

"True."

"But, it is what it is. I can't allow what he does to affect my peace."

"Yes, I feel you on that, sis. So, how's the single life?"

"Honestly, it's great." Camille smiled, thinking about DJ.

"Is that a smile? So, who's the guy? Do I know him? Where did ya'll meet?" Candace shot off questions after questions

"Candy, it's crazy. I met him last year on my anniversary. The night Kameron asked me for a divorce. Honestly, it was a one night stand. I left early in the morning before he could even wake up and I never saw him again."

"Hmmmm, let me find out miss perfect has a little hoe in her."

"No, I will never be a hoe. I was just living life. Being free for once and not little miss perfect, like you call me. But anyway, I haven't spoken or seen DJ since the night at the bar. That was until we ran into each other a few weeks ago on his birthday."

"So, that's ya new boo?" Candace asked, "Let me see a picture of him."

"I don't have any appropriate pictures of him that you can look at. Plus, it's not that serious, He's ten years younger than me. We're just having fun."

"Bitch, you out here robbing the cradle." Candace joked, looking at her sister sideways. "He's Cassie and Caddie age. I know this divorce was a life changer, but you will find somebody that's our age and on our level."

"I said it's not serious. Anyway, how are the twins?" Camille asked, changing the subject. Candace started talking about her kids and Camille tried to get through the lunch without having to slap her sister. Camille didn't even know why she would try to open up about her little fling with DJ. Out of all people, she knew Candace wouldn't understand.

Even though she kept telling herself that it was just a fling with DJ, she had to admit, she seemed to be her happiest when he was around.

11

MOTHERLESS CHILD

*P*aul **Robeson:** *Sometimes I feel like a motherless child. A long way from home.*

"Good practice, today," one of DJ's teammates said as they walked out of the stadium.

"Yeah, it was," DJ responded before dapping him up and telling him that he would see him later. Walking to his car, he saw someone standing next to it, but their back was toward him so he couldn't see their face to tell who it was. He was silently praying that it wasn't Yazmine. Their little talk at his birthday party hadn't seemed to work. In fact, he had to recently change his phone number because she wouldn't stop calling him. It was to the point that she was being a borderline stalker. She would show up to all the places he would be at. He even had to get security to escort her out of the stadium one time.

DJ didn't need any distractions. It was pre-season, and they had their first pre-season game next week.

"Excuse me?" DJ said to the lady. When she turned around, it was like the air was knocked out of him. He couldn't believe the woman that had abandon him for her own personal good was standing next to his car.

"Dion… Son, look at you," Cynthia exclaimed, reaching out to give her son a hug only for him to grab her hands and gently push her away from him. It had been years since she had last seen him, but his rejection slowly but surely broke her heart.

"I'm not your son. You lost the right to call me that when you pawned me off to live the best life," DJ expressed to his mother.

There was definitely tension between them. Ever since he could remember, Cynthia always had a problem with putting men before him. Cynthia was a hopeless romantic, and sometimes her search for love caused her to make some of the poorest decisions.

Growing up, Cynthia's life was handed to her on a silver platter. She was the daughter of a judge down in Texas. She had everything she wanted in life. That was until she fell in love with Dion Sr. Cynthia had met him one night at a bar. She was out celebrating one of her girl-friend's promotions at her job. She was a secretary at Powers Law firm. After the first night at the bar, which ended with them in bed together, Cynthia and Dion Sr. were inseparable. So, imagine her surprise when she found out that the man she had fallen in love with was married and had a daughter.

Not wanting to be a homewrecker, she bowed out gracefully, but Dion Sr. never made it easy. Cynthia was a release and break from his reality. Dion Sr. was a man who wanted to change his past. He was once a promising football player in Philadelphia, but he cut his own dreams short when his high school sweetheart, Nikki, got pregnant with their daughter, Reign. They got married right out of high school, and instead of pursuing his education and taking one of the many athletic scholarships to several universities, he decided to get a job to provide for his family.

Dion Sr. never wanted to see his wife and daughter on welfare. Things were good, until they weren't.

Cynthia never knew the monster that truly lived within him. He had put on façade, not wanting to run her away. Yet, he almost lost Cynthia once due to the fact that he was married, only showed her the loving and caring side of him. As he filled her heart and head up with empty promises that he knew he would never live up too. While Cynthia had her head up in the clouds, Nikki and Reign was living in the house of horrors. But little did Cynthia know, her perfect little world would go crashing down when she realized she was pregnant.

When Cynthia announced that she was pregnant with DJ, things started to take a turn for the worst. Dion Sr. told Cynthia that she couldn't have the baby because he was married and was not losing his wife over an outside child.

Cynthia, once again, tried to bow out gracefully. She tried turning to her parents down south, who were prominent people in their community, and the judge also had a long bloodline of being a racist to anyone of color, so finding out she had a baby by a black man was the ultimate sin. There was no way they would accept her half white half black child into their lives.

They did what they knew best and gave her an ultimatum. Her father told her that she could either return down south, just her, returning to a life of privilege, or she could go back up north to be a mother to a nigger.. Cynthia knew she couldn't leave her baby with Dion Sr. So she made the harsh decision of leaving everything she knew to go back to be with Dion Sr., being as though that was the only family she and DJ had, despite her having to be his mistress for the next eight years.

During those eight years, Dion Sr. went to being a full-blown alcoholic. Things got so bad that he lost his job at the construction site for crashing one the cranes he was operating. He failed the Breathalyzer test with flying colors. After losing his job, things turned from bad to worst.

Dion Sr. became physically, emotionally, and mentally abusive. Cynthia rarely saw that side because he only got abusive with her when she tried asking him to leave his wife, or asked him to be attentive to DJ. In his mind, he could care less about her son, and he did his best to not connect with him because he was just another burden that he couldn't afford, like his sister, Reign.. Every night that Dion

Sr. was in a drunken, it would end up with Nikki being physically abused as their daughter watched hopelessly.

Nikki remained in the marriage because he had separated her from her own family, and she was too embarrassed to seek help from the ones she'd turned her back on. Nikki truly loved Dion Sr. and wanted to get him the help he needed. However, no amount of help would help with the amount of self-hate that embedded deep inside of him. Dion Sr.'s life was in shambles. After losing his job, Nikki had to start working multiple jobs to keep them from drowning. Before long, he started using some of her money to help support Cynthia and DJ. The only way he felt like a man was when he installed fear and hurt on the ones who loved him the most.

After years of abuse, Nikki had finally said enough was enough when Dion threatened to harm Reign. No matter how much she loved him, she loved her daughter more, and would never let Dion hurt her. So, she decided to leave. The only problem was Dion made it clear the only way she would ever leave him was in a body bag. Sad, but true. When Nikki gained the guts to leave, Dion killed her and tried to kill his daughter, Reign, then tried to commit suicide.

He went to jail for murder and attempted murder. Receiving a sentence of 10-15 years with a chance of parole. Cynthia was devastated, and once again, she was alone with no family and no man to love her and her baby. As the years went by, she tried her best to raise her son.

She could have been a great mother if she didn't allow the idea of being in love overshadow her needs to be a mother.

When DJ was six, things started to look up for them when his mother met a white man named Connor. He was everything that Cynthia wanted in a man. Conner was tall, white, and a man with a lot of money. He had come from a family of 'old' money. He was also an investment banker, and a very good one at that. Connor wined and dined Cynthia. He even played like he liked her son for a little while. When the time came to ask her hand in marriage, it was then that Connor made it very clear that DJ did not have a place in his life.

His family too would never accept him, and he didn't want to raise another man's child that he couldn't pass along as if it was his own. Hit with another ultimatum, Cynthia knew she couldn't go back to the life of struggles. She wanted to be happy. She needed Connor and all that he offered her. So, she signed her rights over to Dion Sr.'s mother, Barbara, and never looked back when she dropped DJ at her house in the middle of the hood.

Over the years, Cynthia would send two to five thousand dollars a month to help raise DJ. Little did she know, Barbara took all the money and only used it on herself. DJ barely had any clothes or shoes. He had even gone plenty of nights without eating. Barbara hated her grandson, and her granddaughter received the same treatment when she lived with her. Reign was just lucky to have Tasha and Thomas

Harris to save her from the evil lady they called, grandmother.

When DJ turned sixteen, Barbara kicked him out the house. He was living on the streets and jumping from friend to friend house. It wasn't until he was seventeen when he found his sister and things in his life started to change for the better.

Everything DJ went through in his childhood, feeling abandon and abused by his grandmother all led back to Cynthia. He had nothing but pure hate in his heart for the woman who was supposed to love and protect him from the harsh world. But instead, she lived the life of a rich wife and didn't want anyone to know she had a black son. Cynthia past was what it was until her guilt couldn't allow herself to live a lie anymore.

"I'm sorry," Cynthia said, taking a step back, knowing she had just come on a little strong. She looked at her son and smiled at the man he was. "How have you been?"

"What the hell are you doing here? What do you want?" DJ asked, annoyed. So many emotions were running through his body. What was he supposed to say to the woman who'd abandoned him so she could have the life she dreamed of while he was lived in the slums of Philadelphia?

"Dion…."

"Don't call me that. My name is DJ." He hated his name. He hated the man who he was named after.

"Ummm, okay. I know we haven't been close, lately, but I wanted to come back into your life."

"You twenty fucking years late. You left when I needed you the most. You don't know half of the shit I been through, because you decided to let a woman who hated me raise me."

"DJ, if I knew you was being mistreated, I would have taken you away?" Cynthia said, but they both knew that was a lie. He didn't fit into the lifestyle she was building with her husband.

"Where's Connor?"

"He died a couple of months ago," Cynthia sadly said. Once again, she was lonely with no family, and no one to love her. She never had kids with Connor. No matter how much he wanted them. She never had them because she couldn't fathom the thought of loving and raising another child when she couldn't do that for her son.

"So, you had to wait for the muthafucka to die before you could reach out to me?" DJ chuckled. "You're fucking pathetic."

"DJ, I know I did you wrong, but please, let me right them. Words can't explain how much I regret choosing Connor over you. I regret not being the mother you needed me to be. God knows my attention was right. I was a white woman, trying to raise a black man. I didn't know how to do that. Life throws so many curve balls at you because of the color of your skin. How could I teach something I didn't know? But, look at you. I want to be apart of your life again. My family wants to meet you. We can be a family again. "

"Naw, we would never be a family. If you didn't want to

have a black baby, you shouldn't have busted it open for a nigga. There's no coming back into my life. Would you be trying to come back into my life if I was just some regular nigga in jail, or working a nine to five? Naw. You probably seen me on TV and wanted to stake claim, like you raised me. Like you had any parts in my success. Did you think you were going to flaunt me around your rich white friends and family like I was some trophy? Fuck you! The only family I need is my sister, the one whose been holding me down."

"DJ, please just hear me out," Cynthia begged, with tears starting to fall from her eyes. The rejection was too much to handle. She could look into her son's eyes and see nothing but hate. She hated the choices she made. It was selfish of her, and in the end, her marriage with Connor was loveless and cold. His love for her dwindled when she refused to have his kids, and to be honest, the love she had for him turned into hate when she found out he was more interested in men then her.

The whole marriage was a shame. Connor used her as his beard, to hide the fact that he was gay. Then her hate grew when she saw her son get drafted to the NFL. She missed so much of his life that she could never get back. Yet, she had no one to blame, but herself.

"This discussion is over. Don't show your face around here, again. Leave me the fuck alone. Whatever idea you had about us rebuilding a mother and son relationship, dead that shit. Now move from my car before I run your weak ass over."

Cynthia watched her son hop into his car and pull off. She heard him loud and clear, but she refused to accept that he didn't want anything to do with her. Cynthia knew she had no right to barge into his life now that he was very established, however, the guilt she felt over the years would not allow her to accept the defeat. Even if it was the last thing she did, she had to get her son to forgive her.

12

MY LITTLE SECRET

Xscape: If anybody knew that, it was you and your house that I was creepin' to all the time.

"Ahhhh, fuck!" Candace moaned as she felt her little secret's rod slide in and out of her from the back. She was soak and wet, and felt her orgasm building up.

"Shit, you wet as fuck," he groaned while feeling her pussy gripping his dick.

"This the best pussy you ever had, ain't it?" Candace boosted, but he remained silent and just started drilling into her with harder, shorter strokes until she was cumming all over him.

"Come catch this nut," he muttered, pulling out of her. Candace eagerly turned around, taking him into her mouth. She went to work, sucking off her juices. It wasn't long before he was shooting his load down her throat, getting the release he needed.

"Mmmm," Candace smiled as she swallowed everything that he had to offer her. Once she was done and he got up and instantly started putting on his clothes, reality hit her.

"Kameron, you just going to hit and leave?" She screamed as her heart broke, once again. This was the routine with them, but Candace couldn't help the fact that she'd fallen in love with her sister's ex-husband.

"Yeah, you already know why I came over here. Now I have to get back to Olive. We have a Lamaze class to attend," He explained, continuing to get dress.

"First it was Camille, now it's this white bitch, Olive. What the fuck Kameron? For years, I've been your side bitch, picking up where Camille slacked off. When she was so busy working two and three jobs, I was the one who would come and relieve your stress from studying. I was the one doing everything in the bedroom that Camille thought she was too good to do. Threesomes and taking it in the ass to make sure you were satisfied, but you're asking Olive to marry you. Not only that, but she's carrying your baby while I had to abort the child we created together."

"Did you really think I was going to leave my wife for her hoe ass sister?"

"Hoe?" Candace said, highly offended. "That's how you look at me?"

"You're the one still on your knees from just swallowing my nut." Kameron joked, shaking his head. Candace was one woman that he couldn't get rid of, nor did he want too. She was easy and accepted whatever he gave her. She was so jealous of her sister that she would settle for a piece of her life.

"Fuck you! I hate the way you treat me. I was the one who you were trying to talk to first. That was until Millie walked her annoying ass up to us at the party. Ever since that day at the party we've been secretly sleeping together behind Camille's back. What is it about Millie? Shit, what is it about this Olive girl that has your nose wide open?"

"So, you wanted me to divorce your sister, to be with you publicly?" Kameron couldn't understand how Candace thought this was a great idea. He might've been an asshole, but he knew if Camille ever found out about him and her sister, he knew for sure they would both be in body bags.

Camille had a side that he only seen once, and honestly, he never wanted to see it again. It was their sophomore year of college, right after she had told him that she was pregnant. Not sure how to handle it, he broke up with her. Camille was heartbroken. He was the man she was supposed to spend her life with, and he wanted to leave her because he got her pregnant. Two weeks had gone by and Kameron decided to try and date someone to get his mind off Camille and the child that she stated she would not abort.

Long story short, Camille and Kelly caught him at T.G.I. Fridays with a girl name Karmen. Karmen had been after Kameron for quite some time. Camille had cussed

Kameron out and beat Karmen's ass. By the time Kameron and Karmen got into his car, Camille was in her car with Kelly trying to talk her out of the high-speed chase she was surely going to initiate. Kameron and Karmen got two miles down the road before Camille ran him off the road. When Camille ran him off the road, his car crashed into a pole, instantly killing Karmen. Camille just knew her life was over at that moment, but by the grace of God, she didn't have to do any jail time. Instead she had gotten ten-year probation. Camille promised herself to never lose control over a man like that again, but Kameron knew this secret would indeed push her over the edge.

"Yes! What do you think I've been waiting on? I love you, Kam, and when I found out you asked Camille for a divorce, I just knew it was our time to be together."

"When you assume shit, that's when you make a fool out of yourself. Candace, you knew what this was from the start. There will never be a you and me. Even I know how fucked up what we're doing is. What are our kids supposed to be cousins/stepbrother and sister? You want to be an auntie/stepmother? Plus, I see you for what you truly are. You're jealous of Camille and always will be. You want to be her in every aspect, but you can't."

"If I'm such a fucked up individual, why the fuck you keep coming back to me? Huh?" Candace was mad. Kameron words had just hurt her. She admitted, she envied her twin. Ever since they were little, Camille had always seemed to get what she wanted. Camille was always considered the prettier one, being as though they were fraternal twins and didn't look alike. Camille had the longer hair and better body. Camille was the one who their parents were most proud of because she brought home good grades and was always on the honor role.

As for Candace, she barely graduated high school and didn't get accepted to any colleges. Camille was everything she was not, and she hated it.

"I come back because I like the way you suck my dick."

"Fuck you! Get the fuck out of my house! I swear, this is the last time you will ever have a taste of this!" Candace yelled, snatching her robe and putting it on as she walked down the steps and to the front door.

"Yeah, you say that now. How many times we go through this, Candy? You always answer when I call. Just remember, if you still want a monthly deposit hitting your checking account, you shut the fuck up and get with the program." Kameron snapped. He didn't love or have any type of feeling towards Candace. He just loved the way she made his body feel. Candace did things to him and with him that she should have been ashamed of.

Opening the door, Kameron and Candace came face to face with Leon and their daughter, Aleah. Instantly, Candace became nervous as she looked at the confused expressions on Leon and Aleah faces.

"Uncle Kameron, what are you doing here?" Aleah asked, being nosey. She heard her mother plenty of times talking to her girlfriends as to how he and her Aunt Millie had gotten a divorce.

"Oh, hey, baby girl. I was just…" Kameron started, trying to think of a lie but wasn't coming up with one quick enough.

"Aleah, go pack some clothes so I can take you over to the sleepover you were invited too," Leon ordered, and just like that, Aleah forgot she was waiting on an answer and ran up the steps to do what her father told her to do.

"Who house you okayed her to stay the night at without my consent, Leon?" Candace asked with a major attitude. She hated when Leon came over unannounced.

"First, I don't need your fucking consent when the kids are with me. We have joint custody, so chill the fuck out." Leon put Candace in her place. "But if you must know, it's my neighbor, Lashawna's house. Her daughter is having a sleep over for her ninth birthday, and they invited Aleah. Plus, Junior is staying the night at my sister's house to chill with my nephews."

"Oh, so you have my child chilling over ya little girl-friend's house."

"Candace, don't start your shit. You know Lashawna is gay. Plus, she married. Don't try to start an argument with me to divert from the fact that ya'll muthafuckas just got caught red handed."

"Bro, I don't know what you're talking about?" Kameron tried to play dumb. He knew this was a bad look, especially since he was someone Leon considered a close friend. Kameron knew it went against the bro code. Your friend's baby mamas should be off limits.

"Kam, she ain't my bitch," Leon clarified. If one couldn't tell by now, Leon literally despised Candace. "I just thought you would have learned from my mistake, dealing with her scandalous ass. Ya'll know ya'll foul as shit for doing this to Millie."

Leon could care less of what Candace did in her spare time, as long as she wasn't hoeing around his kids, and when she found someone who would take her serious, all he asked was for the man to respect his kids and vice versa.

Hearing Leon speak of her in such disgust brought Candace down to reality. No man she had ever been with actually cared or loved her. She would see other women happy in their relationships and envy the next woman, wanting the same type of love and affection, wanting to be in that woman's shoes. That's why she went after Leon, thinking he would love her the way he loved Kelly. However, all she got in return was a wet ass and two reminders of how her devious plan backfired. The only satisfaction she received about what she had done was the fact that Kelly called off the wedding after she found out that Candace was pregnant with Leon's kids.

The difference between Leon and Kameron was that Leon truly made a mistake and if given another chance, he would never cheat on Kelly again. Leon and Candace hooked up after a drunken night at the strip club.

Candace would always flirt with him, trying to get him

interested in what she had to offer, and he would ignore her every time. She used to work at KINGS, the strip club she cornered him in and asked for a ride home. He was nice and tipsy, causing her to pray the whole ride to her house as he was swerving in and out of the lane. She was even surprised that he didn't get pulled over for a DUI.

When they had finally reached her house, she convinced him to come inside and sleep the liquor off. Little did he know, he had just fell into her trap. Before he could close his eyes, Candace's hand was already in his pants while she straddled him, ready to give him a night of passion that he couldn't refuse. Leon immediately started regretting his actions that morning, making a promise to himself that he would take the night of infidelity to the grave with him. But, his secret was blown when Candace popped up pregnant and didn't have any shame in telling people who fathered her kids.

Leon begged Candace to get an abortion, but she refused. When he realized it was a lost cause, he delivered the heartbreaking news to his fiancée, losing the love of his life. Kelly told him that was something she couldn't forgive him for, and he couldn't do nothing but accept her choice. Candace thought going forward and having the twins would give her the perfect opportunity to become the number one lady in his life. But, she was sadly mistaken. As soon as the twins were born, Leon took her to court and got his rights as a father. They shared joint custody and the only time they spend together as a family was the kids first birthday and

Christmas. The only time he spoke to her was in regards to the children.

Now, unfortunately, now that their children were older and able to have cellphones. Leon had basically cut her out as the middleman a long time ago.

"What Millie don't know won't hurt her," Candace spat, hating the way Leon looked and spoke of her.

"Oh, he is dealing with your bitter ass? What's done in the dark will always come to light. I feel sorry for the both of you when Camille finds out."

"Dad, I'm ready!" Aleah said, running down the steps and out the front door without bothering to say bye to her mother.

"That's my cue," Leon turned around, and left as quickly as he'd come.

"Shit!" Kameron yelled. "Do you think he's going to tell?" He was now pacing back and forth.

"No! You heard him. He don't fucking care what we do." Candace's voice was filled with hurt. It was upsetting to her that Leon didn't even care that she was sleeping with one of his best friends. He didn't even show an ounce of jealousy. "Why are you so worried about it? Ain't like ya'll married anymore."

"Candace, you always talking big shit. You think because we're divorced this won't hurt her? Shit, you think she beat ya ass when she found out you was pregnant by Leon, imagine what she would do now."

"Not a damn thing, because she's too busy getting

dicked down by her new man," Candace said, laughing at Kameron's expense.

"What the fuck you just say?" Kameron barked, gripping Candace up. He had literally felt a surge of jealousy and anger shoot through his body, not knowing why hearing Camille had moved on bothered him so much. As egoistic as it might have sound, Kameron never thought she would move on. Honestly, he didn't think anyone would want her. She was in her late thirties with two kids. In his opinion, she was damaged good. Kameron had the best years of her life, and all Camille had to show for her marriage was some stretchmarks and a little catering business that she had finally started during their divorce.

"Get the hell off me! You obviously worried about the wrong shit and bitch. Don't you have a Lamaze class to go to with your fiancée?" Candace pushed away from him, pissed that Camille obviously still had some strings pulling at Kameron's heart for him to get jealous. "Get the fuck out of my house!"

Kameron didn't even respond as he stormed out of the house, calling Camille only for her phone to go to the voicemail. That's how most of his phone calls went. Camille truly didn't want to have a civil conversation with him. Glancing down at his watch, he silently cursed realizing he was already thirty minutes late to the Lamaze class, and he knew Olive wasn't going to allow him to hear the end of it.

13

24/7

Meek Mills: *Lovin' the shit out you, fuckin' the shit out you. For seven days straight, and now I can't even live without you.*

"*I*'m tired of this shit," Leon hissed as he got out of bed to put on some ball shorts. He and Kelly had just finished two rounds of intense lovemaking, and here she was, gathering his clothes in an effort to tell him he had to bounce.

"Tired of what?" Kelly responded, dumbfounded, handing him his clothes. Camille was dropping Kyron and Kasie off so she could go on her date with DJ. So she didn't want Camille seeing him there.

"Kelly, you know what I'm talking about, sneaking around like we're some fucking teenagers."

Kelly and Leon had been messing with one another on

the low for the past six months. They saw each other at the market one day, and exchanged numbers. That was the beginning of their late-night session booty calls, but Leon wanted more than sex with Kelly. He still loved her and honestly, he wanted to work on them being a couple again.

"Leon, what you want me to do?" Kelly sighed in frustration. For the past couple of nights, this had been the routine, Leon fussing when she made it a point that he couldn't stay the night at her place, or when she would hurriedly leave his.

"I want you to stop bullshitting. I've been patient with you, Kelly, but you're treating me like I'm some trick."

"I'm not treating you like a trick, Leon. Now you're doing too much," Kelly rolled her eyes as she started to put her clothes on.

"Then what do you call it? You basically only hit me up so I can dick you down. Then you jet right after we're done. I try to take you out to eat or on a date, and you always declining my invitation. Yo, what are we doing?"

"We're chilling and enjoying each other's company. I just need you to leave because I'm watching Kyron and Kasie for Camille tonight, and the last thing I need is for them to see you leaving my house."

"Why would that be such an issue? Nobody have a say in what we do in our lives, but us." Leon couldn't wrap his head around the fact that Kelly wanted to keep them a secret.

"The last thing I need in my life is drama, especially

from ya baby mama. Do you know how stupid I would look to people, and my family, if I gave you another chance? You humiliated me. Not only did you cheat on me, but you had twins with my best friend's sister."

"That's what you care about? What others may think. Nobody's perfect, and I'm not telling you to forget the past, but I'm trying to move forward. I don't fuck with Candace scandalous ass. I never have after the one night I cheated. I got my rights for my kids and I barely speak to the bitch. I love my kids, but Candace shouldn't have been their mother. I should have never cheated on you, but I can't change the past."

"Can we do this another time? Camille will be here in a couple of minutes," Kelly peered down at the clock on her nightstand. She didn't realize that it have gotten that late. Leon chuckled, angrily, as he walked pass her and down the steps. He was over Kelly and her childish games. He knew his past actions was foul, but why rekindle and react on old feelings just to take it nowhere?

"Leon... Leon, don't be mad."

"I'm not mad. I'm just done," he said, swinging the door open to find Camille and the kids about to knock.

"Hey, Leon." Camille was caught off guard but gave him a hug. She honestly felt bad about the whole situation with him and Candace. She believed him when he said it was a mistake and he would never do it again. She knew her sister had been after him since the day she laid eyes on him, not even caring that he was Kelly's fiancée. Camille knew

Candace was a jealous person and always wanted what the other person had.

"Wassup, sis? Damn, ya'll getting big. How are you, princess?" He greeted Kasie, causing her courtesy like a princess. "You still got that arm on you, Kyron?"

"Yeah, you have to come see me play this season. They got me starting."

"Most definitely. I'm trying to get Junior into football, but he's more into basketball.

"I know ya'll see ya'll Auntie over here," Kelly said, causing everybody's attention to go on her.

"Hey, girl," Camille said, giving Kelly the side eye.

"Alright, ya'll. Kyron, don't forget to tell me when your football games are. I'm definitely going to pull through. Alright, Camille, sis, you're looking good?"

"Thanks." She appreciated the compliment and Leon made his way to his car.

"Kasie and Kyron, put ya'll things in the guest bedroom and then get ready for dinner. I already ordered us pizza and hot wings," Kelly told them as she and Camille sat on the sofa.

"So… Are you going to explain Leon?." Camille asked.

"Girl, I don't even know how I got back into dealing with him." Kelly shook her head.

"What's the problem with Leon? Kelly, I know what happened in the past was fucked up, but I can look at that man and tell you, he still loves the ground you walk on. I don't think he's even been serious with anyone since ya'll called it quits, and he hates Candace guts. So she's not an issue if that's what you're worried about."

"So you say. But how would I look dating him again after all he done."

"You can't date him, but you can fuck him." Camille said, shaking her head at her best friend. "Shit, I know ya'll wasn't in here holding hands. How do you really feel?"

"Even though Leon did me dirty in the past, I still love him. That shit never went away and the feeling just got stronger since we've reconnected. I just don't want to be out here looking like a fool."

"You're not looking like a fool because you want love. Go ahead and miss out on happiness because you're afraid of what other people may say or think."

"Okay, best friend, I hear you preaching, but when are you going to take your own advice?" Kelly caught Camille off guard with that.

"What are you talking about?"

"You and DJ been talking for how long? A couple of months now, and you don't see a future with him?"

"My situation with DJ is different. He's ten years younger than me. Still in his twenties. Still living life, and honestly, I'm not looking for anything serious. I just got out of a marriage."

"Hmmm."

"Hmmm, what, Kelly?"

"Girl, you know you just spit some bullshit out to me. Camille, this is the happiest I've seen you in years. When you're free from the kids, you spend all your time with him. If it's not that serious, why didn't you just hit and quit?" Kelly asked a good question. Honestly, the question of them taking things farther than what they were already doing had never come up. DJ was just good company, and he was definitely helping the healing process of the divorce.

"Do I like DJ? Yes. But honestly, I care too much for him to be a rebound and vice versa. This past year he had just gotten out of a bad relationship, and even though he spends a lot of time with me, I know he out there doing him." Knowing DJ was probably entertaining other women did bother her, but she tried to keep her true feelings at bay.

"Okay. But tonight, he's taking you as his date to his charity event. Girl, you are going to be amongst his family and friends and coworkers. Like, what he do for a living anyway?"

"Honestly, I don't know. It never came up," Camille said, instantly feeling awkward. Here she was, secretly catching feelings for a man she barely knew. "But I also catered the event, too. So, I'm sure that's the only reason why I was even invited."

"Keep trying to downplay what ya'll have going on. Yes, he hired you to cater the event, but he also made you hire a head chef to take over while you sit and enjoy the event. If he didn't want to share this moment with you, you would be in the back with your chef hat on." Kelly pointed out the obvious.

"Speaking of the devil." Camille smiled before

answering her phone. It was DJ letting her know that he was outside.

Walking out the front door, he was standing against the car in a Black Armani suit with black Gucci shoes, holding a bouquet of roses.

"Damn, you look beautiful," he said, walking towards Camille. She had on an off the shoulders black tight fitting dress that showed off all of her amazing curves.

"You clean up pretty well yourself." Camille smiled back. It was just something about seeing him dressed up in a suit and tie that had her ready to do some ungodly things to him.

"Ya'll have a good time tonight," Kelly yelled from the doorway.

"We will, and thank you," DJ said to Kelly, knowing the only reason Camille was able to get away, was because Kelly had offered to watch the children after Kameron kept ignoring her phone calls. Kameron was really starting to take being a father to a whole dead-beat level. The only time he spent time with the kids was during the weekend. However, he extended his practice hours so he worked weekends, leaving him not able to hold up his part of the custody agreement.

"Are you ready for your big night?" Camille asked.

"Yeah," DJ smirked. He had finally started his charity, something he always wanted to do when he was in position to make a difference. Last year, he chose three high school seniors who had come from a similar background as him and wanted to further their education. Those three students were now receiving a full ride due to the Dion 'DJ' Roberts Scholarship Foundation. DJ wanted to start the charity sooner, but dealing with the drama and negative exposure from Yazmine and her pregnancy, he didn't want anything to overshadow the moment.

"Well, I want you to know that I'm proud of you. You're doing big things. Your helping these children heightened their chances of success, giving them financial backing of furthering their education. You are a one of a kind man, DJ, and thank you for allowing me to be a part of it."

"Thank you." DJ grabbed her hand and kissed it. "I got something for you." Going inside of his suit jacket, he pulled out three tickets to the Eagles first game of the season. All in the skybox. "So, I know you was trying to get some tickets to take Kyron to the Eagle game."

"Yeah, I tried to get some tickets the other day and they were sold out, which made me so upset because I wasn't the one who promised Kyron I would take him to the game. But of course, Kameron never comes through on his promises, and Kyron been taking the divorce and his father's engagement very hard. This was supposed to had been a step in the right direction to get their relationship back on track."

"Well, you don't worry about that. Honestly, it's not your job for Kameron to be a father to his son, or get their relationship back on track. Kameron did the damage and now he has to be the one to fix it. But I know you said Kyron was really looking forward to being at the game so, I have three tickets for you, Kyron and baby girl if she want to go or maybe one of Kyron friends."

"DJ, you didn't have to do this," she said, looking at the tickets. "Skybox seats? Oh my God. These are way too much. I have to give some money towards these."

"Don't insult me." DJ eyed her like she was crazy.

"I'm sorry. It's just, I know these cost a lot of money and you bought three."

"You do know what I do for a living, right?" DJ asked, wondering how she thought those tickets was too expensive for him.

"No. We've never really talked about it, but it's obviously a really good job if you're paying for three student tuitions."

"I work for the Philadelphia eagles organization. So, I get a little discount. Trust me, it didn't break my pockets. I just want ya'll to enjoy yourselves."

"I'll try. I know nothing about football beside what Kyron tried to teach me, but thank you, again. You don't even understand how happy this will make him."

"No problem." DJ said as Camille leaned over to kiss him.

"So, what do you do for the Philadelphia Eagles?" Camille asked, now curious.

"Mr. Roberts, we're here," the driver announced before DJ could answer the question.

The event was being held at the Drexelbrook Special Event Center. Inside was beautiful. He had gotten Teddy's wife, Kennedy, to decorate the banquet hall. They had cameras capturing every moment.

"DJ, can we please take a picture of you?" One of the photographers asked and Camille let go of his hand.

"What are you doing?"

"I'm letting you take the picture they are asking for." Camille smiled, wanting him to have his moment.

"Girl, you're his date. Get in the picture with my brother," Reign said with a warm smile as she walked up on DJ and Camille. She had been waiting to meet this mystery woman that had DJ's nose wide open.

"Okay, then," Camille said, chuckling. You would of thought Reign was a proud mama taking pictures on her phone. More photographers started to gather around, and it seemed like they were more pressed than anything, especially when they started asking questions about their relationship. DJ ignored them and took a couple more pictures before walking off to get the night started.

Camille was sitting at the table with DJ, his sister Reign and her husband Pharaoh. Pharaoh brothers and their wives, their sister Queen with her longtime boyfriend, Kelz, was also at the table along with Pharaoh parents Maria and Royal. Sitting at the table next to them was Angelo, Cream and Ira with their ladies and Teddy and his wife Kennedy.

"Congratulations, DJ. You know we're proud of you."

"Thanks, Mama Maria. I appreciate everybody for coming," he said as Camille just stood beside him.

"No problem." Everybody said at once.

"So, are you going to introduce us to your date." Reign asked, being nosey. Ever since the Yazmine situation, she knew DJ had decided to become a little man whore. However, lately she had noticed he would only speak about one lady and the lady standing next to him face seemed quite familiar. She actually remembered her from the night of DJ's birthday party.

"This beautiful lady right here is, Camille. Camille, this is my sister, Reign, and her husband, Pharaoh...." DJ introduced as he went around the table introducing her to everyone then walked her over to the next table to do the same.

"It's nice meeting everyone," Camille said with a pleasant smile. She was nervous meeting DJ's family. She knew the age difference was noticeable and she didn't know how they would react.

"Girl, I'm happy to finally meet you. DJ was keeping you a secret," Reign said.

"So, I was a secret DJ?" Camille asked DJ, jokingly, with one eyebrow raised.

"Naw, you wasn't a secret, I just didn't know if I wanted you to meet her crazy ass, yet. You might get ghost on me for real," DJ said, making everybody laugh. Reign had been pressuring him on meeting the woman who he had been spending his time with.

As the night started, dinner was served and people started to speak amongst themselves. Tonight was a huge night. Not only were the three students receiving full scholarships, but there were a few sponsors that were interested in donating towards the scholarship fund as well. The room was field with prominent people with lots of money to give to charity.

"DJ, are you ready to network?" The event planner went over to the table. She had everything set to go off without a hitch.

"Yes, Daria. If you will, please excuse me."

"Camille, I must say, everything smelled and tasted delicious. You did your thing with the catering. I also have some people asking for your business card. They are interested in you catering some of their events they have coming up," Daria said, handing Camille some of the business cards that were given to her to give to Camille.

"Thanks, let me go in the back to make sure everything is good with the desserts."

"No, that's why you hired Jose. I want you to enjoy the night. No, work," DJ whispered in her ear, pulling Camille into him.

"Yes, Sir." Camille smiled and sat back down.

"Now, DJ, I have a couple of people that I will like you to meet. They are invested in donating towards the charity."

DJ walked around the room and pitched to the sponsors why they should donate to his charity. Camille kept stealing glances at him. She loved seeing him in that atmosphere. The conservation she and Kelly had before she left her house kept replaying in her head.

Was she ready to move on? Was it too soon to move on? Did DJ even want to make more of their situation? Camille thought while stealing another glance at the same time DJ was stealing one at her. Winking, he flashed her his famous smile.

"So, my brother seems to really like you," Reign stated to Camille, bringing her out her thoughts. She had been sitting back, watching the interaction between DJ and Camille throughout the dinner.

"You think so?" Camille asked.

"Girl, I know so. If he didn't, he wouldn't have brought you around his family," she said, causing Camille to look around the table at his family. "DJ is not in the habit of bringing random females around the people he love. So, I guess whatever ya'll have going on is serious to him. DJ had only brought one girl around us, which was his ex. Ever since that disaster, he's been very selective. All it took was fifteen minutes of me being around that girl and I kindly showed her to my front door."

"I can tell you, my feelings are definitely mutual, and I guess I'm on ya good side because I haven't been showed the door, yet." Camille joked, causing them both to laugh.

"Yes, I like you. I can see you balancing him out." Little did Camille know, before her coming into DJ's life, DJ was becoming known as NFL bad boy. He was constantly in the blogs, TMZ and other gossip site being seen with a different woman. However, being with Camille seemed to have slowed him down.

"I guess you can say the same thing about me when it comes to him. My best friend just told me she hadn't seen me this happy in years. Sad part about it, I was married. But what did homegirl do to get kicked out in fifteen minutes? DJ doesn't talk much about his past relationship. All he told me was that it ended badly."

"What didn't that girl do? When I first met Yazmine, she walked inside my house without speaking."

"And you waited a full fifteen minutes before kicking her out?" Camille said. "Yazmine wouldn't have even gotten pass the threshold." Camille felt like that was the most disrespectful thing a person could do, walk into your house without speaking.

"I tried to be nice. You know, everybody wasn't raised with manners. Plus, DJ seemed to have really liked her, and that was the first girl he had ever brought home. I didn't want to come off as the overbearing big sister, but honey, fifteen minutes was all I needed to see her true colors. She was nothing like DJ described her to be. I guess it was all a front. With the life DJ live, it can either make or break a relationship. Yazmine allowed DJ's success to go to her head, and she started feeling herself. When your relationship is in the public eye, you have to be careful, and it's easy to fall for the bullshit, thinking the grass is greener on the other side."

"Public eye?" Camille asked in confusion.

"Excuse me, Camille" Queen said, interrupting Reign and Camille's conversation. "Your food was amazing."

"Thank you."

"We're throwing my parents a surprise dinner for their

30th wedding anniversary, and I would love for you to cater the party."

"Yes! Of course," Camille said, handing Queen her business card. She couldn't believe how many opportunities were opening up for her just from catering DJ's charity event. "Just let me know when you're ready for a taste testing."

"Perfect." Queen said, smiling. That was one thing off her checklist for this party.

"So, I own a day spa. You should come join us next Friday. Every third Friday, I shut the spa down early for me and my family to enjoy a much-needed spa treatment."

"Wait. You're the owner of Reign's Day Spa?" Camille asked, putting two and two together. "I heard so much about the spa. I'm definitely down." Camille had wanted to treat herself, but running her business and taking care of the kids while picking up Kameron's slack, she never really found time for herself.

"Cool. Before we leave here, I'll get your information so I can hit you up and give you the details." Reign said before they joined the conversation at the table. So far, Reign did like Camille, but she needed to get a better feel for her. Reign was super overprotective of her brother, and vice versa. Reign refused to allow DJ to have a repeat of Yazmine.

14

IT'S JUST US AGAINST THE WORLD

DJ KHALED & SZA: BACKS AGAINST THE WALL, MIDDLE FINGER IN THE AIR.

"*D*J, you're doing great. I just want to personally introduce you to one more person before you go up to do your speech, and the recipients could give their acceptance speech. Then people can mingle for the remainder of the event and go home," Daria explained as they walked around the room. The event was going lovely, and she had to give herself a pat on the back. The turn out was absolutely amazing.

"Now, the person I'm about to introduce you to is Judge Roberts. He's from down south. His wife Carolyn personally reached out to me for an invitation to the gala. Carolyn is very huge on charities. So, for her to personally reach out to contribute to your charity is a good sign."

"Cool." DJ loved the fact that his charity was ringing

bells. He was honestly honored that Mrs. Roberts reached out to be apart of his big day.

"Judge Roberts and Mrs. Roberts, I wanted to formally introduce you to the man of the hour. This is Dion 'DJ' Roberts. DJ, this is Judge Roberts and his lovely wife that I was just telling you so much about."

"Thank you both for reaching out and attending my first annual charity gala," DJ greeted them as he shook Judge Roberts hand. Mrs. Roberts just went straight in for a hug, catching him off guard, but he returned the love.

"No problem, son. My wife is huge on charities. Happy wife and happy life. Plus, I'm a huge football fan. I've been watching you play since you were in college," Judge Roberts admitted, literally pulling Carolyn off of DJ. It was like she didn't want to let him go.

"Oh, yeah? That's wassup? I definitely have to get you some tickets to the next game."

"That would be great…"

"What are you doing here?" DJ asked his egg donor when he saw her walk up to them. He was beyond pissed that he couldn't even hide his disdain for her. In all honestly, he wanted to kick her out of the Gala, but he didn't want to give the press anything negative to talk about.

"DJ," Daria hissed with widen eyes. She couldn't believe how rude he was being, especially towards Judge Roberts and Carolyn's daughter, Cynthia. The Roberts were prominent people and their donation would be a great contribution to the charity. A good word from them, they could introduce other people to the charity. The more money that was raised, the more scholarships could be given out to students in need.

"Dion..." Cynthia started but quickly corrected herself. "DJ, we're not here to start any trouble or butt into your life. We're just here to support you."

DJ stared at them through cold, darkened eyes as he grinded his teeth in an effort to calm down. At that moment, he realized why Carolyn was hugging him like, had she let him go, he would disappear. They were his grandparents. DJ couldn't understand why Cynthia thought popping up to his charity gala would've been such a great idea. He'd already told her to stay away from him, and he damn sure didn't want to meet his rich grandparents who didn't want anything to do with him when he was a child. His grandmother, Barbara, who was his father's mother, never hesitate to remind him he was a piece of trash that his father, mother nor rich grandparents didn't want. She was his last and only family member, and living with her was like hell on earth.

"Listen, I'm not going to allow you to ruin my night and the night of my recipients. I already told you there's nothing for us to talk about, nor is there a chance that we can build our relationship," he expressed to Cynthia who had tears forming in her eyes. Cynthia just wanted DJ to know she was coming to him from a genuine place, and honestly, his rejection was starting to become too hard to bare.

"If you want to donate to the charity, great. Do it

because you truly want to make a change in a young person life. I don't want you to think donating to my charity will give you the slightest chance of becoming apart of my life. You didn't want me when I was younger, so don't want me now. Keep the same energy. I'm the same black grandson you turned your back on."

"You think those thugs over there are your family?" Judge Roberts asked looking over at the Black family along with Angelo and Cream. "You surround yourself with a whole bunch of drug dealers." He knew exactly who they were. How could he not? He was one of the judges that the Blacks didn't have in their pockets. Judge Roberts didn't like DJ's rejection and now he was pissed. His entitlement blinded him to the fact that DJ had a valid reason as to shun them from his life.

"Patrick!" Carolyn hissed, knowing her husband was making matters worse. She knew their rejection of him would bite them in the ass.

"Your true colors showing. I guess all black men who have tattoos and are successful by not throwing a football or basketball are thugs. I guess I'm a thug, too. You don't know my life. The sad part about it is, I would probably be in jail or dead if it weren't for my sister and the people sitting at the table. Enjoy your night." With that, DJ walked off, livid.

"How dare he talk to us like that?" Judge Roberts hissed, embarrassedly, as he looked around the ballroom to make sure no one had seen the interaction.

"I know. All we wanted to do was support him and this is

the treatment we get," Carolyn co-signed, snidely. She too was a little upset by the way DJ handled them.

"What did you expect? You thought you were going to get a warm greeting with a bunch of hugs and kisses when he realized exactly who you were?"Cynthia asked.

"No, but that boy can show a little more respect," No one had ever in Judge Roberts life spoke to him in that manner.

"You have to understand his anger. I abandon him when he needed me the most. I abandoned him because the things I wanted could not include him."

"That's the past!" Carolyn hissed. She honestly believed that DJ was making a huge deal out of nothing. In her eyes, his life turned out to be great.

"DJ has every right to feel the way he does. I told you guys this wasn't a great idea. I told you I had to be the one to make amends with my son first. Then introduce you to him. He hates me and this probably just pushed me back ten steps." Cynthia said. For her parents meeting DJ and coming into his life was just for show. They wanted the bragging rights of saying they were his grandparents, but Cynthia just wanted her son back.

"Are you going to tell me what that was about?" Daria queried.

"No, they are irrelevant. Lets continue with the event because I'm ready to get up out of here."

"Okay. Are you okay?"

"Naw, but I will be."

"Well, I want you to go up there with a clear head. We can switch the program around and have the recipients give their scholarship first and allow them to give their speeches. Then you can come up," Daria suggested.

"Yeah, that would be good." DJ agreed before heading over to his table with his family and Camille.

"You okay, babe?" Camille asked, noticing his vibe was off.

"Yeah. My sister was grilling you, wasn't she?"

"Really, DJ," Reign asked, appalled.

"No. I actually think we hit it off pretty well," Camille said as he kissed the back of her hand. Just seconds ago, he was fuming on the inside, but just being around her presence seemed to had calm him.

The entire room was filled with emotions as the guest listened to the recipients give the acceptance speeches for the scholarship. Hearing the life experiences of the students that were chosen made the goal of his charity very clear. Those children had come from nothing, and the only way they could move forward was to go to school. The recipients were so grateful, and it gave DJ great pride to had been a helping hand. Everybody's not good at sports, but that shouldn't be the only way a child should not go to school free of debt.

"Now, I will like to introduce the man that made this all possible. Not only is he the quarterback for the Philadelphia Eagles." The crowd cheered. "He is also one of the bleeding hearts behind the city of brotherly love. When he became successful, he didn't turn his back on his community. Instead, he's been uplifting the community in every way possible. Please give a warm welcome to, Dion 'DJ' Roberts!" The announcer said as DJ stood to walk to the stage.

Philadelphia Eagles Quarterback.

Camille silently thought. She was pretty sure the shock expression was displayed on her face. When DJ said he worked for the Eagles organization, she never thought he was the quarterback. Now everything Reign was talking about having a relationship in a public eye had became very clear. Thinking back to the night she and her sisters went out, Cassie did say it was a Philadelphia Eagles football player's birthday party. She shook her head for not putting two and two together. Now she had more questions swarming her head.

Why would DJ not tell her about his profession? Was she ready for a relationship in the public eye? She was just getting use to dating a younger man. Was she ready to have the world judge her for her choice in men?

"I know that look," Mama Maria whispered into Camille's ear. She could tell just by the look on her face that she didn't know exactly who DJ truly was.

"What look?"

"The look of doubt. Listen, baby, DJ is a great man and is very private. The only reason why his last relationship was in the public eye was because his ex was an attention whore and loved the fame that came with him.

"He's younger than me," Camille said, looking at Mama Maria.

"You see that fine man sitting next to me? Well that's my husband, Royal, and he's five years younger than me. Trust, if I cared what people thought about him being younger than me, we wouldn't have the beautiful family or a successful marriage. Listen, you can't allow other people opinions to stop your happiness. You and DJ are grown people. Most of the time people are just jealous, and trust me, misery loves company." Mama Maria voiced, and Camille listened to every word before turning her attention to DJ.

"I want to thank everybody that came out tonight and who donated to the charity and to the recipient. Nyla, Rasheed, and Kirk, I am very proud and honor to have you as the first recipients of the **DJ Roberts Scholarship** fund. You're strong people that overcame many obstacles. Please give them a round of applause because they definitely set the bar high for the next years candidates. They truly deserved this scholarship plus more." DJ started and everyone applauded the young students.

"This is my first charity and it means so much to me. Just like our recipients, I too had a hard life. It wasn't until I was seventeen years old that I was shown love from a family and had a true support system. I was a son of a man who could care less about me. I don't remember having any type of relationship with my father. All I remember was him being abusive towards my mother. He went to jail for murder of his wife and the attempted murder of my sister. My mother and I was his second family, one he didn't claim."

DJ eyes locked on Cynthia who had tears in her eyes. Not only was she embarrassed, but she also hated that was the only memory he had of his parents being a family.

"A couple of years after my father went to jail, my mother fell in love with a man who liked her more. He was her race and had lots of money. However, the downside of wanting the life her husband could provide was he didn't want her black son to be apart of their life. Instead of being a mother, she shipped me off to a place of hell. She sent me to live with my gambling, alcoholic, abusive grandmother. This lady was my father's mother. She hated me. Even though my mother was sending her a couple of thousand dollars a month to support me, I went without food, clothes and she barely let me wash my body. Things got so bad that I eventually became homeless. She wanted me to suffer, because in her eyes, I was one of the reasons why her son was in jail. My father's wife was trying to leave the abusive relationship with my sister, and he killed her when he realized she was serious. My grandmother put that burden on me at a young age. It had gotten to the point where I would do anything to survive. Football was my safe haven, but as soon as practice was over, or we won the game, my cold reality hit like a ton of bricks.

Money and gifts was the way my mother dealt with her guilt. For years, I hadn't seen her, but she came to Philadelphia on my sixteenth birthday with a brand-new Benz. I was a sixteen-year-old with a car that men in my neighborhood couldn't even afford. By the time I was seventeen, I was fully homeless. I put on a front so the school or my coach wouldn't know. The last thing I wanted was to be placed in the system. My own grandmother treated me like this, so I could only imagine how someone else would've treated me. It's crazy how I met my sister, Reign, but as you all know, she is the biggest blessing God had given me.

It wasn't until I found my twenty-five-year-old sister, at the time, that I learned the true meaning a family and love. Since the first day I came into her life, she had been my support system and she changed my life. I was no longer living under the bridges in my car. I had my own bed and room, I didn't have to sneak into the high school to shower and handle my hygiene before practice and after school let out. Reign, you saved me," DJ vented.

He had never been shy to talk about his life experience.

"I know you hate when I give you praise, but the world deserves to know what you did for me. Not only did my sister come into my life, but so did my brother-in-law, Pharaoh Black. He also helped me stay on track. If it wasn't for him, I was probably about to blow this whole football thing. I actually want to give the whole Black family, and Angelo and Cream, a huge shout out for not just accepting my sister, but allowing me to be apart of their family. These people are my support system. Without them, I wouldn't be here. However, everybody's not as lucky as me. Everybody doesn't have a support system, let alone a million-dollar arm that could get them to be the first draft pick in the 2014 NFL draft." He turned to the recipients. "This is why I started this charity. I want to be a support system for people in need. This charity is not just for the students who want to go to college or a university. Any student can apply even if they are applying to trade school. This charity is for you, too. It's not always as easy as some people try to portray it to be. I know the struggle, and with my charity, I hope we can change one-person's life at a time. Thank you."

There wasn't a dry eye in the room. Listening to DJ's hard knock life had Camille in tears. Being in DJ's presence, one would've never thought he had been through any of this. Now it was clear why he was so humble. On the other side of the room, Cynthia had to excuse herself as she felt like shit. Money and gifts was the only way to show her love, especially since her husband Connor wouldn't allow him to live with them. Carolyn got up and walked over to her grandson before he could reach his seat.

"DJ…" Carolyn called his name, silently praying that he didn't cause a scene

DJ looked at the little white woman in front of him with cold eyes. Granted, Carolyn or Judge Roberts didn't have to do anything for him because that was Cynthia's job, but they weren't there for him either, and didn't even try to make an effort to get to know him or make sure he was good.

"This check is for you, to go towards the charity. I love

the difference you are trying to make in these young people lives," Carolyn said, personally handed him a check for twenty thousand dollars.

"Thank you for your contribution," DJ said, coolly.

"I understand why you wouldn't want anything to do with us. Your life was horrific, and we could have done something about it. However, the past is the past and we can only move forward. Hopefully, you find it in your heart to learn to forgive so we can build a relationship." She too felt like the worst person in the world. She couldn't imagine what DJ was doing to get the money he needed to survive.

"Thank you. Enjoy your evening." DJ dismissed them before walking away. It might've been easy for Carolyn to say the past is the past, but that's only because she didn't live the life he lived. Before Reign came into his life, DJ was a straight up jack boy, and it would've been only a matter of time before he ended up dead or in jail. DJ was okay leaving the past in the past, however, the past was trying to become a part of his future and that's where his problem lies.

"I'm so proud of you," Royal said. Mama Maria and Royal loved the fact that he didn't hide the fact that they were his family. The Black name rang bells and it wasn't always for the best. Pharaoh and his brothers were the connects of Philly. Anything underground illegal went through them. Being as though DJ name was a brand, it would've been easier for him to distance himself from them when he was in the public eye.

"Thanks. I meant everything I said up there," DJ voiced

before he saw Judge Roberts and Carolyn leave the ballroom.

"DJ, I'm proud of you, too, and a little shock as to who you really are," Camille whispered in his ear.

"I liked the fact you were genuine interest in me and not my money or my status. Just me. Now that you know I hope things don't change."

"Nothing will change. You still the same DJ I met at the Jameson Hotel. The man who is slowly but surely becoming my peace," Camille said, completely understanding why he would keep his job a secret. She just hoped things didn't change drastically in her life.

15

JUST MIGHT

Summer Walker: Keep playing, loving is a losing game, and I just can't take it anymore. That love is a losing game. So I just might be a hoe.

Olive waddled into the break room to find a group of nurses talking only to get silent when she walked in. That was a clear sign that they had been talking about her. Something that had been going on since she and Kameron came out as the newly engaged couple.

"Don't worry about them," Jessica said as she walked in behind Olive. Jessica was a nurse that basically stayed to herself. She didn't befriend coworkers because she knew the girls at the job could be messy.

"Okay," Olive said, holding her head up high as she walked to the refrigerator to grab her and Kameron's lunch.

"Homewrecker." Someone in the group voiced loud enough for Olive to hear.

"How about you mind the business that pays you. Talking trash like she doesn't have the pull to have you fired. Stop being some miserable, bitches, because she got the man ya'll wish ya'll had," Jessica said, shutting the nurses right on up. After getting her lunch out the refrigerator, she headed out the break room, heading to her car where she usually ate lunch and talked on the phone with her sister.

"Hey, Jessica... Thank you." Olive said, stopping her. Since she and Kameron had come out as a couple, things had been bad. Not only had family transitions been hard, but the friends she did have at work seemed to have a sense of loyalty towards Camille.

"No problem."

"Do you believe what you said in there?" She asked, causing a look of confusion to plaster on Jessica's face. "You know, about them being jealous of my relationship with Kameron."

Jessica looked at Olive and then shook her head. "Honestly, no. I just don't like bullies. They too old to be doing that high school crap, but, listen, most of the staff has been here from the beginning. They've worked with Camille when she worked as the receptionist. It's just as much of Camille's blood, sweat, and tears in this office as Kameron's. You need to gain some tough skin. Regardless of what you think, you were part of the reason for a marriage failure.

Most of the women in here are married, and knowing you was Kameron's side chick for however long before he divorced his wife, they're not going to be cool with it. They will never like you or invite you out. Not because of their loyalty to Camille, but because they can't trust a woman like you around their men."

"I don't want their men," Olive said, offended. What happened between she and Kameron was the first time she had ever dealt with a married man, or any man that was in a relationship for that matter. In her mind, she wasn't this homewrecking woman that everybody was trying to pin her out to be.

"And, I'm sure when Camille convinced Kameron to hire you, she didn't think you would be the reason why their marriage went down the drain. Ya'll foul as hell. But this was ya'll decision. I'm not judging you. Just grow a pair of balls. People are going to judge you and talk shit about you. That's just life. But it looks like you taking Kameron cheating ass off her hands was a blessing in disguise, because now her catering business is doing well. Plus, she may have found someone better. The Shade Room just posted a picture of her and DJ Roberts. It's just gossip, but they announced that she was the caterer at his event."

"So, she was the help?" Olive slipped and said in a nasty tone. She knew she shouldn't have been the one that disliked Camille. It should've definitely been the other way around, but it just seemed like since the divorce, things had change drastically between she and Kameron. So she blamed Camille for all of the changes in their relationship. Kameron seemed disinterested in her. He had been forcing himself into work and their sex life had become damn near non-existent.

"The help? Hating is not a good look sweetheart. Camille has her own catering business and already catering events for celebrities. You have the man you wanted, right? Anyway, DJ Roberts probably dropped a big ass check on her. He's the quarterback for the Eagles. And she's definitely more than the help. They have people wondering if they are a couple. They were seen cozied up with one another at his charity event. It might be the start of a budding romance. If it is, all power to her, because she definitely upgraded," Jessica said, heading out the door to sit in her car in the parking lot while Olive headed over to Kameron's office with their lunch.

"Candace, I'm not doing this with you. I cannot come over later on tonight because Camille is dropping the kids off." Olive heard Kameron as she opened his office door. Her heart dropped at the thought of him cheating on her.

Who is Candace?

"I'll call you back, somebody just walked into my office," Kameron said, rushing off the phone while looking at his fiancée. "Why didn't you knock before entering?"

"I didn't know I had too. I brought you lunch. I made chicken casserole last night for dinner. The dinner you were supposed to join me and my parents," Olive said, but it looked like he had brought lunch already from a soul food place called Crafty Soul.

"I wish I would have known. I wouldn't have bought this, and I told you I had a thing with the kids," Kameron lied. The truth was, he was with Candace, getting a much needed release. Kameron loved Olive, but ever since she'd became pregnant with his son, he had became less attracted to her. He didn't know what it was, but the spark in their relationship was gone. Truth be told, Kameron loved the excitement of having a forbidden relationship.

"Who's Candace?"

"She's Camille's twin sister. I promised her that I would mount her TV on the wall." The lie rolled off his tongue with so much ease.

"Why do you still have communication with her?"

"Just because me and Camille didn't work out don't mean I can't help the family out."

"Okay." Olive didn't really believe the answer he had just given her, but she decided not to go further into the topic. The last thing she wanted to do was start an argument. That would only give him a reason to stay away.

"So, when are we going to move in together? Junior will be here in a couple of months, and I hope you're ready to raise him as a family. A family that lives in the same house."

"This weekend I was thinking about looking at houses. We need a new house that's going to accommodate all of us. Kyron, Kasie and Junior."

"Okay, will the kids be there this weekend, or will this be a me and you thing?"

"Camille is supposed to be dropping them off after school," Kameron answered and he could see the disappointment in Olive's face. It wasn't that Olive didn't want his kids to be a part of their lives, it was just, Kyron really left a bad taste in her mouth and she tried her best to stay away when he was around. "Olive, how are we supposed to be family if you have a problem being around my kids?" Kameron then asked.

"I don't have a problem. I just know that Kyron doesn't like me, nor does he hide the fact."

"Kyron don't even like me right now, and maybe if you let me go about things the way I planned than he wouldn't have such a dislike for you. Kyron is like his mother. He can hold a grudge, but at the end, he will eventually forgive the both of us."

"Okay. Maybe I can stay the weekend with you guys, and we all do something fun." Olive said, thinking of a solution. "What does he like to do?"

Kameron thought about her question, and he honestly couldn't tell her. He believed providing for his children was what a good father consisted of. He felt like he had given his children a way better life than he ever had, and that alone made him feel like a great father, not realizing kids made memories off of the time they spent with their parents, and not the materialistic things that Kameron kept giving.

"I know he likes football. I was actually supposed to get

him the tickets to the game today, but I never got around to doing it." Kameron said, shaking his head, knowing his son probably hated him more, especially since he didn't have the balls to tell him that he wasn't taking him.

"How about we do a mini vacation to Atlantic City, or the indoor waterpark that all the kids loved. I think it's called, Sahara Sam's."

"Yeah that sounds cool," Kameron said, liking the idea. "That will give all of us a chance to bond."

"I'll call them now to see if we can get rooms for this weekend." Olive suggested, getting up to make some calls, thinking the weekend was what they needed to get everybody back on track.

The rest of the day at work, Olive took Jessica's advice and decided to ignore the hateful remarks that were being made. Regardless of some considering her a homewrecker, the truth was, the Davidson's home was already broken, way before she stepped in the picture.

DING! DONG!

"Olive, get the door," Kameron yelled. He was in the bedroom packing his clothes for their weekend getaway with the kids. Olive was able to get a room from Saturday to Monday. So, tonight, they were going to go out to dinner and to the mall so they could be ready to leave the following morning.

Opening the door, Olive got very nervous as she came face to face with Camille and Kasie.

"Hello, Camille," Olive spoke, nervously. Camille's eyes ran over her swollen belly that she subconsciously rubbed with her left hand, giving Camille the perfect view of her engagement ring.

"Olive," Camille said as she and Kasie walked into Kameron's house. Camille would never like Olive. In her eyes, she was part of the reason for her divorce, and this was probably the most cordial she would ever be towards Olive. It took a lot out of her to even speak.

"I'll get Kameron for you. Hey, Kasie," Olive spoke to Kasie, and Kasie automatically ran over to her, gave her a hug and rubbed her stomach. The interaction between them didn't bother Camille as much as she thought.

"Wassup, Camille? Where's Kyron?"

"Kyron is at his friend, Eric's house. I'm taking them to the Eagles game, tonight," Camille answered.

"Well, I had plans this weekend."

"Okay, well I got the tickets to take him to the game that you promised to take him to. Now, I will drop him off after the game." Camille said, not thinking it was much of a problem. Kameron never mentioned anything to her about them doing anything special for the weekend, so that's why she didn't think it was a big deal.

"That should be fine. Kameron, we're not leaving for the trip until in the morning," Olive said, not understanding why Kameron was making such a big deal of Kyron going to the game.

"I wish you would communicate with me," Kameron said, pissed, completely ignoring Olive. He was madder at the fact that Camille was once again picking up his slack, making him look like a bad parent.

"I wish you would have communicated with your son about not taking him to the game. He been looking forward to this game ever since you told him that you was going to get the tickets."

"I was making it up to him this weekend. That's why we're going to Sahara Sam's for the weekend, and coming back on Monday."

"Okay. So are you going to drop them off at school on Tuesday?" Camille asked. She wasn't even going to sit there and argue with Kameron. She had the kids on a strict schedule when it came to school, and she hated for them to miss days.

"I guess."

"Okay. I'll call you when we're on our way back from the game," Camille said before giving Kasie a hug and kiss goodbye.

"I don't even know how she got those tickets. The last time I looked, they were sold out?" Kameron said out loud as the front door closed.

"Maybe her friend, DJ Roberts, gave her the tickets." Olive said, thinking about what Jessica had said earlier.

"DJ Roberts? As in the Philadelphia Eagles quarterback?" Kameron asked, looking at Olive like she had lost her mind. "Camille don't know no damn DJ Roberts. She doesn't even like football."

"Well, she supposedly had catered his charity event. Jessica said it's all over the shade room. They even suggesting that they are a couple." Olive threw that out there to see how Kameron would react to the information.

"Baby girl, put your things in your room," he told Kasie. Once she had disappeared up the steps, he decided to reply to Olive's last statement. "Shade room? That's a gossip blog. There's no way DJ Roberts want Camille."

The mere thought of DJ Roberts having any interest in Camille was hilarious.

"Camille has a good ten years on him. Plus, she's not as attractive as she used to be when we were younger. Her body is not the same as it was before we had children. It's filled with stretch marks and saggy skin. What man wants to see that? I'm positive DJ has women his age throwing themselves at him."

Olive cringe at the way Kameron spoke about Camille. From the looks of Camille's picture in the shade room, her body seemed tight. There were no pudge showcasing in the picture, and when she was standing in front of them, she didn't look like she had two kids. Olive was now nervous that Kameron would soon lose interest in her after the baby was born, especially if her body didn't snap back to the way it was before the baby.

"Yeah," Olive muttered. "I told Jessica she couldn't believe everything on the Internet."

"I'm the best thing that happened to Camille! Why do you think she went so hard in the divorce? She will never find another man on my level," Kameron said before walking into the kitchen, leaving Olive standing in the living room shaking her head at his foolishness.

16

SOMETHING REAL

Summer Walker & Chris Brown: I ain't tryna go through Déjà vu. It's some bullshit that I went through. Hope it's not the same with you.

"*T*OUCHDOWN, EAGELS!!!!!!!!" The announcer screamed as everybody in the skybox and stadium erupted in cheers." DJ had thrown the winning touchdown against the Dallas Cowboys. Camille even found herself cheering along with the crowd. She couldn't lie, seeing DJ in his element was such a turn on, and being there was such a great experience for her and Kyron.

"Mom, thanks. This is so dope!" Kyron said, excitedly, as he gave Camille a hug. It was his first time to an Eagles game and he enjoyed every minute of it. He didn't know how his mother had pulled off getting them tickets to sit in the skybox, but he was glad she did.

"Yeah, Ms. Camille, thanks for bringing me with you guys," Eric said. "I can't wait to go to school next week to let everybody know."

"Not a problem at all." Eric had been Kyron's best friend since kindergarten, and with Eric's mom being a single mom, working full time, Camille always tried to include him on the fun things she did with Kyron, and she couldn't think of a more perfect person to join them. "Are ya'll ready?"

DJ had just texted her phone, letting her know he had someone coming to the skybox to bring her down to the locker room. He was going to have some of his teammates autograph a football for Kyron and Eric. Camille was grateful for DJ for making it a wonderful experience. Not only did he get them the tickets, he also bought everybody Eagles gear to wear to the game.

"Camille?" She heard her name being called from behind. Turning around, she came face to face with Tempest and King Black.

"Hey guys," Camille said, giving them both a hug.

"I thought that was you. Are these handsome men your sons?"

"Kyron is my son, and this is Eric, his best friend. My baby girl is at her father's house for the weekend. Is this ya'll son?"

"Yeah, this is KJ, and our daughters Princess and Jamie

are at home. They're not into sports." Tempest explained as KJ spoke and went off to the side with Kyron and Eric to talk about the game.

"Camille, it was nice seeing you again. Babe, I'm going to head out to the car." King said, giving Camille another hug.

"Nice to see you, too," she responded to King before he turned to leave. "Girl, I'm happy to finally see someone I know." She then said, noticing some of the women in the skybox giving her the side eye. "So, do ya'll come to all of the games?" Camille tried to ignore the woman mugging her.

"Yeah, DJ and KJ have a good relationship. So we usually come to all the homes games. Should I be expecting you at the home games now?" Tempest asked with a smile. She could see that DJ and Camille were getting serious, especially since it looked like DJ was about to meet her son..

"Maybe. I've never been all into sports. However, I can't lie, I did enjoy myself tonight, and so did KJ. I know he's going to want to make this a norm," Camille said as she looked over at the group of women who was still staring at her and whispering to one another. "Is it me, or do those women have an eye problem?" She said loud enough for the group of women to hear, causing them to look in another direction.

"Girl, just ignore them. They're salty because they know DJ is the one who invited you here. They're his ex's friends."

"Why the hell they clocking me? And how do they know DJ invited me to the game?"

"I don't know if you know or not, but you're becoming a social media hot commodity. Everybody wants to know who this mystery woman is in DJ's life."

What?" Camille asked in shocked. She didn't have any social media accounts, and she was never one to entertain the gossip blogs and magazines. She hated how the media and paparazzi invade people privacy.

"You heard me correctly." Tempest gave her confirmation by taking it a step further and showing her the many posts on social media about her and DJ. "So my question is, are you and DJ serious?"

That was the million-dollar question, and honestly, Camille didn't have an answer for it. Her and DJ had never discussed the status of their relationship. She knew he considered them as more than friends with benefits, but she didn't want to jump the guns by saying they were in a relationship.

"I don't know. We've never put a title on our situation. We're both getting out of terrible relationships, so we just been taking it one day at a time, but anybody with eyes can see I truly care about him. It's crazy.DJ don't know it, but he pulled me out of a dark place."

"Seeing ya'll together, I can tell there's some deep feelings coming from both ends. I say life is too short to not to live it. Go for it. Take that step and make him your man...."

"Hey, Tempest," Yazmine said, finally deciding to make her way over to Tempest.

"Yazmine, what do you want?" Tempest asked, getting straight to the point. Out of all the years DJ had been playing professional football, Yazmine had never made an effort to sit or try to associate with his family. So, Tempest knew she was trying to be messy by speaking to her.

"Dang, girl, you act like we're not family." Yazmine faked hurt. She didn't care about Tempest little attitude. She was just her excuse to get close to Camille. Yazmine was seething with jealousy. Being the social media queen herself, of course she kept up with the latest tea, especially when she wasn't in the center of it. So, imagine her surprise when her ex popped up on the shade room and TMZ with a new woman on his arm. In the pictures that the paparazzi had snapped of them at his charity event, DJ seemed to have been truly into the woman, especially since he had brought her around his family.

"Bitch, you know damn well we didn't fuck with you. You will never be considered family. So I hope you just came for the game and then make your way out of the stadium. You need to stay away from DJ."

"Why would I stay away from my man, Tempest? I can't understand why you, his sister, Reign, or anybody else in ya'll little family think it's okay to be in our relationship. DJ invited me here tonight. I know the family don't like me and don't want us to be together, but we have too much history to allow a little hiccup to break what we have built throughout the years." Yazmine said, looking directly at Camille the whole time she talked.

Camille chuckled as she shook her head. Now, she knew why Yazmine looked familiar. Yazmine was the same girl that DJ was arguing with at the club the night they had reconnected. Camille wasn't trying to allow this girl to get her out of character. DJ told her all about Yazmine and how she damn near turned borderline stalker, trying to get him to talk to her. But she couldn't lie, Yazmine presence truly bothered her, especially the words she'd just spat out her mouth. She prayed Yazmine was just talking trash.

"Are you done?" Tempest asked, giving her a round of applause. "Your little speech was cute. You and I both know the only reason why you came over here is because you know exactly who Camille is. I guess you call yourself trying to cause trouble in DJ's relationship, but all you look like is the desperate hoe you are. Yazmine, stop embarrassing yourself more than you already have. What you and DJ had is over. It was over the moment you left him high and dry, thinking his career was over. So just accept the fact that he will never want you again. You need to get your priorities straight. Stop chasing after your ex and take care of the child you have with JoJo. That's the man you wanted. So keep the same energy. Camille, are you ready to see ya man?" Tempest said, dismissing Yazmine, who was low key hurt by the way Tempest had just read her.

Yazmine knew she was the last person that DJ wanted to see. Her goal for coming to the game was to try her luck and try to get him to have a civil conversation with her. All she needed was one serious heart to heart moment to remind him that she was still the same girl he had fallen in love with in college. Yazmine hated that she was now pinned as the gold digging ex, because she truly did and still love DJ, and was secretly killing her to see him actually moving on. Being as though she was DJ's first love, she never thought someone could take her place so quickly, but obviously, she was wrong.

"Boys, are ya'll ready?" Camille called out to Kyron and Eric.

"Yeah. Mom, KJ said DJ Roberts is his uncle. Can we meet him?" Kyron asked, hyped at the opportunity to meet his favorite player.

"Camille?" A security guard called her name, taking her attention off Kyron.

"Yes?"

"I'm Derrick, DJ sent me up here to escort you to the locker room."

"Oh, yeah." Camille completely forgot all about the text message had DJ sent her after the game.

"Ms. Black, you coming?"

"Yeah," Tempest answered.

"Mom, did he say DJ Roberts wanted to see you?" Kyron asked, giving his mother the side eye.

"Yeah, it seems like it. You know, I catered his charity event. That's how we got the tickets. So make sure you thank him."

"Okay." Kyron said, excitedly.

"Lead the way, big homie," KJ said to the security guard, giving him a handshake.

So many thoughts were going through Camille's mind as they made their way to the locker room.

"Listen, don't allow that whole situation with Yazmine to ruin your night. Being with a man like DJ, you have to have tough skin. He's one of the highest paid quarterback's in the NFL. Bitches are always going to try you by throwing themselves at him. Then you have tired hoes like Yazmine trying to get his attention. DJ is a good man. When he's with you, he's with you, and no one will be able to break that up, except you. Why you think Yazmine is salty as shit? She thought the grass was greener on the other side. Now she has a baby by a man who doesn't want her, and she lost the love of her life in the process."

"That's the thing, she thought it was okay to start bullshit with my son a few feet away. I'm too old to be putting my foot up somebody's ass. On top of that, my privacy is everything. My life is not for the world to chime in on."

"DJ will never put you in a negative light. DJ is also a very private person, too. The only reason why he was in the blog is because of the craziness Yazmine created with being pregnant and not knowing if DJ was her baby daddy or JoJo from the Boston Celtics. The media had a field day with her then. So, to see him with someone new is a story within itself. But by next week, someone else will be the topic of discussion. Don't allow an irrelevant chick to make you fall back from your man. Trust, all she wants is time and opportunity to get her hooks into him."

Camille knew tempest was right, but the question that she had yet to answer was, if that was a lifestyle she wanted to live, dating a professional athlete. It wasn't just about her, but she had kids. She was raising a brand that she was building and didn't want to allow the media to run ragged stories about her personal life. At thirty-six years old, and one fail marriage, she was over the drama. Secondly, she needed to figure out where she and DJ actually stood in their relationship. There was no reason to drive herself crazy with unanswered questions if he didn't see a future with her.

As soon as Derrick rounded the corner, DJ couldn't stop the smile that formed on his face when his eyes landed on Camille. Things had been hectic lately. With her booming catering business taking off and her taking care of the kids, along with his schedule being filled with practice to prepare for the game, they hadn't really spent much time together.

"Wassup, babe?" DJ said as he pulled Camille in for a hug and kiss. Kyron stood back with widened eyes, not sure how to react. The last he knew, his mother was single, not dating his favorite NFL player.

"Dog, did you know ya mom was dating DJ Roberts?" Eric asked, just as shocked as Kyron.

"Here I am, thinking I'm about to introduce you to my uncle and look like you're about to become my cousin." KJ joked, laughing at the look on Kyron's face.

"Wassup, sis?" DJ said, acknowledging Tempest, giving her a hug as well. "Nephew."

"Hey," Tempest spoke as DJ and KJ did their special handshake.

"DJ, I want you to meet my son Kyron, and his friend, Eric."

"Wassup, man? Ya mom told me so much about you." DJ gave both, Kyron and Eric, a handshake.

"Wassup? Thanks for getting us the tickets to the game," Kyron replied back.

"Not a problem. When ya mom told me ya'll wanted to come but the tickets was sold out, you know I had to make it happen. Maybe home games can be a regular thing for you and Eric."

"For real! Ya, that's would be so dope," Kyron and Eric said together.

"Yeah, definitely. I actually got some of my teammates to autograph these footballs for ya'll."

"Thanks!" They said in unison, again.

"Mr. DJ, can I take a picture with you? My mom is not going to believe this," Eric said, already pulling out his cell phone.

"Yeah, man."

Kyron looked on. He didn't know how to take his mom dating again, even if she was dating his favorite football player. All Kyron knew was, the breakup she had with his father had really changed her, and the last thing he wanted was for her to go through another heartbreak. But on the other hand, he did want his mom to be happy, especially since his father had moved on.

"Come on, bro, and Ms. Camille, get in." Eric happily said. Camille allowed them to take a few more pictures with DJ by themselves before hopping in. She couldn't help the smile that'd spread across her face as she watched her two favorite men.

"Let me grab my things and we can be out," DJ said to Camille before walking back into the locker room.

As soon as DJ walked back out the locker room, everybody started walking towards the exit of the stadium. Camille and Tempest was having their own conversation about the spa day that Reign had invited her to, while Eric and KJ was still talking about the game, and when all three of them would link up for KJ's birthday party that was coming up. Kyron on the other hand, he kind of stayed back because he wanted to speak with DJ alone.

"So… you and my mom are like a thing, or are ya'll just friends?" Kyron asked, causing Camille to slow her stride, trying to be nosey. She knew her son could get out of a child's place sometimes, and she didn't want him to offend DJ.

"Your mother is my woman. I care very deeply for her," DJ answered. He knew he and Camille had never made it official, but he was tired of not having a title. He wanted people to know, when they saw her, she was his. "I hope you cool with that."

"I guess…"

"You guess?" DJ repeated, cocking his head to the side.

"I don't have a problem with it, but don't you think my mom a little too old for you?"

DJ chuckle at Kyron's question. He was the first person to bring up the age difference, but he knew he wouldn't be the last. "Naw, ya mom not too old to be my girl."

"Well, I'm cool with what ya'll have going on. I have noticed a difference with my mom over these past couple of weeks. I guess we can say it's because of you. She seems happier. I just want her to stay happy. Last year was a bad year. I just don't want to see her down like that again," Kyron voiced. The way his father had broken his mother's heart was part of the reason why he and his father weren't as close as they once were.

"You have my word. Your mom's happiness is my priority. I never want to or will intentionally hurt her."

"Cool. Now that that's out the way, lets talk about that pass you made for the winning touchdown."

Kyron and DJ talk the whole way to the parking lot. They walked Tempest and KJ to their car where King was waiting for them first, then headed over to Camille's car.

"Alright, Mr. DJ, I guess I'll be seeing you around?" Kyron said before giving him a handshake followed by Eric.

"Most, definitely," he answer as they got in the car, leaving him and Camille standing outside.

"I missed you," Camille admitted as he pulled her into his personal space.

"What you about to do?" DJ asked, wanting to spend some time with his lady.

"I'm going to take Eric home then drop Kyron off to his father's house. The kids are staying with him this weekend. He's even taking them to school on Monday. So I'm completely free to do whatever."

"When you done, meet me at my house. Tomorrow we're going to catch a flight for a mini vacation."

"What?" Camille surprisedly asked. "Wait... There's so much for me to do. I didn't even pack."

"Listen, don't worry about packing. I'll buy everything we need when we get there. I'm thinking about Turk and Caicos."

"I can't believe you." Camille was all smiles. Dropping everything just to travel just because it was the weekend was not her. She was one who always had to be in control.

"Just say, yes." DJ knew the trip was unexpected, but he wanted to make the weekend special, especially since it was the weekend to make things official.

"Yes!" Camille said before kissing him passionately, and she didn't stop until she heard her car horn beep.

"Man, ain't nobody trying to see that." Kyron yelled out of the window and then let it back up.

"He's a mess." Camille shook her head, laughing at Kyron.

"Take them where they need to go so I can show you how much I missed you."

"Say no more," Camille moaned, thinking about what

he was going to do to her body. Giving him another kiss, she hopped into her car. DJ was definitely changing her for the better, and she was living life to the fullest.

"Thanks, Ms. Camille. Alright, bro." Eric said, giving Kyron a handshake when they pulled up to his house.

"No problem."

"Ms. Camille, I just wanted to let you know that you're a great mom and Mr. Kameron definitely lost out, and you definitely upgraded." Eric said before walking off. Eric had always been one to say what was on his mind, and Kyron had always talked to him about what was going on with his parents. So he knew what Camille was going through.

"Okay," Camille chuckled along with Kyron.

"He's not lying, mom." Kyron agreed with his best friend as his mom pulled off to go to their next destination. "So, mom, why you didn't tell us you had a boyfriend?"

"What are you talking about, Kyron?"

"Well, I hope he's your boyfriend the way you're walking around kissing him," Kyron stated with a raised brow. "Plus, he told me you was his woman and your happiness is his priority."

"He said that?" Camille asked in shocked.

"Yeah, and I like him for you. He seems to be cool."

"I like him, too." Camille responded with a smile. She was happy that Kyron seemed to have approved of her relationship. Being as though he was so against Kameron and Olive's relationship, she thought he was just not ready for his parents to move on.

"Cool. You have my blessing."

"Boy, you're crazy." Camille laughed at her son. Pulling up to Kameron's house, Kyron sigh when he realized Olive's car was in the driveway.

"Listen, Kyron, I want you to be on your best behavior. I think your father and Olive are taking you guys somewhere fun for the weekend."

"Man, I ain't trying to be around that lady. Can I just stay with you this weekend?"

"Well, actually, DJ is taking me away for a little vacation this weekend. Plus, you already know how your dad is about *his visitations.*"

"Hold up. Mr. DJ starting this family thing all wrong. Why me and Kasie not going on the vacation? And your ex-husband barely commits to his visitations. This our first time visiting him in how long?"

"You're right, but I'm not trying to deal with the headache that comes with your father. He even had a problem with me not dropping you off with Kasie. Answer this question, why are you okay with me and DJ and not Kameron and Olive?"

"It's just the way they went about everything. When dad first came to us about the divorce, I asked if he cheated and he told me, no. Ya'll taught us not to lie, and as a man, he lied in my face. I would have respect him more if he just told the truth. Then, Ms. Olive just popped up pregnant, telling us that they were engaged the day after y'all divorce. It just wasn't cool. She didn't even care how we would take the news or if we were hurt behind ya'll divorce or not. To me, she's just a selfish person. But with you and Mr. DJ, ya'll waited, and honestly, it's good to see you smile for once. He's changing you back to your old self."

"I completely understand where you're coming from. Unfortunately, this is something that you have to get use too. Ms. Olive is engaged to marry your father. So she's obviously going to be around. Just be respectful and cordial. Who knows, you may actually enjoy yourself this weekend. What happened between me and your father is our situation. I don't want you choosing sides or putting yourself in the middle of it."

"Alright..." Kyron said, shaking his head. He didn't respect his father or Olive, but to keep the peace, he was going to be respectful and cordial. "Mr. DJ said I could come to the home games."

"That's cool. I think I want to go to more games, too. Tonight was fun."

"It was. Thanks again for following through on the promise that my father was supposed to come through on."

"No problem, baby. Now go in the house before I have to cuss your dad out," Camille said, rolling her eyes at the fact that Kameron had been standing at the door since they pulled up.

"Alright, mom, have fun," Kyron said, giving his mom a kiss on the cheek before hopping out of the car.

Now it's time for some alone time with my man. Camille thought as she pulled off.

17

AGAIN

Kehlani: *But there was blood from your heart on my hands again. Though I swore I washed it off in the waves. And I wish I was sorry, damn I wish I was sorry. That's I don't know how to stay away.*

"Welcome to Reign's Day Spa! How may I help you?"

"Hello, my name is Cynthia. Is it possible for you to get the owner?" Cynthia asked the receptionist.

"Sure. One moment, please," The receptionist said before disappearing toward the back.

Cynthia patiently waited for Reign in the lounge area. It was going to be her last and final plea, hating that she had to go through Reign, especially when the young lady probably hated her guts due to the affair she had with her married father. But, Reign was her last resort to get close to DJ.

"Hello, my name is Reign. I'm the owner of the spa. How may I help you?" Reign said, walking up to Cynthia with her hand held out for a handshake.

"Hello, Reign." Cynthia stood, shaking her hand. A feeling of guilt shot through her like a wave. Reign looked exactly like her mother, Nikki, and Cynthia hated that she wasn't strong enough to leave Dion Sr. alone. She could only imagine the horrors that Dion Sr. had put her through. She honestly used to envy Nikki because she had the family she always wanted. That was until she saw on the news the horrific things Dion had done to her and her daughter. That's when she realized she had actually dodged a huge bullet.

"Was your service not to your liking?"

Reign rarely got any complaint when it came to her staff or their service, so she really needed to know why this lady had to speak with her, personally.

"I'm not here to complain," Cynthia started.

"Okay. Not to be rude, but I got off a conference call to speak with you. So what can I do for you?"

"I'm sorry to come to you, but this is my last resort. I'm Cynthia, DJ's mother."

Reign looked at the white woman in front of her and wanted to cuss her out. The woman who unknowingly and uncaringly caused so much pain in her brother's life. DJ was a really damaged person due to his mother's actions.

"I don't believe there is anything I can help you with."

"Please!" Cynthia begged out loud, causing a few stares their way. "Please, just hear me out."

"Come to my office," Reign suggested, turning to walk away. Her spa was very classy and the last thing she wanted was for her customers to see or hear the tongue lashing Cynthia was about to receive. Reign knew her brother like the back of her hand, and she knew he had probably told his mother to kick rocks.

"Thank you," Cynthia said, appreciating Reign for giving her a moment of her time.

"Don't thank me, yet. After all of these years, why the hell you think it's a great idea to show your face now?"

"It's not what you think."

"I don't know what to think, Cynthia. You abandoned my brother with the devil herself, and now you want to pop the fuck up like you've been a loving, caring mother. What do you really want?"

"I didn't come back because DJ is now this big successful football player. I want my son back in my life. I want to be apart of his."

"Aren't you a couple of years too late? Listen, I'm not one to judge, but personally knowing what my brother encountered with our grandmother, Brenda, I can't respect you. You left him in the care with a woman you didn't know. Just because they shared blood didn't mean she had his best interest at heart. See, my mother was murdered. You were perfectly capable of taking care of him. He didn't have to go through the abuse. He didn't have to rob drug dealers and jack boys to survive. DJ was on a slippery slope to self-destruction while you were enjoying life in the Hamptons with your rich husband."

"Believe it or not, my life stopped the day I dropped DJ off at Brenda's house. Everyday was a living hell," Cynthia admitted as Reign gave her the bitch please look. "I mean, the guilt of leaving my only child was a huge burden."

"What are your intentions with my brother? And don't tell me you just want to be apart of his life. And why the hell are you coming to me with this sob story, instead of DJ?"

"My only intention is to be apart of his life on his terms. I know it may not seem like it, but I do love my son. I allowed a man to come in between me and him due to my own selfish needs. We were struggling and Connor was our way out of poverty. You have to understand. I truly thought Brenda would take good care of him. Even though Connor said DJ didn't fit into his life, he still took care of him financially. Well, at least I thought." Cynthia ranted, feeling more like shit.

God knew her heart, and she thought she was doing the best for her and her son, but then again, she knew leaving DJ should have never been an option. And any man that claimed to have loved her should have accepted her child, too.

"Hmmmm. I can tell you now that breaking through to DJ is not going to be easy."

"I figured. Plus, I tried to speak with him but he didn't

want to listen. That's why I'm here with you. I was thinking maybe you could put in a good word for me. I just need a moment of his time."

Reign sighed, shaking her head. The last thing she wanted to do was get in the middle of DJ and his mother's drama. She completely understood why DJ didn't want anything to do with Cynthia. She wasn't there when he needed her the most. However, the look in Cynthia's eyes screamed sincerity.

If Reign had another chance to have her mother back in her life, she would jump on it. Granted, Nikki didn't abandon Reign, but she did allow her to endure mental and emotional abuse at the hands of her father. She even had to watch her mother be beaten day in and day out. That alone could take a toll on any child. When Nikki had finally built up the strength to leave, she was murdered. Watching her mother die at the hands of her father was something that Reign would never forget. Yet, if she had another chance with her mother, she would let the past be the past and try to enjoy the time they could create together.

"I can't put a good word in for you because I don't respect what you done, and I'm talking about from a mother perspective. But, I can try to set up a date and time for you and DJ to talk. Let's clear one thing about me, I don't like to be made a fool out of. You seem truly sincere and genuine and I truly hope your intention are pure, because it will be nothing to make you disappear."

"Thank you," Cynthia said, grateful for whatever help

Reign was willing to give, but Reign's threat didn't go unnoticed. Cynthia was well aware of who Reign Black's husband was and his family. So, she didn't have any doubt that if she disappointed DJ she would come up missing.

I CAN'T BELIEVE HE'S MESSING WITH THIS BITCH! YAZMINE thought as she looked at DJ's Instagram pictures, noticing he had taken Camille on a mini bae-cation to Turk and Caicos. Yazmine swore she could feel her whole body turn green with envy. She knew after their very public break up, DJ would've eventually moved on, by sleeping around with multiple women. However, what she didn't think was that he would actually take someone serious.

Seeing DJ and Camille's pictures and all the likes and people calling them the *new it couple* and saying how he had definitely upgraded from her made Yazmine want her man back. The saying *you never know what you have until it's gone* rang true for her. Now, she was full of regret, but in her mind, she felt DJ still had love for her. How could he not when she was his first love?

"You don't hear our son crying!" JoJo snapped as he walked into the room with baby Joey on his chest. He was fuming on the inside. He had just come home from practice only to hear his son screaming at the top of his lungs, and Yazmine was nowhere to be found.

"No, I didn't hear him," she lied. The truth was, she was

so busy cyber stalking DJ that her son cries didn't mean anything to her. In her eyes, he was the wrong baby that had survived. She wished he was DJ's child so that she would still have a reason to be in his life. "I thought Grace had him. I asked her to keep an eye on him so I could get a minute to myself."

"She's the fucking maid. Not a nanny!" JoJo yelled, causing Joey to cry again. He was over Yazmine and her ways, and honestly, his patience was starting to run thin.

"I'm sorry. Give him to me. He's probably hungry." Yazmine instantly felt like shit as she looked at her son.

When she had gotten pregnant, she was happy. Mainly, because she was having a baby by a baller and she thought she would be set for life. She'd always heard how NFL players ex's or baby mamas always seemed to come off on top with the child support payments. With that money, she planned to live the best lifestyle that DJ's money could afford her to live. So, when she found out she was having twins, nothing could bring her happiness down.

Never in a million years did she think DJ would ask her to have an abortion. He was all about family so she couldn't understand why he wanted to destroy his chances of having one of his own.. She expected that response from JoJo, mainly, because he was her side nigga that never wanted the main nigga's responsibilities. Refusing to abort her babies, Yazmine went through her pregnancy alone. The happiness she once felt quickly turned into bitterness. She spoke with every gossip magazine and social outlet, dogging DJ until his lawyer sent her a gag order.

The day she went into labor was supposed to have been the happiest day of her life. Instead, it was filled with embarrassment and sorrow. Neither DJ, nor JoJo showed their faces or support. The only person who stood by her side as she pushed out her beautiful twins was her judgmental mother, who couldn't see how her daughter could be so stupid to mess up her relationship with DJ and now didn't know who the father of her children could have possibly been.

Sorrow filled her heart when the doctor told her that one of the babies had came out stillborn. Losing a child was a hurt that no woman would truly recover from. When she notified DJ that she had the babies, he went to the hospital only for a DNA test. When he found out his baby had died, he left the hospital without even making sure Yazmine was okay. His actions alone broke her heart. Did he hate her that much that he couldn't even check on her to see if she was okay?

All Yazmine knew for sure was, the day DJ walked out the hospital, he had also walked out of her life, for good.

"Yazmine, you need to get it together. I don't know if you're still suffering from post-partum depression or what, but the way you're treating our son is not acceptable."

"I'm trying," she shot back as Joey finally latched onto her nipple. Even though Yazmine wished Joey was DJ's son, she still loved her son, even if she had a funny way of showing it.

"You're not trying hard enough."

"Parenting is not as easy as you think. Being as though you're always on the road, or spending all of your free time with a whole bunch of random bitches you wouldn't know that," Yazmine spat. When she was creeping on DJ with JoJo, JoJo couldn't keep his hands off her. Now that she had Joey and was living with him full-time, that had drastically change. He didn't even bother to sleep with her. Between him and DJ, Yazmine had never felt so unwanted in her life.

"The only concern you need to have when it comes to me is our son. Don't worry about who I'm fucking."

"But you could have a little more respect for me and your son, and stop bringing your hoes to the house we lay our heads at."

JoJo knew Yazmine was right, but he didn't plan on changing his lifestyle because she decided to have a baby by him and force his hand to live in his mansion. His current living arrangement was not how he thought he would be living in his twenties.

"Yazmine, this is my house! If I want to have company, that's what I'm going to do. If I want bitches walking around butt booty hole naked, that's what's going to happen in the house I pay the bills for. If you want a say so on how I do things, you need to put up some coins to go toward these bills. If you can't do that, your feelings about what I do in my home is irrelevant. You knew the type of person I was before you went along with this pregnancy."

"I didn't think you were the father!" Yazmine shook her head, regretting ever sleeping with this man. "But you are the father and you're not even open about becoming a family."

"Everything don't have to be traditional. I love my son, but you and me both know, baby Joey was never supposed to happen. I was ya side nigga, and I was cool with being that on the low. I had no commitment to you, but common sense been told me not to wife you up, not even for my son's sake."

"So I'm good enough to fuck, but not wife up?" Yazmine asked for clarification. JoJo had honestly offended and hurt her feelings.

"Yaz, you're foul as shit. Why would I trust you? You been with that nigga DJ since college. When most men dropped their girl once they got drafted so they could live the life as a rookie with no strings attached, that nigga brought you along. He never did you dirty or had you out here looking dumb. You cheated because he wasn't spending a lot of time with you due to his career. Not only were you cheating on him, you made that shit public. Paparazzi never came around us or caught us out together until you left him after he'd gotten injured and thought his career was over. Then had the nerve to get mad because the nigga wasn't claiming the babies when you were pregnant. So, instead of keeping a low profile, you threw dirt on his name like he was the scum of the earth. So to answer your question, yes you're good enough to fuck. Trust the pussy is A1, but wifing you up, that's going to be a hard pass for me. If you did that to the man you proclaimed you loved. I can only imagine what you would do to me. A nigga you're just trying to use to pump fake like you have a happy family," JoJo ranted as he watched Yazmine roll her eyes.

"This coming from a man that disrespected him by sleeping with his girl."

"I don't know that nigga. I don't owe him any loyalty. Plus, if you throwing the pussy at me, I'm damn sure going to catch it."

"Whatever. Just like you don't want this, neither do I. DJ was supposed to be the father of my children. This—" Yazmine said, pointing around the room. "—is not how I planned my life."

"I bet you thought I was going to be the replacement nigga when you thought his career was over." He flashed a knowing smirk.

"I wish everybody stop saying that! I didn't leave because I thought his NFL career was over. I planned on being by his side through it all, but when DJ got hurt, he changed, and not for the better. He became mean and bitter, and I personally wasn't going to stay around to be his verbal punching bag."

"Naw." JoJo shook his head, not believing a word she'd just said. That was Yazmine's problem. She always wanted to play the victim to the situations she created. "You got nervous and left homie without a real explanation, and you thought a Dear John letter would be okay. You told me that all the letter said was that you could no longer be in that relationship. If he was treating you the way you just said he was, why not tell him. Instead of keeping it one hundred with ole bul, you popped up in the tabloid with me the next day. "

Yazmine sat there as she watched JoJo chuckle and shake his head like he had her all figured out. On the other hand, JoJo knew he had read her like an open book. He knew Yazmine had realized her mistake, but it was too late. To make matters even worse, DJ knew who she truly was.

"Whatever. I don't even know why we're speaking about DJ."

"Probably because you ignoring our child's needs, because you're too busy snooping on your ex's social media."

"What…" She tried to play dumb only for JoJo to walk over to her and snatch her phone out of her hand. Just as he expected, she was on DJ's Instagram. He didn't care about what Yazmine did or who she dated, but he didn't want his child neglected in the process.

"JoJo, I'm not going to sit here and allow you to act like I'm this horrible mother. I love my son, but did you ever think that, just maybe, I might be still grieving. I was supposed to have twins."

"I understand that, and I'm sorry for your loss, but at the end of the day, you can't neglect one child because his twin didn't survive. You still have to be a mother to baby Joey." An awkward silence fell in between them. Yazmine knew she could and needed to do better as a mother, and now that it was being brought to her attention, she knew she needed to change her ways. Her worst fear was for her son to hate her the way DJ hated his mother.

DJ had confided in Yazmine plenty of times about the hurt and hate he held for his mother, and she always made a promise to herself that she would never be like that, or even worse, like her mother, Louise. Louise was what you called a kept woman, a gold digger. She lived off of her husband and never worked a day in her life. Love wasn't and priority in her life. So you could only imagine when Yazmine messed up with DJ how disappointed Louise was. As much as Yazmine hated to admit, she was definitely going down the paths of both women.

"How about me and Joey move back to Philly?"

"Naw... I'm not comfortable with that," JoJo stated. Yazmine easily ignored Joey now. JoJo didn't know why she would think in a million years he would be okay with her taking his son back to Philly.

Listen.... You're the one with the life in Boston. Being here, I'm separated from my family and friends. My whole support system...."

"Your ex." JoJo said. "Yazmine cut the bullshit. You're not worried about no family, friends or support system. Keep it one hundred with me. If that's the case, why you come all the way to Boston in the first place."

"Yes, DJ is in Philly, but I'm not worried about him. He seemed to have moved on with his senior citizen." Yazmine couldn't help but throw a dig at Camille. Truth be told, Camille was breath taken and she hated she was receiving the love and care that she once received from the love of her life.

"Where's your salty ass going to stay?"

"I was thinking you could set us up in a nice house."

"So, I still need to provide for you." JoJo shook his head.

"News flash, Joseph, we share a child. So the next eighteen years you will be helping me. Now, it can be voluntarily or involuntarily. I wouldn't mind taking my NBA Player baby daddy to court for child support, but I really don't want to go that route. I want to co-parent. Also, I don't plan on depending on you forever. Once I touch down in Philadelphia, I plan on looking for a job in my degree. Everybody has this false perception of me. I'm not a gold digger. I want to be able to provide for my son myself and not depend on someone else for our lifestyle. I'm serious from now on. Joey will be my only priority."

"Okay, I will have my realtor look into some properties for you."

"Are you serious?" Yazmine didn't think he would go for it so easily.

"Yeah, like you said, your family is in Philadelphia. You don't have anyone here besides me to help you, and with the season coming up, I'm going to be traveling a lot with away games and everything. I'm going to support you in this move." Yazmine couldn't help the huge smile that was spreading across her face.

"But if I find out you only going back to Philly to be on some sack chasing shit, you will feel my wrath. I honestly don't give a fuck what you do in your personal life or who you date, but don't have my son in the middle of some paparazzi bullshit, or neglected because you trying to get back with that nigga, DJ. And I'm going to hire a nanny to help, especially since you say you're trying to work."

"Okay!" Yazmine rolled her eyes. Everything that she'd said about changing and putting her son first was true, but the move to Philly was to get close to DJ, too. She truly wanted to rekindle their relationship. DJ was the love of her life, and the only man who genuinely cared for her. DJ always said action spoke louder than words. So she thought maybe if she showed him that she was still the girl that'd graduated at the top of her class, he would give her a second chance.

Yazmine felt like she had never fought hard enough. She should have toughened it out and weathered the storm with DJ after his injury. That was going to change when she touched back down in Philly. There was no way she could live with him giving his love to another woman. Everybody had secrets, and she felt it was only going to be a matter of time before Camille's past caught up with her and skeletons started falling out her closet.

"I told you, this move is strictly for the betterment of me and Joey," Yazmine assure JoJo in more of a hushed tone.

18

RIGHT MY WRONGS

Bryson Tiller: *Tell me how can I right my wrongs. That's something I should know.*

"*H*ey, DJ," Larissa flirted as soon as DJ walked into his sister's spa. Larissa was one of the receptionists and she had been having eyes on Reign's little brother since she had taken the job, but DJ had never taken the bait.

"Wassup, can you tell my sister that I'm here to pick her up for our lunch," DJ said, completely ignoring Larissa's flirtation. He saw right through her and the dollar signs she had in her eyes.

"Oh, just go in her office. I'm pretty sure that's not a problem," she suggested, picking up her cell phone to scroll through social media, not bothering to do her job, making DJ shake his head at her actions. He was definitely going to tell his sister that she needed to start looking for her replacement.

Walking towards the back, in the direction of Reign's office, he thought about how Reign made him take time out of the day so he could take her to lunch. With the football season and spending all of his time with Camille and her kids, he definitely hadn't been making much time for his sister. Knocking on the door after opening it to let himself in, he found his sister on top of her desk with her husband fucking the shit out of her.

"What the fuck, yo?" DJ barked, covering his eyes with his hand, trying to get the image out of his head. Reign looked back in total shock to see her brother at the office door.

"Oh, shit, babe." She tensed up. " DJ!" She called his name as he slammed her office door shut.

DJ was well aware that Reign was sexually active, but he damn sure didn't want to witness it. Heading back up front, he was going to give Larissa a piece of his mind for sending him back there.

"Babe… wait… stop," Reign said, completely embarrassed that her brother had walked in on her in that compromising position.

"Stop?" Pharaoh respected in confusion, not missing a beat.

"Fuck! No, baby, right there!" Reign threw her head back as Pharaoh took her to ecstasy. She loved his mid- day pop ups. As of lately, his little surprise visits always seemed to end with a mid-day quickie. Pharaoh was secretly on a mission to get his wife pregnant again. The twins were five years old, and now he was ready for more babies. He loved seeing his wife barefoot and pregnant.

"Damn, Reign," Pharaoh moaned as his wife's wet pussy felt like a vice grip on his dick.

"Baby, pull out," Reign demanded as she felt both of them getting ready to reach their peak.

"I didn't marry you to pull out." Pharaoh hissed, hitting her g-spot with every long stroke. Reign wanted to say something smart in return, but the way her husband was fucking her, the words couldn't get pass her throat. The only thing that was audible was the soft moans of her calling out his name. Making sure Reign legs were in a death grip, he pounded her middle until they both came together.

"RoRo," Reign whine, knowing her husband had just disregarded what she asked him to do.

"Don't call me that shit!" He hissed before kissing her on her lips. Pharaoh hated that nickname she had given him many years ago.

"You know you on some straight up hood rat shit. You really trying to trap me?" Reign pouted, causing Pharaoh to laugh. Reign loved her kids to death, but she honestly wasn't ready for more, yet. She wasn't totally against the idea because she did want more kids in the future, but as of now, she was focused on her business and creating more business deal for the spa. She now had five spas. Two free standing, and three that were all connected to different resorts.

"You're my wife. How am I trapping you?" Pharaoh chuckled at her little theory. In his eyes, he wasn't trapping his wife. He didn't know why Reign thought he would pull out when he had raw dogged her the first time they ever had sex and he didn't pull out.

"Baby, you know I'm not ready for more kids, yet. Maybe when the twins turn ten I'll be ready."

"Yeah, you tripping. You might as well get use to the idea. I'm definitely dropping another set of twins in you before then."

"You better not!" Reign couldn't even think about being pregnant with twins again.

"Who the hell walked in on us?" Pharaoh asked. He was so into their quickie that he didn't hear her yell out DJ's name.

"Oh, shit. That was DJ." Reign said. She had completely forgot that DJ had walked in on them. "But my question is, why Larissa didn't page me to let me know he was on his way to the back."

Larissa had been working at Reign's Day Spa for about three months now, and she had to have been by far the worst receptionist she had ever hired. She'd received complaints multiple times about her attitude and lack of customer service, but her sending DJ back there without paging her was definitely the last straw. Reign didn't care if DJ was her brother. No one was allowed to just walk in the back to her office. The only person who had that right was her husband.

"I told you to fire that sack chasing hoe when you first hired her," Pharaoh said, coming out of Reign's personal bathroom that was in her office, holding a warm wash cloth to wash his wife up. Larissa rubbed him the wrong way when she tried to flirt with him, not knowing he was the boss's husband.

"Trust me, that's on the top of my list as soon as I get back from lunch with DJ, that you tried to make me late for with this pop up visit."

"Did you tell him what you're doing?" Pharaoh asked, already knowing his wife answer.

"No. He just think we're going to lunch to catch up with one another. If I told him the truth, he wouldn't be here."

"Reign, you need to mind your business," Pharaoh warned, knowing his wife would do the opposite.

"It's too late." Reign looked in the mirror and rolled her eyes at the freshly place passion marks her husband had left on her neck.

"Babe, you look fine," he told her, giving her her coat as they headed out of her office.

"Ya'll muthafuckas just going to finish and act like I didn't walk in on ya'll," DJ fussed as soon as he spotted his sister and Pharaoh walk into the waiting area.

"Hell yeah. I ain't getting blue balls for no fucking

body," Pharaoh replied before giving his brother-in-law some dap.

"Larissa, I need to talk with you when I return."

"I hope you're finally going to fire her dumb ass," DJ muttered.

"Okay," Larissa said in just above a whisper, silently praying she didn't lose her job.

"Let's go, brother. I missed you," Reign said, giving DJ a hug.

"Hmmmm. You know lunch is on you, right?" DJ told Reign, irked at the fact that he couldn't get the image out his head of her and Pharaoh. He was truly traumatized.

"You're so petty," Reign pouted before they all walked out the door of the spa together.

"Babe, I'll see you when you get home." Pharaoh pulled his wife into his arms, kissing her passionately. After all these years, Reign was still the most beautiful woman in the world to him, and he couldn't keep his hands off her.

After going their separate ways, Reign and DJ hopped in his truck to head to the restaurant. The closer they got to it, the more nervous Reign became, knowing it wasn't going to be a normal lunch. Reign had invited Cynthia, and she didn't know how her brother would react to his mother joining them. As soon as they were seated at Del Frisco's, they placed their drink orders in.

"So, brother, how's everything going?"

"Football, good."

"And your love life?" Reign truly liked Camille for DJ.

The day she had came to the spa day for the ladies outing, she fitted right in, unlike Yazmine.

"Sis, I'm really feeling shorty," DJ admitted, smiling from ear to ear as he thought of Camille and how she was everything he wanted in a woman. He even found himself thanking God for allowing her husband to fuck up and not see the diamond he had in front of his eyes. Not only was Camille perfect, but her kids had truly grown on him. He never thought he would be a stepfather, but for Kyron and Kasie, he would gladly take that role. "I never thought I would feel this way about anyone after Yazmine. The way I felt for Yazmine doesn't even compare to what I feel for Camille."

"Are you in love, DJ?" Reign asked her brother.

DJ thought hard on her question, and he could honestly say that he was very much so in love with Camille. "I am."

"Do you think you would want kids?"

It was no secret with the age difference between DJ and Camille. With Camille set at the age thirty-six and her oldest child being sixteen, Reign doubted Camille wanted to start over with a new baby, especially being so close to forty.

"I don't know. I never really thought about it. My child-hood was so fucked up that I wouldn't even know how to be a parent. But being around Kyron and Kasie, I wouldn't mind being a father."

Reign looked at her brother with concern. She would hate for him to put his wants on hold.

"Don't look at me like that. All I'm saying is that having

kids or no kids won't be a deal breaker in my relationship with Camille. To be honest, I don't even know if I want to continue the bloodline of my parents. They both were some fucked up individuals, and the last thing I need is to pass along some fucked up traits."

"Okay." Reign said, silently praying Cynthia got cold feet. Now she wished she had listened to her husband and stayed out of DJ's relationship with his mother. As soon as the waitress came back, they ordered their food.

"I would ask you how your love life is, but unfortunately I saw that ya'll was good in that department."

"I'm so sorry about that," Reign apologized, turning red from embarrassment.

"So, I'm trying to pick up Baby Nikki and Royal this weekend. Camille's daughter, Kasie been asking for them to come over and play." DJ said, thinking about the promise he'd made to Kasie the last time he had spent time with Camille and her kids.

"You know you can take them whenever you want. That's not a problem." Reign said at the same time a nervous Cynthia approached their table.

"Hello," Cynthia spoke, bracing herself for her son's reaction.

"Why are you here?" DJ hissed after looking up to see his egg donor standing there. He was tired of Cynthia popping up on him and didn't know what else he had to say, to let her know that she was dead to him.

"DJ, a couple of weeks ago Cynthia came by the spa…"

Reign tried to step in and be the mediator, but DJ cut her off.

"So since you couldn't get to me, you bothered my sister with this nonsense, at her place of business."

"No..." Cynthia answered, looking at Reign for her help.

"DJ, Cynthia did come to the spa to ask if I could get you two together to have a conversation." DJ looked at his sister with a knowing look, and Reign completely understood his frustration with her. She had definitely blindsided him and overstepped her boundaries. "Just hear me out. I know you're pissed but I think you should hear your mother out."

"Why?"

"Because you actually get to have another chance to have your mother in your life. DJ, I know what she did was beyond fucked up, and nothing will change the past, but aren't you tired of living with that anger? I'm not saying you have to be the mother and son dynamic duo, but forgiveness is the only way to let go of that hurt."

"Sis, I know if the shoe was on the other foot, you would hop at this opportunity, but Cynthia abandoned me by choice. She didn't die." DJ didn't want to disrespect his sister, but their situation was not the same. Plus, she only stayed with their grandmother, Brenda, for one year before her mother's best friend, Tanya, and her husband, Thomas, rescued her from that hellhole.

"Your right..." Reign said, throwing her hands up in a

surrendering motion. She was now stepping out of the situation. She had stayed true to her word and created a time and opportunity for Cynthia to speak to her son, but now she wanted no parts of it.

"DJ, please, don't be mad at your sister," Cynthia voiced, feeling bad for putting Reign in the middle. "DJ, you have every right to be mad at me. I fucked up. I made a horrible decision but you have to understand, my decision was not based off any selfish malicious reason. I don't know how much you remember of the time that we were living together before Connor came into the picture…"

DJ just looked at his mother with an emotionless face, waiting for her to explain her leaving him wasn't selfish.

"Before I met your father, I use to work at a law firm downtown Philadelphia, as a secretary. When I met your father, he never let on that he was a married man with a family. It wasn't until I had gotten pregnant with you that he told me the truth. I tried to leave Dion. I went back home down south only for my father to shut the door in my face because I had a baby by a black man. I was stuck with Dion Sr. because he was my only support system, and he didn't even want you. When Dion did the unspeakable and went to jail, it was just you and me. My father took away my trust fund because he refused for me to use the money he saved to help raise you. And when word got out that Dion was my lover and child's father, my job let me go. Not wanting the negative publicity to ruin the law firm's reputation."

Reign remembered her father's trail. It had made headlines. It was one of the biggest trials in Philadelphia. She remembered Brenda cussing up a storm because some white bitch had testified against Dion about the abuse. Reign knew the white woman was a vital part of getting Dion locked up, and now after all these years, she now knew the white woman was Cynthia.

"I tried my best as a mother to raise and support you, but once I was fired, I got a job at Fresh Grocer as a deli clerk. That's where I met Connor. When he came into our lives, things change for the better. We were no longer struggling. We were never hungry because there was no need for me to sell the food stamps to make sure the electric and gas stayed on. I didn't have to sell the food stamps to make up for the money that I was short on for rent…"

As much as DJ hated to admit it, he knew his mother struggle before Connor came into the picture, and even though in the beginning, Connor may have been God's sent, he was also the main reason for his misery.

"I know you may think I was being selfish when I dropped you off at Brenda's, but I made a choice that would have benefited the both of us. At least I thought I was making a good choice. I gave Brenda five thousand dollars a month to keep you fed, clothes on your back and help with her household expensive. Remember when I first dropped you off? I would visit every weekend. The visits stopped because I couldn't handle leaving. The guilt would kick in, but I knew if I had brought you home, Connor would leave me, and without him, I would not have had the money to help you and we would've gone right back to living in the projects, barely making it. Even though the visit had stopped, I called you every day and Brenda would answer and tell me that you didn't want to speak with me. I understood that as hard as it was for me, it was harder for you. So I stopped the calls and only called on your birthdays and holidays. I knew my decision hurt you, but if I knew you were being mistreated, I would have easily made the decision to go back to the projects and struggle. When I came to give you your car, you never let on that you were homeless or being mistreated. I just wished you have said something."

"For what!" DJ shouted, banging on the table. "You leaving me should have never fucking happened! I would have rather been hungry, cold, and struggling, receiving your love and care that a child supposed to have, instead of being intentionally starved and unable to bathe because my grandmother blamed me for my father going to jail. She told me I was the reason why Dion pulled the trigger that killed my sister's mother and why he tried to kill my sister. From what I was told, Nikki found out about me and when she tried to leave him, he killed her and tried to commit suicide. She told me this at seven years old. For years, I held the burden that some blood was on my hands."

"I'm sorry," Cynthia said as the tears rolled down her and Reign's face. Brenda had really done a number on him.

DJ was so conflicted on the inside. Apart of him wanted to get from the table and never look back at Cynthia, but after allowing her to say her piece, he hated that he understood why she did what she had done. The truth was, Cynthia had also sacrificed the love and relationship with her child in hopes to give him a better life. The only problem was, she entrusted the wrong person to take care of him.

"Listen…" DJ started, trying to get his words together. "I'm fucked up on the inside. I've always been in survival mode until I met my sister. When she came into my life, that was the first time in a long time that I could actually be a kid and act my age. I didn't have to worry about where my next meal was coming from. I didn't have to risk my life by robbing drug dealers and other jack boys so I can have some money to occasionally stay at a motel, instead of sleeping in my car. For once, all I had to do was go to school and play football… I now know what you did wasn't for your own selfish gain. I know you gave Brenda money, so I take that into accountability. Those checks were clearing, so you thought I was being well taken care of, and you're right, I never opened my mouth to tell you what was going on. So, with that said, I do forgive you."

"Thank you." Cynthia said, mustering up a smile. DJ couldn't even imagine what those words meant to her.

"We need to take this one day at a time. I'm not saying we're going to pick up our relationship and act like this never happen.

"I understand, but I do want to get to know you better. One day you may have kids and get married. I would love to be there to witness some of the positive things that happen in your life. I don't have any family and would truly like a second chance at being a family with you."

"I would like that, too, but like I said, one day at a time."

"Of course." Cynthia completely understood that she was on his time.

"I'll give you my number." DJ said, writing his number on a napkin.

"I'm proud of you," Reign whispered to her brother. She knew it had to have taken a lot out of DJ to forgive the woman that'd abandoned him.

"Thank you." Cynthia said to Reign before grabbing the napkin. She was getting ready to leave as the waitress returned to their table with their food. "I'll call you later. I promise not to blow up your phone. Thank you. You don't know what this second chance means to me."

"Cynthia," DJ called out to her as she turned to walk away from the table. "How about you join us for lunch. My treat."

"Sure." Cynthia rushed back to the table. The smile that was plastered on her face could light up a room. As she ordered her Caesar salad and water with lemon, the smile never left.

"So, how did you link up?" Cynthia asked. She had been wondering that for the longest being that she remembered when dropping DJ off Reign did not live there.

"It's a long story," Reign said, shaking her head and letting out a chuckle. For a long time, she couldn't laugh about how she met DJ, but now she could. "God have a crazy way of placing people in your life."

"So, I was about to rob her with these two niggas I used to consider friends...." DJ started the story, and Cynthia's eyes got as wide as saucer as she silently listened to the crazy story that had brought the brother and sister together.

19

FIGHT FOR YOU

Rico Love: You better hope that nigga down to fight for you. Cause I'm down to fight for you. Now I've got to deal with another man in your face.

"Our 2019 Homecoming King is, Kyron Davidson!" Principal Tate announced as the crowd erupted into cheers.

Everybody had come out to show Kyron some support at his homecoming football game. Usually, it would've been, Camille, her sisters, Kelly, and Caddie's boyfriend, Matthew, supporting Kyron at his games, but this year, he had the full support of his family and DJ's family. Camille was so surprised when DJ came squad deep, with The Black family, along with Angelo and Cream. Even Kameron and Olive were at the game, sitting a few bleachers away.

It seemed after the spa day Camille had with the women of the black family, along with Tracey and Brooklyn, she had been inducted into the family. Even Kyron and Kasie called the Black family aunts, uncles and cousins.

"Ya'll heard that, my boy, Kyron, is the homecoming King!" DJ was on Instagram live, congratulating Kyron. Over the last couple of months, their bond had grown tight. It was sad to say that Kyron respected DJ more than his own father. Mainly because he'd never seen his mother so happy in his life. He had watched how DJ pushed her to reach her goals. He spent time with him and Kasie, and even took the time out of his busy schedule to work with him on bettering his skill in football. Even his coach and teachers had seen the change in Kyron's attitude and behavior since last year.

"The family out here showing support," DJ said, flipping the camera to show the Blacks and Camille's family. "My beautiful girls repping my youngin, too." Camille leaned to the camera with Kasie on her hip, screaming, *that's my brother!* DJ couldn't resist, he had to kiss his woman, and it caused his followers to go crazy with the likes and comments.

Angie_Martina1008: *Ya'll are so cute! Congratulation, Kyron!*

ShayShay1992: *Relationship goals. Love how families come together to support the young King.*

Meli_Christina: *Blended Family! Baby girl is so cute. Congratulation, Kyron!*

0527_Allie_Marie_0302: It takes a village to raise a child. And Kyron definitely has a strong village.

After halftime, the game continued with Kyron's school winning, 21-7.

"Let's go!" Kameron hissed at Olive, who in return looked at him like he was crazy.

"Okay…" She then said, growing tired of Kameron's funky mood. He had been in a funk ever since he realized DJ was there with Camille. "Kyron just text us telling us to meet him in the parking lot."

"We can see him another time. They're coming over next weekend. I ain't trying to be around Camille and her annoying ass sisters."

The whole game Kameron barely watched his son dominate the field because he was so busy watching his ex-wife smiling in her new man's face. Hearing that Camille and DJ was an item was completely different from seeing them together. Before seeing Camille with DJ, he made it a point to believe it was just gossip. Even when his own children made him aware of their mother's new boyfriend, he told them to stop lying. Kameron could not understand why a man of DJ's caliber would want a woman like Camille.

In his opinion, she was used up and not worth a damn.

"I don't want to wait until next week. Kyron invited me here and I'm not leaving until I can tell him good game." Olive was surprised she received a personal invitation to Kyron's homecoming game, and the last thing she wanted to do was disappoint him by leaving before she could speak.

"Okay," Kameron replied back, shaking his head. He did not want to be around Camille and her sisters. He knew they all hated him, and with Candace being in her feelings lately, the last thing he needed was for her to show out at his son's game and put their secret on blast.

Walking into the parking lot, Kameron easily spotted Camille and her new boyfriend because there were so many people asking for his autograph.

"Daddy!" Kasie yelled, pulling away from her mother and running toward her father.

"Hey Sweet pea." Kameron picked her up and threw her in the air. No matter how much people paint him as the bad guy, his daughter's love for him never withered.

"Hi, Kasie," Olive spoke as Kameron put her back down.

"Hi, Ms. Olive." Kasie gave Olive a hug then rubbed on her stomach. She was so excited to be a big sister.

"Hey, ya'll," Camille spoke. "Kasie, you know better than to run off like that. This is a crowded parking lot, not a playground. Anything could have happened."

"Sorry, mom."

"It's okay. Kyron should be out soon," Camille said before turning away to head back to her family. As soon as Camille reached them, she wrapped her arms around DJ and leaned into him as they waited for the homecoming King.

"Daddy, you want to meet Mr. DJ? He's so cool. He'll

probably give you an autograph, too, if I ask him," Kasie innocently asked.

"No, baby girl. I'm okay." Kameron fought the urge to not cuss Camille out. He hated that she had this man around his kids, and what hurt the most was that his children seemed to truly like this DJ character.

After ten minutes of waiting, Kyron finally came out to the parking lot. Kameron watched as DJ's family showed him mad love. He had never seen his son so happy.

"Kyron!" Kasie screamed, excited to see her brother. Kyron was her everything. Her own personal superhero.

"Let's go over there," Olive suggested.

"No he didn't!" Cassie hissed as she saw Kameron and Olive making their way over to the family.

"Stop, Cassie. Kyron invited Olive here. Please be on your best behavior. This is a fun night. We don't need any drama," Camille said, warning her sisters. She was actually proud of her son for inviting Olive. It seemed like he had taken her advice and he found out that Olive was kind of cool.

"Oh, so you just happy with being disrespected? That shit couldn't be me," Candace hissed. She was really mad that Kameron had the audacity to show up with his fiancée when he had just left her bed that morning. She hated that not only did she have to come second to her sister, but she was coming second to Olive as well. She couldn't understand why he would never choose her. Now he was being disrespectful by flaunting Olive in her face. She had told

Kameron that she was coming to the game tonight. So the least he could have done was left his fiancée home.

"He's not being disrespectful. Kameron bringing his fiancée to the kids event is their reality," Caddie said, trying to deescalate the problem

"Plus, she just said Kyron invited her personally, and Camille's not worried about them. She's being cordial like she should be when her kids are involve," Kelly added, coming to her best friend's defense. Candace got on her nerves.

"Kelly, nobody was talking to you!" Candace snapped,

"Bitch, but I was talking to you. You sitting here pissed the fuck off like Kameron is your ex-husband," Kelly shot back, causing Candace's eyes to get as wide as saucer. Only if they had known the truth in her statement, all hell would've broke loose.

"Ya'll, chill," Camille told them, not trying to be in the middle of those two fighting.

"I'm just going to say this. My sister ain't worried about Kameron or his bitch. Did you see that fine ass young nigga by her side? Millie definitely bossed up and got a real nigga?" Cassie pointed out, causing them to laugh because it was the truth.

"Wassup, dad?" Kyron spoke, making his way over to his father and Olive after speaking with DJ. Being as though Kyron had made it a point to speak and acknowledge DJ's presence before his had truly pissed Kameron off. "Hey, Olive." Kyron said, giving her a hug.

"Kyron, I must say, you dominated the field today. Thank you for allowing me to enjoy this day with you," Olive said.

"Thanks for coming."

"Not a problem. I would love to come to more games if that's okay with you."

"Yeah, that's cool," Kyron said.

"Go call your mom over here so I can speak with her for a minute," Kameron told his son. He had some words that he wanted to say to Camille. "Olive, go wait for me in the car."

"Why?" Olive asked as she looked at Kameron. Not only was she upset that he was shooing her away like he was ashamed of her, but she wanted to know what was so important that he needed to speak to Camille about that she couldn't hear. Little did Kameron know, his true color was showing and he was turning green with envy.

"Wassup? Kyron said you wanted to speak with me." Camille walked over and said.

"Yeah, I wanted to know when was it okay for our kids to be a part of a fucking circus act?" Kameron fussed, causing, both, Camille and Olive to look at him in shock.

"What the fuck are you talking about?" Camille asked, trying to keep her composure.

"Kameron, why are you starting trouble? Everybody just had a good time." Olive was just as confused as Camille.

"Olive, go to the car. This has nothing to do with you!" Kameron snapped. Camille wanted to feel bad for Olive, but this was the side of Kameron that Olive had unknowingly signed up for. That's why it was never okay to sleep with married men. They gave you the glitz and the glamour of being with them until you truly had them. Then you're being disrespected by the man who claimed to love you.

"Kameron, what is your problem?"

"My problem is you and your little boyfriend parading my children all over social media. You really know how to rob the cradle. You're a fucking cougar now!"

"Naw, she's my fucking woman! Now lower your fucking tone when speaking to her," DJ said, walking up to Camille and Kameron. He had noticed Kameron staring at him the entire game, and he figured he was Camille's ex.

"Excuse me?" Kameron said, caught off guard.

"Nigga, your heard me. Our relationship status don't have shit to do with you. I see you here with your woman. So what's the fucking problem?" DJ asked the question everybody wanted to know.

"Camille, I dismissed Olive. Please dismiss your little boyfriend."

"Kameron, he's everything, but little. I don't know what your problem is, but you need to get out your feelings. I'm not dismissing my man like he's a fucking child! Whatever you have to say to me, you can say in front of him, because I'm pretty sure he's the topic of discussion," Camille stated.

Kameron was frustrated and now all the attention was on him. He couldn't lie, the way DJ along with the men in his family were looking at him, it had him a little shook.

"Bro, you good?" Pharaoh asked. He never wanted DJ getting his hands dirty. DJ had too much to lose, but it was nothing for him to handle a situation with the quickness.

"We good?" DJ asked Kameron with a smirk. He could see the fear radiating off him. Kameron simply nodded his head. "We good, bro."

"Alright! Everybody heading to Teddy's bar and Grill to celebrate," Pharaoh announced, telling them the move.

"Babe, I'm going to be over here," DJ said, pointing only a few feet away from them, letting her know he was going to be close. He never planned on going over there, but he decided to make his presence known when Kameron thought he could talk to his woman any kind of way.

"Okay."

"You think it's okay to have our kids around a man like that? His family basically just threatened to harm me in front of our kids? Do you even know who his family are?"

"Yes, I know who his family is, and they accepted our children and myself into their family. Why is my relationship with DJ bothering you so much?"

"So you're okay with our kids being around known criminals?"

It was no secret who DJ was related to. Every time he talked about his support system, he talked about his sister and the Black Family. Throughout his career he had always been asked questions about his connection to the Black family and did he sell drugs for them. Everyone in the city of Philadelphia knew about the Black Brothers, and it was rumored that they were the Connect when it came to drugs, guns, and contract killing. Even though some might've thought they were true businessmen.

"I don't say shit when it comes to you and Olive, so please show me the same respect. The only time you have a right to say anything about my relationship or who I can have around my children is if we are being mistreated. And as you can see, Kyron and Kasie love him. You have a great night. Thanks for trying to ruin your son's night." With that said, Camille walked away to go be with her man and kids. She couldn't believe Kameron had acted the way he did, but he wouldn't be Kameron if he didn't make the night about him in some shape, way or form. Walking to the opposite side of the parking lot, Kameron was fuming. As soon as he reached his car, he hopped in, not even bothering to say two words to Olive.

"So are you going to explain why you were so upset? Tonight was supposed to be fun and it really bothers me that you tried to start a fight with Camille." Olive finally spoke up after fifteen minutes of driving. Kameron behavior really was driving her crazy.

"Olive this has nothing to do with you. You're not a parent yet. So you can't possibly understand where I'm coming from?"

"Just because our child haven't been born, yet, don't mean I wouldn't understand your point of view. But to be honest, you did wrong. And the only thing I see is that you are jealous."

"Jealous?" Kameron glance at Olive before laughing, like she was Kevin Hart or somebody. "I could never be jealous of Camille. Just look at her. She's ridiculous. She's stooping so low that she's dating a man ten years younger than her."

"I don't see anything ridiculous about that. They're both adults, and she actually looks happy, and the kids seem to have a great relationship with him. So, again, what's the real the issue?" Olive asked again. Deep down, she knew what Kameron's issue was, even if he didn't want to admit it out loud or to himself, she knew.

"Olive, DJ Roberts may be this great football player, but the people he's related to are dangerous people, and I don't want my kids around him or them. I see the look on your face, and I don't want to deal with the insecurity shit right now. Olive, I don't care that Camille's dating. I'm happy she finally moved on from our marriage. She was all depressed and shit, and that was affecting our children. So, thank God she moved on. It's just the person she moved on with isn't a good fit." Kameron explained, grabbing Olive's hand and kissing it.

Kameron said those words trying to convince himself more than he was trying to convince Olive. He never thought Camille would move on after him, especially with a younger and more financially stable man. He liked the fact that he thought she secretly wanted her marriage with him back; but the proof was in the pudding. His ex-wife had leveled up in ways he never imagined she would.

Not only did it bother him that he had to watch her with another man, but he also wondered if DJ satisfied her in ways he could never do, but the smile that graced his ex-wife's face was a smile he'd never seen. She was becoming the successful businesswoman she always wanted to be, and it killed him that he couldn't take any credit in her success, unlike she could with his.

20

WASTED LOVE

Jhene Aiko: Put that on my life, everything I love. Never crossed no line. It was all because I dedicate my life to lovin' you right

"So, You don't have the flu or a stomach virus. Candace, you're pregnant." Doctor Fisher excitedly announced as she walked back into the exam room where Candace was currently waiting, anxiously, silently praying that wasn't the cause of her nausea.

"Pregnant?" She repeated, not knowing what else to say. Apart of her wanted to jump for joy but the other knew Kameron would never allow her to have his baby.

"Yes. Would you like to do an ultrasound to see how far along you are?"

"Sure." Candace laid back down and placed her legs in the stirrups while Dr. Fisher prepared to do her ultrasound.

"Now, we're doing a vaginal ultrasound so we can get an accurate dating of your little peanut."

Candace swore it was like Deja Vu. This wasn't the first time she and Kameron had slipped up. The first time was literally a month before he and Camille's wedding when she called him to let him know the news. Watching her sister marry the love of her life was heartbreaking enough, but it was even worse because she was one of the bridesmaids. Kameron begged Candace to get an abortion.

The only person who knew the truth of Kameron and Candace affair was her mother, Colleen, and as she got ready to hear the heartbeat of her unborn child, the only thing that ran through her mind was the conversation that had changed her and her mother's relationship forever.

"What's wrong baby girl?" Colleen asked as she walked into Candace's room. Camille had just called and told her that she had just missed the fitting. "Your sister is upset with you, that you missed your dress fitting. Why didn't you call her and tell her to cancel the appointment? This the second time she will have to reschedule for you."

"Mama, Camille will get over it. She can just reschedule. It's not that deep." Candace rolled her eyes because she had bigger problems to deal with.

"Rescheduling an appointment may not be as deep to you, but you made it deep when you didn't take time out your day to cancel the appointment and had your sister leave work to meet you at an appointment that you didn't even show up to. All of the other bridesmaid were fitted for their dresses, and picked them up. It's a month until your

sister's wedding and you haven't been fitted. Sometimes alteration takes longer than you expect. I don't know what's going on with you, but you been the only one causing problems this whole process, and I hate to say this, but it's coming off as jealousy. It seems like you been doing everything in your power to ruin this happy time in your sister's life."

Colleen looked at her daughter with concern. It was never a secret that Candace always wanted to have one up on Camille. Colleen and her husband, Peter, always made sure to show all of the girls the same amount of love. Favoritism was never played in their house. So they could never understand why Candace always felt the need to be in competition with Camille.

"I'll make the next appointment, but you coming at me when Camille has been acting like a Bridezilla during this whole process. Anyway, I have a lot going on, too, mama. Maybe you and daddy would notice it if ya'll wasn't so concerned about your precious Millie."

"Watch your tone, little girl. Now what's going on with you that your father and me haven't noticed? You act like we see you every day. It's nothing for you to disappear for days at a time. Plus, you working down at the club, stripping. I never see you. So stop playing the victim. If you think we have a better relationship with your sisters, it's only because they make sure to visit us on the regular. Not when they need something."

Colleen was tired of Candace always playing the victim.

"Whatever, mom," Candace muttered just before jumping out of bed as a wave a nausea washed over her. Her sneakiness had finally caught up to her and now she was in a big dilemma. Colleen walked

243

into the bathroom that her daughter had just run into and watched her puke her guts out.

"Candy, don't tell me you're pregnant," Colleen said, shaking her head. The last thing Candace needed was a child to take care of when she couldn't take care of herself.

All Candace could do was cry. She was indeed pregnant, and it seemed like Kameron had dropped off the face of the earth. She told him about the baby as soon as she left the doctor's office only for him to tell her to get an abortion. Every time she called him, he would answer only to ask if she got the abortion, yet, and when he received the answer that he didn't want, he would hang up on her.

"What's wrong, child? It's going to be okay. I know this wasn't planned, but we have to make do. Who is the child's father?"

Even though she knew Candace was in no shape to become a mother, who truly was. Most pregnancies weren't not planned? But, that wouldn't stop her from being her daughter's support system, just like they were with Camille. Candace heart started to beat extra fast when her mother asked about the father, not sure if she wanted to tell her the truth. But at that point and time, she had no one to help her.

"Kameron," she admitted in just above a whisper.

"Who?" Colleen asked, knowing she couldn't have heard her daughter correctly.

"Kameron…" Candace said again, only for her to feel the sting on the right side of her face from her mother's slap. Colleen then slammed the bathroom door, not wanting anyone else in the house to hear their conversation.

"What the fuck you mean it's Kameron's baby? Ya'll muthafuckas been fucking around behind your sister's back?"

Candace cried hard, not able to answer her mother's question.

"Don't fucking cry now! You wasn't crying when you was allowing that nigga to fuck you. Now do he know you carrying his second child, that he cannot afford? Do you not understand it's your sister holding shit down while he's in school?" Colleen stressed, not understanding how stupid Candace could be. "Do you really hate your sister that much that you have to sleep with her man when there's a lot of niggas out here slinging dick?"

"Mom, I love him!"

"Candy, you can't be serious, baby. Your sister been dating this boy since high school." She eyed her like she was crazy.

"Don't look at me like that, mom. Kameron was supposed to be mine. I was talking to him first, but it was like as soon as he saw Camille, I was like a thing of the past. Camille always gets what she want. Everybody thinks she's so much better than me."

"Did Camille ever know ya'll use to talk?" Colleen asked. One thing she knew about her daughter, Millie, was that she was loyal and sometimes her loyalty could be a flaw. So she couldn't imagine Camille going against the girl code because of some boy. Camille had always wanted a close knit relationship with her twin, but. Candace never made it easy.

"No, but that's not the point," Candace said, feeling foolish. She knew she was holding a grudge against her sister, for years, for taking a man that she didn't even know she liked.

"Camille is going to kill y'all," Colleen stated with tears in her eyes. Camille was the sweetest person you'll ever meet, but when she was pushed to a limit of no return, she could be easily blinded by rage. Colleen couldn't understand for the life of her why Kameron would try

to put his life on the line like that. One would have thought he would've learned when Camille drove him and another young lady off the road. "Get an abortion!"

"Get an abortion?" Candace repeated. "So Camille can have a baby but not me!" She couldn't believe her mother's suggestion. Did she think Colleen would jump up and down in joy with the news of her baby being Kameron's? No. But she thought her mother could consider abortion as the last resort.

"Candace, do you hear yourself. Why would you even want to have a baby by this man? And if I didn't fear Camille going to jail for a double homicide, I would tell her. But that truth would have me losing two children."

"I want my child."

"Go head. You think you know so much. Have this child and watch he disappears. Do you think he will leave your sister and be with you?"

"I don't know, probably."

"No he will not! I bet he told you to get an abortion, too." All Candace could do was put her head down because she knew it was the truth. She couldn't even get Kameron to speak to her.

"I'll tell you this. Keep your pregnancy and I bet when the truth comes out, Camille would probably beat the baby out of you, and Kameron will still be chasing after your sister. Candace, this is not the way you find love. Accept the fact that you allowed that boy to play you like the fool you are."

"Well, this is not your decision?" Candace huffed, standing up. This was her decision to make and she didn't want to give up her child.

"Girl, you keep that child, I'll wash my hands with you. You have

the one type of evil to bring misery to others, especially your own sister."
Colleen said before walking out of the bathroom. After that day, they
have barely spoken two words to each other. In Candace's eyes, if it was
that easy for her mother to wash her hands with her, then there was no
need to be in her life.

After two weeks of being completely ignored by Kameron, Candace
finally got the balls to pop up at the apartment he shared with her sister.
She knew Camille was at work and Kameron was at home with Kyron,
who had just turned one. That night, she planned on laying everything
out on the table, asking him to call off his wedding and become a
family with her. However, that night Kameron sweet talked her right out
her lace panties by filling her head with empty promises, only for him to
tell her that if she truly loved him, she would get an abortion.

The next day she set up the appointment only to go through that
process alone, and only to watch him marry her sister, two weeks later.
Heartbroken was an understatement, but for some reason, he still had
his hooks in her.

Hearing her baby's heartbeat loud and strong brought
tears to her eyes. Candace refused to allow this opportunity to pass. She was having the baby and Kameron
couldn't do nothing but accept it. She had given the ultimate sacrifice of aborting her first child trying to prove
her love to him, and in return he made her sit on the side-
line, watching him make the next woman happy. First it
was Camille, now it was Olive. Candace refused to disappear into the background to make his life easier this go
round.

"Sounds healthy. You're measuring out to be ten weeks

pregnant," Dr. Fisher informed her, printing out the pictures.

"Okay."

"So go ahead and get dress. I'm going to prescribe you some prenatal pills. I'll have everything ready for you at the front desk when you check out."

As soon as Dr. Fisher left the room, Candace grabbed her phone to take a picture of the ultrasound pictures and sent Kameron the text of the good news.

Candace: *Congratulations daddy. We're ten weeks pregnant.*

Kam My First Love: *Candy, I don't have time for your shit. My fiancée is due in a couple of weeks. Get a fucking abortion. I'll cash app you the money. Why the fuck would you want to have a baby? Do you know what this will do to me and my fiancée? Even worse, your sister and my kids?*

Kameron response had literally broke Candace's heart into a million pieces. Why couldn't he love her the way she wanted? What didn't she have that Camille and Olive did? When was she going to get her happy ending? Her sadness instantly turned into anger as she dialed his number only to be sent to the voicemail.

Kam My First Love: *Do not contact me until you get rid of the fucking baby. I don't know what you want from me, but get it through your thick skull, you will never be anything to me but a fuck. And since you can't handle that, I'm done with you!*

Candace: *I'm keeping the baby!*

Kam My first Love: *Keep that baby and I'll kill you myself.*

Candace vision was so blurry due to the tears that

wouldn't seem to stop flowing. How could a man that she did everything for threaten her like that? Right then and there, she decided she would not get another abortion to satisfy him or save his ass. Candace was no longer going to be Kameron's secret, no matter what the truth might cost her.

21

MY SONG

H.E.R: *Everything that you've told me, I thank you every day for. All the things you wanted me to be is everything I've prayed for.*

*C*amille was on cloud nine as she walked through the airport to baggage claim. She had just spent the past two days out of town meeting with executive from the Food Network for an opportunity of a lifetime. She never thought her catering business would take her this far, and she owed everything to DJ for giving her the confidence and push she needed to start the business.

DJ was the first big client that gave her the opportunity to work for many different celebrities and people. He had taught her how to use every platform. For an example, her social media pages for Instagram and Twitter had over 1.1 million followers. She even started a YouTube channel that had over 500k subscribers. On her channel, she cooked many different meals. She even had DJ and the kids to join her to make the show more interesting. They even had little contest that her viewers suggested, and they picked the winner.

All of his advice and encouragement lead her to the point she was at now. Now she had just signed a deal to have a cooking show that would be aired on the Food Network.

As soon as she walked into baggage claim, her eyes lit up as DJ stood there with her bags and Kyron and Kasie holding up a sign with her name on it. The past six months had been the best months of her life. Camille was genuinely happy and so were her kids. Even though Kameron tried on multiple occasions to try her about her relationship with DJ, he soon got the point that DJ was not going anywhere. Plus, him meddling in her relationship was causing a strain in his own relationship with his fiancée.

"What are you guys doing here?" She asked in surprise, giving each and every one of them a hug.

"We were so anxious to figure out if you have good news or bad news," Kyron said as they made their way to DJ's Range Rover.

"Whatever the news may be, we're still celebrating. Camille, you don't know how proud I am of you," DJ said as he opened the door for her to get in the car. "So, where you want to go to eat?"

"Let's go to Ruth Chris steak house," Camille suggested with a smile. The last time she had stepped foot in her favorite restaurant was when Kameron asked her for a divorce. She initially never wanted to go back, thinking the restaurant would only bring back bad memories that she wanted to forget. But, she wanted to share her great news at her favorite restaurant with her favorite people.

"Sounds good to me."

They headed to Camille's house to drop all her luggages off and for everybody to get freshened up and changed for dinner. Slowly but surely, DJ and Camille started leaving clothes at each other's houses. Even the kids had clothes at DJ's house when they all spent the night over in his mansion.

"So, what's the verdict?" DJ asked as soon as they placed their order in with the waitress. He had been trying to be patient, but he wanted to know what happened with the big meeting.

"Well…. The meeting went great. They loved my YouTube channel and they told me they could see me with my own cooking show."

"Wait, mom, you're going to be on TV?" Kyron asked.

"Yes! Well, I have to do a pilot first to see how that goes. If my pilot does great, then they're offering me a deal for five million dollars for two years of my own show on the Food Network.

"What!" Kyron said with his mouth wide open.

"Mommy, you are black girl magic," Kasie said, giving her mom a hug. All Kasie knew was that her mom was going to be on TV like a superstar.

"Damn, babe, I'm so proud of you," DJ said, smiling. It was nothing sexier than seeing his woman being a go-getter and making boss moves. When he met Camille, all she had was dreams of owning her own catering business. Now her dreams were taking her further than she ever expected.

"Thank you, babe, but I want you to know you're such a huge part of my success story. This has been a dream for years, and after one conversation with you, I decided to put myself first and put some action behind my dreams, making it reality." DJ lifted up his glass and clinked it with hers.

"Babe, this is all you." He refused to take any credit. He may have given her words of encouragement, but at the end of the day, she was the one who had put in the work.

"So, what's next, big baller?" Kyron asked his mom. He was also proud of her. Growing up, he would always hear his mom talk about her catering company. To see her dream in completion made him believe he could accomplish anything. It also taught him that sometimes things did happen if you have the right people around you. Hearing his mom give DJ thanks for giving her the push that his father never did made him respect him a little bit more.

"I don't know. The sky is the limit. I was thinking about writing a cookbook with all my recipes, but my ultimate goal is owning a restaurant."

"I like that," Kasie said, making everybody laugh.

DJ's laugh was cut short due to his phone ringing. Pulling it out, it was another number that he didn't recognize, so he pushed the ignore button as a heavy sigh left his mouth. Even though he didn't know the number, it didn't mean he didn't know who the caller was. He knew exactly who it was.

"Is everything okay? Your phone been going off since you picked me up from the airport."

"Yeah, everything's cool. The call not important," DJ assured her before taking a sip of his drink. He knew Camille's question had an underlying meaning. So far, Camille had not dragged her insecurities and baggage from her past relationship into theirs, but he knew a lot of things would easily make her speculate cheating, and he knew he wasn't doing a great job of easing her mind.

Not once since they had been together had he purposely ignored a phone call, especially when people called him back to back. He answered just to make sure everything and everyone was okay. So his actions at the moment were definitely out of the norm. Hearing his phone ring again, he pulled it out and turned it off to avoid any other distractions.

"You sure?" Camille asked with a raised eyebrow. DJ never gave her a reason to question him, but the feeling in her guts was telling her that something wasn't right. Some would've thought she was doing too much, but she refused to get played again.

"Positive." DJ answered with finality, letting her know that they weren't going down that road.

DJ was irritated. Not so much at Camille, but at Yazmine. For some reason, for the past couple of days she had been calling him nonstop, leaving several voice messages asking if they could meet up to talk. DJ was annoyed at the fact that someone had given her his number. He wanted to change his number, but that would cause too much of a hassle trying to make sure everybody had the new number, and with the ignored phone calls Yazmine still seemed like she couldn't catch a hint. In his opinion, there was nothing to talk about. They both had moved on with their lives. Now her constant calling was starting to have Camille look at him sideways.

"So, mom, are we still doing the dinner before thanksgiving?" Kyron asked. Since he had been chilling with KJ, he'd met Charlie, and they had been talking on the low for quite some time. Charlie was the niece of Queen's fiancé, Kelz, and he wanted to invite her to the dinner.

"Dinner before Thanksgiving?" DJ asked.

"Yeah, it's our little family tradition. We host our big thanksgiving dinner the day before thanksgiving so that allows my sisters to spend thanksgiving with their significant others instead of having everybody split the holiday between multiple households."

"That's wassup."

"So, to answer your question, yes. Why?"

"Cuz I wanted to invite Charlie over for dinner," Kyron said, shocking Camille. She knew her son had little girl-friends here and there, but not none he wanted to invite over for a family gathering.

"Charlie…" Kasie sang her name in a teasing way before making kissing faces.

"Charlie, huh?" Camille smiled. She had met Charlie before at one of the Black family's event, and she was a complete sweetheart.

"Yeah, I like her," he admitted

"Alright. You know you have to come correct with her," DJ said. Kelz didn't play when it came to his niece.

"Definitely."

"You coming, right, to the dinner? You can help me make my cookies." Kasie asked DJ.

"Of course, baby girl." DJ answered, pinching her cheek, causing her to laugh.

"You know he's not missing an opportunity to get down on moms cooking." Kyron cracked.

"You damn right."

"Plus, he can't miss our first holiday together." Camille was just as excited that DJ was spending the holidays with her. "So, babe, you know you going to be helping with the cooking. All three of you."

"Yeah… sure." DJ said, knowing damn well he wasn't cooking. That was unless she wanted dinner to be burnt. "So are you ready for this driving test, tomorrow?"

"As ready as I'm going to be," Kyron replied back, hyped up. DJ had been taking him driving for the past couple of weeks. He already had three lessons and just wanted to practice some more before the test. Being as Camille was a horrible teacher, Kyron barely spoke to his dad after the whole thing at his football game, but he did keep in contact with Olive to check in on her with the baby. Surprisingly, he was anxiously waiting for the arrival of his little brother.

"Good!" Camille said with a smile. She loved the fact that Kyron was trying to gain more independence. She had been back and forth about buying him a car if and when he passed the driving test, but DJ already had the perfect car in mind for him, his Benz. The first car he ever had. The one his mother had bought for him. Once DJ was able to buy his own car, he never drove it again. It was still in perfect condition and that was the car he had been using to teach Kyron how to drive.

"Oh, Olive just sent me a text. She had the baby," Kyron said, looking at his phone then passed it to Kasie so she could see their little brother.

"Look, mommy!" Kasie said, excitedly showing Camille the picture of her new baby brother.

"He's handsome." Camille smiled, answering honestly.

For the first time, she realized she had let go of the hurt and pain that Kameron and Olive had caused. Looking at the picture of Kameron newborn son did not faze her one bit. She thought when Olive had the baby she would feel some type of emotion. Like, anger, sadness, even envy. But all she felt was content.

Looking across the table, she stared in the eyes of the man who help heal her broken heart. The man who taught her how to love again and that she was worth being loved the right way.

The rest of the dinner was fun, and they enjoyed each other's company. After leaving the restaurant, Camille decided that they would spend the evening at DJ's mansion, especially since the kids wanted to use his indoor pool. When they got there, Kyron and Kasie both went into the guest bedrooms they stayed in when they spend the night.

"Babe, you sure you want to take Kyron tomorrow morning to his test? I know you have practice. I don't want you to run late." Camille asked, walking out of the master bathroom in nothing but a towel. She had just gotten out the shower.

"I'm good. I told him I'll take him so that's what I'm going to do. I'm a man of my word."

"I know, and thank you," she said, climbing on the bed and straddling him. Kissing his neck, before she leaned back to see his face, she could tell his mind was somewhere else. "What's wrong?"

"Nothing," DJ said, trying to unwrap her towel but she stopped him.

"Babe…"

"So, you know Reign set up a lunch for me and my mom to talk…" DJ started and Camille nodded her head, yeah. "Well, that day at the lunch I forgave her. Even though I didn't agree with what she did, I understood her reason. Now she want to know what I'm doing for the holidays."

"Okay…"

"I know I forgave her, but I still feel some type of way. I can't really explain it. I know I need to leave the past in the past, but I think it's too soon for her to be spending the holidays with us and shit."

"If you forgave her, you need to let go of that hurt. No one can change the past. So if you think this is too soon, the right time will never come for you. All you can do now is make new and better memories. So why not start by inviting her to our pre-thanksgiving dinner party."

"Alright, I'll call her in the morning."

"Good, now I want and need all you attention on me so we can celebrate the right way," Camille said, finally allowing her towel to drop. Tonight was far from over as the two lovers explored each other's bodies, making up for lost time.

22

U + ME (LOVE LESSON)

Mary J. Blige: *You plus me was a love lesson.*
In too deep without imperfection.

Kameron sat next to Olive on the sofa as she breast fed their baby boy, Kameron Davidson Jr. Watching Olive give birth to his second son was such an amazing experience. He knew he needed to handle Candace as soon as possible before she tried to ruin everybody's happiness. For the life of him, he could not understand how she got pregnant, because he always wrapped up or pulled out when they had sex, but lo and behold, she was pregnant and was trying to pin the baby on him.

"Babe, you mind if I make a run really quick? I want to check on the kids. I really don't like where me and Kyron stand in our relationship," Kameron lied using his children as an excuse to get away.

"No. Sure," Olive said, completely understanding. She had even developed a relationship with Kyron, but Kameron really seemed to piss him off at the game when he tried to start an argument with Camille because of DJ. "My mother is here to help me, so we're good."

"Cool. Do you want anything while I'm out?"

"No, I'm okay. Just tell Kasie and Kyron I said hey and I can't wait for the to meet baby Kam."

"I will."

Kameron gave baby Kam and Olive a kiss before grabbing his car keys and heading to the front door. As soon as he got in the car, he tried to call Candace for the umpteenth time only for his call to go straight to voicemail. He needed to know if she had gotten the abortion that he asked her to get. He had cash app her fifteen hundred dollars to get the procedure done, and buy herself something with the extra cash to make her feel better, but she had yet to contact him or answer his call to verify that the deed was done.

After driving for about twenty minutes, Kameron pulled up in front of Camille's parents house. That was the house Candace lived in with her twins. Kameron got out the car, silently praying that none of her nosey neighbors recognized him or his car. He quickly walked to the door and used the key that Candace had given him to let himself in when he came over for a late night quickie.

"What are you doing here?" Candace asked as soon as Kameron made his way into her house.

I need to get these locks changed, ASAP! She silently thought, regretting giving his ass access to her home.

"You know why I'm here. Why haven't you been answering my phone calls?"

"There's nothing you need to say to me that you didn't say in those text messages."

"Did you handle your problem?" Kameron asked the question that led him there in the first place. All he needed to know was that she had taken care of the problem and he promised he would go about his day and stay out of her life. The last thing he wanted or needed was for Candace to be a mother to one of his kids.

In Kameron opinion, she shouldn't add on another burden of being a mother to a third child. Candace was far from an independent woman. She survived off child support she received from Leon and welfare. The house she lived in was paid for, and her sisters were the ones that paid the property taxes. Candace was comfortable with living off the back of her sisters and Leon, and he refused to be another one of her sponsors.

"My problem?" she asked, hurt by his choice of words. She couldn't understand why Kameron couldn't see their child as a blessing.

"Yes, Candace. I'm not playing with you. I don't even know how ya Houdini ass got pregnant. I always strapped up or pulled out. Plus, you said you were on birth control."

"What are you trying to insinuate? Kameron, obviously your pull-out game is not as good as you think," Candace yelled, throwing a pillow at him. She was on birth control but the last time they had sex, she had forgotten to get a refill. So mistakes happened, and now she was pregnant by a man who acted like it was the worst thing that could've happened in the world.

"Whatever? Just give me an answer. Did you get the abortion or not?" Kameron's patient was wearing thin.

"Why having a baby by me is such a problem? I'm a good mother. My kids never want for anything."

"I don't want you to be a mother to my kids because you have nothing to offer them. Just like you have nothing to offer your kids that you have with Leon. You sit here and refuse to get a job because you're comfortable with living off Leon's child support. I'm not one to judge, but there's not one moral bone in your body. You're just a grimy bitch who want what the next woman has. All you teaching your daughter now is how to trap niggas and your son is learning how to not trust bitches like you. So, fuck no. You can't have my child. It's not going to turn out to be messed up like you."

"Nigga, are you serious right now? Camille was a stay at home, bitch, not doing shit with her life but living off your money. Or did your dumb ass forget that? That hoe Olive don't have any moral when she was sleeping with you while you was married. Fuck you for looking down on me, and you're just as grimy and fucked up as me."

"Your sister turned into a stay at home mom, but she had always held shit down, even when I couldn't." Kameron admitted. He may have talked shit about Camille, but it truly bothered him to hear Candace talk down on her. "So, watch your damn mouth! You act like Camille isn't the reason you're staying here, because you know damn well ya mom didn't leave this house to you. As a of matter fact, you weren't even in your parents will. So show some respect to the one who's helping you and your kids survive, because your bum ass think living off welfare is the way to go."

"That bitch ain't do shit for me!" Candace exclaimed with tears in her eyes. Her parents were a sore subject for her, and it hurt her everyday that they left this world on bad terms.

"Listen, I didn't come over here to argue or point out the truth in your life. But you're not thinking rational. You have to know you having that child is the worst thing ever that you could do. How do you think your sister would react to this? Or my fiancée who just gave birth to my son?"

"I don't give a fuck about those bitches! Why the fuck you care so much about Camille's feelings?"

"I don't, really, but at the end of the day, she's the mother of my children. If she's not good, my kids won't be good, and most likely, if she ever found this out, she'll probably go to jail for murder. You know her temper as well as I do, and trust me, I'm not trying to see that side of her. Plus, I'm on my last thread of hope of repairing my relationship with Kyron. I'm not going to lose my fiancée or my kids over you. Do all of us a favor and don't keep this baby."

Over the past couple of days, Candace had been going back and forth about taking the abortion pills that was prescribed to her. Glancing at the CVS bag on the table, she shook her head. She knew the consequences that would come if the truth ever came out about her and Kameron. Candace might not of had a close relationship with her sisters, but the baby she was carrying would definitely make their relationship nonexistent, and sad to say, they were the only family she had left.

Kameron followed her eyes to the coffee table to see the CVS bag on there. Without hesitation, he grabbed the bag and opened it to find the prescription for her abortion pills.

"Why are these still filled? Why haven't you taken them?" He snapped. He was tired of playing games with Candace. Walking into her kitchen, he got a glass of water. Candace was about to take the pills, voluntarily or involuntarily.

"I don't know why you're getting me a glass of water like I'm about to take these pills. I made my decision to keep my baby, and I'll be damn if I get an abortion to satisfy you or the next bitch," she stated, rolling her eyes. "So you can let yourself out of my house and leave the key."

Kameron calmly ignored her and open the pill bottle. Candace gave him no choice but to shove the pills down her throat. Gripping her jaws, Kameron shoved the first one into her mouth.

"Get the fuck off of me!" Candace screamed, and before he could grab the water to make her swallow it, Aleah and Leon Jr came walking into the house, catching Kameron off guard.

"Ayo, what you doing to my mom?" Leon Jr yelled, charging over to Kameron. The situation in front of him didn't look right.

"Uncle Kameron?" Aleah called out, wondering why he was there, yet, again. And why it looked like he and her mom was about to fight.

"What are you doing to my mom? And why are you here?" Leon asked, about to pull out his phone to call his dad.

"Listen, me and ya mom was just playing. Alright, Candace, I'll catch you later," he said with a smile, but his eyes were dark and cold. Telling her that he was very displeased about this situation. He didn't even bother saying good-bye to the kids before walking out and slamming the front door behind him. Now, not only did Candace make a decision to keep the baby, but now he had to worry about Leon and Aleah opening their mouths to the wrong person and have things blowing up in his face before he could prepare himself.

"Mom, why was Uncle Kameron over here?"

"Because we're still friends, and he wanted to talk to me about something?" Candace lied, and by the look on her son's face, she knew he wasn't buying it.

"Why are you friends with Uncle Kameron when nobody else in the family is?"

"Just because him and auntie Millie got a divorce doesn't mean that I have to stop being his friend."

"Well, why was he gripping you up? I'm about to call my dad to handle him," Leon Jr was beyond pissed at what he had walked in on, and he knew they weren't just playing.

"Stay out of grown folks business, Junior, and what happens in this house stays in this house. Do you understand?" Candace fussed. The last thing she needed was to have everybody in her business. She was going to keep the baby, but she was going to disclose to anyone who her baby's father was. Just a little hush money from Kameron every month on top of child support would do just fine. She wanted to live in a big house like Camille and Olive, and she didn't see why she couldn't now that she was pregnant with Kameron's baby.

⚭

"ARE YOU NERVOUS?" KAMERON ASKED OLIVE BEFORE THEY got out of the car.

Tonight was the night of the family dinner that Kameron's mother, Sandra, had set up so she could meet her new grandson. The whole Davidson's clan would be in attendance, and Kameron had been putting off the dinner for the longest. Everybody wanted to meet the famous, Olive, the woman who'd stolen his heart from Camille. But now with the holidays coming and the arrival of Baby Kam, Kameron knew he had to get the meet and greet out of the way. Plus, Olive was starting to plan the wedding and they had officially set a date.

"Yes, a little," Olive answered, looking around her surroundings. Kameron didn't grow up in the suburbs that they lived in now. He was raised smack dead in the hood. "So this is where you was raised, and your family still live here?"

Olive subconsciously clutched her purse closer to her. That one moment made Kameron want to turn around and head back to the car, already knowing the dinner was about to go left. His parents loved his neighborhood and took pride they'd raised their children there. The only person who seemed to have been ashamed of his upbringing was Kameron, being the reason he rarely visited.

"Yeah," he answered, clearing his throat. They walked towards the house and rung the doorbell. Everybody knew that Kameron was bringing Olive over for dinner, but that didn't mean they would be on their best behavior, especially if Olive pulled some bullshit like clutching her purse again like somebody was about to rob her.

"Hey, son!" Kevin, Kameron's father said answering the door and inviting him and Olive into the house.

"Hey, dad. Ya'll have it smelling good up in here?" Kameron said as his stomach rumbled. It had been a whole year of him not having some soul food cooking. Olive was on this health trip, and only cooked healthy things. Now that he thought about it, the last time he had a good home cooked meal was the last time he slept with Camille.

"You know how your mother get down. She have fried chicken, ham, mac and cheese, greens, yams, rice, butter rolls and for dessert she have my banana pudding." Kevin said, running down the food menu.

"Sounds delightful," Olive said, making her presence known.

"You must be Ms. Olive, and this here have to be my youngest grandson, Kam?" Kevin said, reaching for the baby to take him out of his car seat.

"Oops, I have some hand sanitizer. Can you put some on before picking him up?" Olive said, pulling it out of her bag, causing Kevin to stop and look at her like she was crazy. He understood new parents wanting everybody's hands cleaned before touching their baby, but all he was trying to do was help.

"That's fine. I'm going to let everybody know you're here," Kevin said, shaking his head because Olive was definitely probably going to get cussed out by tonight. "Put ya'll coats and everything in the guest room."

"Okay," Kameron said as he walked to the guest room. As soon as he reached the room, he started in on Olive. " Olive, what is your problem tonight?"

"What are you talking about?" She asked, oblivious as to how she was being rude.

"When we first got here you were clutching your purse like somebody was going to run up on us and rob us. Then you stopped my father from picking up my son. You never made your mom or father put hand sanitizer on before picking up Kam. I'll tell you now, keep that shit up this will be the worst dinner you ever attended. Matter of fact, let's leave."

Kameron could see the disaster dinner happening even before it got started. His father, Kevin, was the easiest person she would be able to get along with, and she had done offended him. Everybody else was team Camille. Even Kevin was team Camille, but he stayed out of his kids business. Kameron had made his choice to leave his ex-wife, now everybody just had to get use to the woman he chose.

"Wait, no. I'm sorry if I offended your father. I will be more conscious of what I do. I just don't want the baby getting sick," Olive explained, not wanting to make a bad impression, but it was too late because she had already done that with Kevin.

"Okay." Kameron sighed, knowing he should've just left.

"Well, hello, my long lost brother who act like he don't know anyone," Kameron's sister, Sierra, spoke.

"Wassup, Sierra?" He said, pulling his little sister in for a hug. Sierra used to look up to her big brother like a hero. She used to be proud to say her brother was a doctor, but that ended when a little bit a money made him forget where he had came from.

"Wassup, bro? Where my niece and nephew?" Kyler asked, giving his brother some dap.

"Man, Kyron on a date with his girlfriend and Kasie is

271

attending a sleepover with one of her friends. They already had the date and sleepover planned and I didn't want them backing out of their prior commitments."

"Understandable," Kyler said, bobbing his head.

Olive stood off to the side holding Kam in her arms, noticing how Kameron's sister and brother completely ignored her and her son.

"Ummm hmmm," she cleared her throat.

"Oh, babe, come here and let me introduce you to everybody at once. Mom, Dad, Kyler and Sierra, this is my fiancée, Olive, and our son, Kameron Jr. We call him baby Kam or Kam."

"Well, hello, Olive. It's nice to finally meet you." Sierra said dryly, and everyone else spoke too.

"Well, now that the introduction is out the way, lets sit down and eat."

Dinner was going great. Olive just sat back and watched Kameron in the comforts of his family home, and she was totally amazed at how he was acting. It was like he was finally letting loose. He was drinking, cussing, and joking around. He honestly looked to be happy and enjoying himself. Sad to say, Olive was jealous because he never seemed that happy around her.

"I must say, the food was delicious and this banana pudding is to die for. Ms. Sandra, you will have to share your recipe," Olive said, trying to join the conversation.

"It is to die for, but this is not my recipe. I didn't even make it. You know, Kevin have a sugar tooth, and he called

Camille right on up and asked her to make him her famous banana pudding."

"Yeah, you know my daughter-in-law loves me. She made me two pans. Kyron brought it by yesterday when he introduced us to his girlfriend," Kevin said, not meaning to throw shade at Olive, but he would always consider Camille as his daughter in law.

"So you guys still keep in contact with Camille? That's nice," Olive said, forcing herself to not roll her eyes.

"Why wouldn't we? She's the mother of my niece and nephew. Just because Kameron and Millie got a divorce, that doesn't change our relationship with her," Sierra responded, waiting for Olive to say something in return. Everybody had been trying to be on their best behavior, but when Kevin came in the kitchen and told his wife what Olive did, they were all ready for the dinner to be over.

"Oh, it's not a problem. So ya'll met Kyron's girlfriend. I haven't even met her, yet." Kameron joked, chuckling, hating the way his relationship with his son seemed to be unraveling.

"Yes, she's such a pretty girl," Kevin said before the doorbell rung and he excused himself.

"Hello, family!" Uncle Kendrick said as he walked into the house. Uncle Kendrick was Kevin's brother.

"Hey, Kendrick!" Sandra said as he made his way around the dining room table to give everybody a hug. "Let me go make you a plate."

"Thanks, Sandra. Goddamn! Hell must have frozen. Boy, what the hell your boujee ass doing in the hood?"

"Wassup, Uncle Kendrick? I came down so everybody can meet my fiancée and son, Kam," Kameron explained, laughing at his uncle. He didn't find what he said offensive because he knew once he made it out the hood he wasn't turning back.

"Your fiancée and baby? Well, hello, beautiful. I'm Uncle Kendrick and this my nephew…"

"Kam." Olive said with a smudge smile.

"Well, welcome to the family, baby girl. So Kameron, I guess that fine ass ex-wife of yours finally gave you your walking papers?" Kendrick said, causing everybody to laugh except Kameron and Olive.

"Naw, I was the one who asked her for a divorce." Kameron made clear in a matter of fact tone.

"So, Olive, how did you meet my nephew?"

"Oh, I'm a pediatrician at his practice," she said, smiling, loving that she could throw out there that she was a doctor. In her opinion, Camille was a housewife that had lucked up in the divorce and was now using her new man's status for her successful business. Olive tried not to be jealous of Camille, especially since she had the man that they both wanted, but hearing Kameron's family speaks so highly of her turned her envious because she knew she would never have that relationship with them.

"The practice his wife helped him build from ground

A YOUNG RICH BOSS CAPTURED MY HEART

up? Damn, nephew, you one cold muthafucka." Kendrick said, laughing.

"He's bold as shit, right?" Kyler co-signed, joining in laughing.

"Well, the best woman won." Kameron said. He hated how his family was looking at Olive like she was the other woman. The truth was, his marriage with Camille was over and he fell in love with Olive.

"Damn right she won. Camille out here looking like a whole snack. Her business is flourishing. Kyron just told me she got an offer to have a cooking show on the Food Network, and she's dating the young man, DJ Roberts, from the Philadelphia Eagles. So when you say the best woman won, I have to agree with you, honey." Sandra said, placing Kendrick's plate in front of him.

"Yesssss, mama. My big sis definitely leveled the fuck up! Olive, you might not have seemed like a blessing to Millie at first, but girl, you took away the person who was blocking all of her blessings," Sierra voiced, causing Kyler to laugh.

"Sandra and Sierra," Kevin called their names, trying to smother the smoke before it turned into fire. He'd seen this argument coming a mile away.

"Naw, dad, let them speak their peace. But the truth is, Camille was boring and a moocher, and I gave her her walking papers because she was no longer on my level, and Olive was."

Sandra loved her son, but what she was not going to

allow was for him to disrespect Camille to make Olive feel better about herself.

"Kameron, don't get ahead of yourself, son. Camille was on your level when she was working multiple jobs to help put you through medical school and open up that practice of yours. So don't try to downplay her role in your achievements. Let's be real, if it weren't for Camille pushing your dreams while putting hers on the back burner, you probably wouldn't be a doctor or have this practice. And Olive, you wouldn't have had the chance to hop on a married man's dick." Sandra bluntly stated, but she wasn't done. "Also since you going to be getting married to Kameron, Olive you need to grow the fuck up and woman up. I don't care if you guys get married and be married for the rest of your lives, you will always be the other woman who turned into his wife. Own it and don't make excuses about it. This is what you wanted, no matter what it took or who it broke in the process. This will always be the narrative of your love story."

"I think we will be going now." Kameron had heard enough and didn't know what else to say. Just like he thought, dinner was a disaster.

"That's okay. You can make your way up out of here. You honestly lasted longer than I thought, but let's make something clear. If you don't want us to be apart of Kam's life, don't bring him over here. That fiancée held him so tight like we were going to kidnap him. She already offended your father when he tried to bond with his grandson, and didn't even apologize. So just keep the same energy and don't get mad when Kam's brother and sister know us, and he don't.

"How do you think that's even fair? And correction, I didn't mean to offend anyone. Kam's a newborn and I don't want him getting sick. So let's make this right, if you're not in Kam's life, that's because of the choice you made, not us." Olive clarified, tired of how they were trying to make her and Kameron out to be the bad people.

"Olive, you're probably wondering why we have such a close knit relationship with Camille. That's because when they made it out the hood, she never forgot about us. She's the reason why we have a relationship with his other kids, not him. I'm his mother and I don't even know where he lives. Like I said, keep that same energy," Sandra said, getting up from the table to walk in the kitchen.

Nobody said another word as Kameron and Olive got their coats and placed Kam in his little snowsuit and headed out the door.

"I can never replace her," Olive said as soon as Kameron pulled off from the house. This was not how she thought the dinner would go.

"I'm not marrying you to replace Camille. Don't let what they said get to you. All that matters to me is you and my kids. I don't need any extended family," Kameron stated.

He heard his mother loud and clear and he was going to keep that same energy. He didn't need their negativity in his life.

23

WHATEVER LOLA WANTS

Sarah Vaughn: *I always get what I aim for*
And your heart and soul is what I came for.

"Yo!" DJ barked into the phone. He was just leaving practice and all he wanted to do was relax and chill. Practice had literally worn him out.

"Why are you yelling?" Yazmine asked like she wasn't bothering him with all of the excessive phone calls and messages.

"Yazmine, what the fuck you want?" He asked, hopping in the car.

"DJ, I didn't think you were going to answer." Yazmine tried getting her thoughts together. She had been calling him for the pass couple of weeks with no answer or call back. So she was shocked that he had even picked up this time.

"I only answered to tell ya stalking ass that I'm about to get a restraining order against you. Why are you blowing me up like this?"

"A restraining order? Really? This is what we have come to?" Yazmine sounded really hurt.

"Yaz, what do you want?" DJ asked, calming himself down. He'd already made up his mind that his phone number would be changed today.

"DJ, all I want is a moment of your time. I know you're in a relationship and trust, I'm not trying to mess that up, but I think we both need some closure when it comes to our relationship."

"I don't need any closure. I gave you the world and you did me dirty, end of story. I took it as a lesson learn," DJ stated. The last thing he wanted was to keep rehashing his past relationship.

"DJ, it's not all black and white. Please just let me have this one moment to explain and apologize. Can you meet me at Crafty Soul Food?" Yazmine was referring to the little Soul Food restaurant they used to go to all of the time when they were in Philly. "DJ, please. After this, you will never hear from me again."

"Alright. Meet you there in twenty."

"Great!" Yazmine said, excitedly, before DJ hung up in her ear.

DJ knew he was going against his better judgement

about meeting Yazmine, but if that was what it took for her to not contact him again, so be it. Plus, as much as he hated to admit it, he was truly interested as to what she had to say, and he drove straight from the stadium to the restaurant.

"Yo, sis?" DJ answered his phone as he parked his car. He just pulled up to the restaurant.

"Where you at? You trying to go to lunch?" Reign asked as she walked into her office at her shop.

"I'm actually at Crafty Soul Food right now, about to get something to eat. You want me to grab you something? I can swing by the spa when I'm done here?'

"Yeah… Wait. Why are you at Craft Soul Food? You live nowhere near there?" Reign asked. He loved their food when he was younger, but he wasn't driving across the city to get it.

"I'm meeting Yazmine here," DJ admitted before the line went silent. "Hello?"

"Nigga, now you know this is a bad idea. Why the fuck are you meeting up with that bitch?"

"Man, she talking about some closure."

"Fuck that hoe closure! DJ, I don't have a good feeling about this. You made it perfectly clear that you were done and there was nothing to talk about."

"Reign…"

"Naw, how you think Camille would feel about this? Yazmine already tried to be messy before and Tempest had to put her in her place."

"Camille knows I'm loyal and I would never give her a reason to doubt me, and I would never disrespect her."

"Alright, do what you want. But order me the fried fish platter, seafood mac n cheese, greens, candy yams, and rice with gravy." Reign ran down her order. DJ was a grown man and he could do what he wanted. However, she was letting him know that it was a bad idea. Yazmine was messy and she wanted him back. So in Reign's eyes, DJ was currently giving her the opportunity to cause problems in his current relationship.

"Damn, Reign. What, you eating for two?" DJ joked only for Reign to buss out crying. "What's wrong with you?"

"Your brother-in-law done knocked me up, again. And this baby is giving me hell. I'm throwing up every day and all day. Crying over everything. I swear I'm getting my tubes tied," She complained, causing DJ to laugh at her expense.

"You already know Pharaoh not having that," he voiced as he saw Yazmine walking to the restaurant carrying a car seat and a diaper bag.

"Whatever… and since you think it's funny, stop at Fresh Grocer and get me a fruit salad, too."

"Alright, let me get this shit over with?" DJ said, before hanging up with his sister.

"DJ!" Yazmine called, waving her hand so she could get his attention.

"Wassup, Yazmine?" He said, sitting at the table. For some reason, he looked down at the car seat that Joey was sleeping peacefully in. For the first time in a long time, he thought about their child that had passed away. Even though having a baby by Yazmine was the last thing he wanted, it didn't stop him from wondering how his son would have looked and what type of personality he would have had. DJ never took the time to grieve his death. He just simply pushed it to the back of his mind.

"His nanny had a doctor appointment. So I brought him with me," Yazmine explain Joey's presence.

"That's cool. He's getting big."

"Yeah he is. Thank you for coming to meet me."

"So, Wassup? What do you need to get off your chest?" DJ asked, getting straight to the point.

"DJ, first thing first. I want to say I'm truly sorry from the bottom of my heart."

"The only question I have is, why? Why the fuck you disrespect me? I'm a grown ass man. If you didn't want to be in the relationship anymore, you could just been a woman about it. But instead, you had a secret affair with that nigga, JoJo. Having the whole world laughing at me like I'm some fucking sucka. I never did you dirty or had you looking stupid. I gave you everything you wanted."

"But that was it. You gave materialistic things, DJ. That wasn't enough."

"That wasn't enough but you ain't never turn shit down. You changed, Yaz. You weren't the same girl I fell for in college. My money changed you for the worst. Out of everybody besides my family, I never thought it would change you. You was supposed to be the one solid thing in my life when fake ass people was surrounding me."

"You're right. I'm not going to lie. You spoiled me. I loved the idea of being taking care of. You were everything I wanted in the man, but you change, too, DJ."

DJ looked at Yazmine, wondering how she figured he had changed. What could he have possibly done for her to have an affair? He didn't cheat on her. Women never came at her wrong with anything that concerned him.

"DJ, you forgot about me?"

"What the fuck are you talking about? You fucking lived with me."

"I mean once you got drafted. There wasn't an us anymore. You didn't do all of the things you did in college. Your main focus was football and football only. You cancelled dates with me. We no longer spent quality time together. Not to mention, your family hated me. I was alone. So I started to seek attention elsewhere. It was fucked up of me and maybe I should have come to you about how I was feeling, but the truth is, you were barely there for me to have a sit down and tell you anything.

"I was barely there but you could get in contact with me when you needed my black card. Come on, Yaz. Am I supposed to believe that shit? The truth is, you started hanging around a whole bunch of sack chasers. Not real-izing you was on a whole different level than them. I'm not saying you couldn't have friends, but you already had at home what those bitches was searching for."

Yazmine knew DJ was right. The crowd she hung around was always on a mission to get with the next baller, but that didn't take away from the way he made her feel.

"DJ, just because you fell like you didn't do anything wrong don't mean you didn't. I'm just being honest with you. JoJo was there as a place holder I don't love him, nor do I want to be with him. He just gave me the attention you weren't."

DJ knew Yazmine had a valid point. He couldn't tell her how she felt.

"Okay, but you left me when I was at my worst. You want me to believe that you genuinely loved me but you left when it was a possibility that the lifestyle I provided for you could disappear. Not only did you go that route, but you was all in the tabloids and shit with that nigga JoJo. Then you popped up pregnant."

"I hate that you would think I'm that kind of person. I never been with you because of your money and you know that. DJ, lets be real. You always had money. Ya sister made sure you stayed with a couple of stacks in your bank account while we were in college. Your money never impressed me. When you got hurt, you changed. Not only were you miserable, but you treated me like shit in the process. Talked to me any kind of way. You were emotionally draining me and I was starting to resent you, so I left."

DJ looked into Yazmine's eyes and she looked to had been telling the truth, but what did he know when she looked him in the eyes everyday and carried on with a whole affair? Still, there was a lot of truth to her statement, even if he didn't want to admit it.

When he got injured, his world change, he change, and it wasn't for the better. Football was his life. Everybody was counting him out and he had even started to believe he couldn't make a comeback. That was until Reign snapped and told him to man up and prove his haters wrong, and that's what he did. Honestly, he should give Yazmine some credit because her leaving pushed him into beast mode, and his come back was better than ever.

"You're right. I wasn't myself, and I apologize for the way I treated you." DJ was man enough to admit when he was wrong.

"And I'm sorry, too. About everything, especially dragging you on social media and the gossip sites. I was just salty as hell when you didn't want anything to do with me when I told you I was pregnant. DJ, I love you and for you to treat me like I was some hoe off the streets broke my heart. So I acted off pure emotions, trying to damage your image only to hurt myself in the end."

"It is what it is. There's no hard feeling. Yaz, I just want you to live your best life. Do what's best for you and your son." DJ forgave her, and was no longer holding on to that hurt.

"So, this Camille…"

"Not up for discussion," He said, shutting down that topic.

"I just want you to be careful. Everybody has a past. Just

make sure her past doesn't interfere with your future," Yazmine stated like she knew something that DJ didn't, but he didn't give her the satisfaction of entertaining the bull-shit. Instead, he changed the subject as soon as their food came. The rest of lunch went smooth and it seemed like Yazmine had really changed and was on her grown woman shit.

"Naw, but I'm proud of you? Getting a job and making sure you and ya baby straight. That's wassup," DJ said, meaning every word. The waitress bought him Reign's platter and they stood to get ready to go.

"Thanks, it means a lot coming from you," she said, trying to lift up the car seat along with her doggy bag, purse and diaper bag.

"Damn, let me help you," DJ offered, taking the car seat from her. He walked Yazmine to her car and made sure Joey was secured in the back seat.

"DJ, I just want to say thank you for meeting me today. I needed you to know the truth. I know your perception of me changed, but I am trying to get back to my old self."

"Take care, shorty," was all DJ said, opening her driver side door. Yazmine took that as her chance to give him a hug, and to her surprise, he oblige. Pulling away Yazmine couldn't resist. She just had to kiss his lips one more time, knowing it would be the last time she would be that close to him.

"Yo, what the fuck?" DJ barked, shaking his head and pushing her away.

"I'm sorry. I just got carried away," Yazmine confessed.

"Take care." He said before walking away to his car.

Yazmine smiled, sneakily, as she got into her own car. Unbeknownst to DJ, he had just given her all of them ammunition she needed to set her plan into motion to destroy his relationship with Camille.

24

KNUCK IF YOU BUCK

Crime Mob: Yeah, we knuckin' and buckin' and ready to fight, I betcha I'm'a throw dem thangs. So haters best to think twice.

Tonight was the night of Camille's thanksgiving dinner. It was 5:00pm and everybody was starting to make their way to her house. It would be the first holiday she share with DJ and she was excited for her family to finally get to know the man that she had fallen in love with.

"Babe, my mom just texted me saying she was outside." DJ said, kissing Camille's neck before heading to the door. Camille was putting the finishing touches on everything. Dinner was ready and now they were just waiting for the rest of the gang to arrive.

"Hello, Ms. Cynthia," Camille spoke as soon as DJ and his mother appeared into the kitchen.

"Hi, Camille. I can't thank you enough for allowing me to be apart of you guys' thanksgiving celebration. I brought two bottle of wine. I hope that's okay."

"Yes, thank you. Babe, take her coat. Ms. Cynthia, can I get you anything?"

"No. Can I help with anything?"

"Sure. If you like. I'm about to start placing the food on the table. You can help me with that. My sisters should be here in a second. Then we can eat."

Cynthia and Camille got to know one another through small talk while setting the table and placing the food on there.

"Can we eat, yet?" Candace asked with an attitude. She was in one of her funky moods. She haven't heard from Kameron since he left her house, and now she had to sit in front of her sister and her new man looking so happy. All Candace wanted was a relationship that would make her happy, but it seemed like God didn't want her to have that.

"We can eat in a moment. Kelly said she was five minutes away," Camille answered as she sat up the kids' table. As soon as she told the kids to come sit down, her doorbell rung and DJ went to get the door.

"Happy Pre-Thanksgiving, ya'll," Kelly said, shocking everybody in the house when Leon walked in with her.

"Hey, best friend, and Leon," Camille spoke, giving them both a big hug. She had no clue that Kelly and Leon had decided to finally make their secret relationship public, but she was happy.

"Wassup, dad? Hey Ms. Kelly," Leon Jr said, followed by Aleah, giving Kelly and her father a hug. That pissed Candace off even more.

"So when the fuck did this happen? So you want my sloppy seconds, Kelly? You that desperate that you had to get with my baby father?" Candace snapped, causing everybody to look at her like she was crazy.

"Bitch, do you have amnesia? Leon was my fucking fiancé before your hoe ass slept with him. Bitch, he was never yours to begin with!" Kelly clarified, ready to take Candace's head off.

"Kids, get out the room." Caddie said.

"Candace, you need to chill the fuck out. You know me and you have never been in a fucking relationship. I don't come at your neck about who you talking to, so you need to come fucking correct when you speak on mine," Leon roared, putting Candace in her place. He knew she would probably be salty about him and Kelly, but she needed to accept it and mind the business that pays her.

"So you just have random bitches around my kids?" Candace yelled. Honestly, she didn't know why she was causing this big scene when she had never cared what Leon did when it came to his personal life. Yet, seeing him walk in with Kelly was another slap in her face. The man she wanted to love her so bad, didn't, and now he was back with the woman that she tried to take him from.

"Ain't shit random about Kelly, Candace, and you know that. Get the fuck out of your feelings, embarrassing yourself in front of your kids. Now they know your hoe ass like sleeping with other people men." Cassie chimed in, adding her two cents while shaking her head.

"Can we all act like adults and eat dinner? Like, what the fuck?" Camille voiced, walking out of the dining room to pour herself a drink.

"Babe, relax." DJ told her as he followed her, taking the drink from her that she just made. Her sister Candace had been annoying him since she got there, giving him a bad vibe.

"All I wanted was a nice dinner. This is our first holiday together. The first time I'm meeting your mother and Kyron's first time bringing his girlfriend to the family gathering. I just wanted this to be perfect but everybody decided to be ratchet."

"Listen, lets just go in here and eat this delicious meal you cooked."

"Okay," she muttered as DJ led her back into the dining room with her family and friends.

"Listen, Millie, if it's too much drama for me and Leon to be here, we can leave," Kelly suggested, hating that she could've potentially ruined her best friend's dinner. Kelly and Leon never thought it would be a problem.

"No, you will not leave. Candace, Kelly is my best friend and truth be told, Leon was her man before ya'll had a little one night stand that he could barely remember. Now if seeing them together is going to be a problem for you, then you can leave."

"Really, Millie? It's just like you to take Kelly's side."

"Candy, you heard what she said. If you can't handle it, you can bounce. Now, somebody tell the kids that they can come back down so we all can eat," Matthew, Caddie's boyfriend said, deading the whole situation.

Candace rolled her eyes but didn't get up to get her things so everybody went on about their business. Camille said grace and everybody started to dig in.

"Camille, I must say, you have a beautiful home," Cynthia complimented.

"Thank you."

"It just ought to be breathtaking, it cost your ex a pretty good penny," Candace muttered under her breath, but Caddie heard it and hit her on her leg.

"You need to chill. You been on one hundred since you walked through the door," Caddie whispered. " You know you don't want no problems with Millie."

"Whatever, nobody is scared of Camille's ass," Candace said rolling her eyes.

"So, babe. You're going to tell them the good news?" DJ asked to brighten the moment.

"What good news, best friend? You holding out on us?" Kelly asked as everybody waited with anticipation.

"Well, as you know, this year has been full of blessings. I started my catering business, which sky rocket overnight and I'm all booked up for the rest of the year. So, I created a

YouTube channel, which is also a success and is gaining the attention of some of the producers at the Food Network. So a couple weeks ago, I had a meeting and I did my first pilot for my cooking show. Now they've offered me a two year deal to have my own cooking show on the Food Network."

"That's so dope, Ms. Camille," Charlie said as everybody else congratulated her on her newfound success.

"Thanks, Charlie, and everybody. I'm just excited for this new journey. Who would have ever thought I would have so many blessings after a year like last year."

"And you deserve every one of them, sissy." Cassie said.

"Damn, sis. You sure know how to pick them? First it was Kameron. He got you up out the hood, and now Mr. DJ here is putting you in positions to be a fake ass self-millionaire," Candace assumed.

"Naw, shorty did all of that on her own. Don't try to take away the accomplishment of her hard work. I ain't have shit to do with anything but be her support system every step of the way," DJ said, refusing to allow Candace to ruin the moment.

"DJ, don't worry about her. She always been a hater," Camille stated, daring Candace to say something back to her.

"Well, I'm not a hater, twin. I just speak facts. I think it's cool that you have men in your life that supports you. So, congratulations." Candace raised her glass as too give her sister a fake ass toast.

"Anyway, Camille not the only one with good news. I'm

pregnant, again," Candace said, thinking she was going to get the same response.

"Who the damn daddy? Nobody even knew you were seeing anyone," Cassie was the first one to speak up, asking the question everybody wanted to know.

"Damn, I can't get one congratulation?" Candace said, shaking her head.

"No you can't! You just told us you were pregnant because you wanted to be the center of attention once again. Why can't you just let Millie have her time to shine for once." Caddie chimed, catching everybody off guard. Caddie was usually the peacemaker of the family, but Candace had been getting on her last nerve.

"I see this is gang up on Candace time. It never fails when we all get together."

"Mom, you're pregnant?" Leon Jr asked.

"Is that why Uncle Kameron was so upset the other day when he was at the house?" Aleah asked the million-dollar question.

The entire room got silent as all eyes went to Candace and Camille. It was so quiet you could've heard a mouse piss on cotton. Feeling everyone intense stare caused Candace to wish she could have disappeared. She couldn't believe her own damn child had just outed her biggest secret.

"What the fuck was Kameron doing over your house, Candy?" Cassie asked. Camille could feel her anger rising and rising to a point of no return.

"Fuck it. Since I'm the fucked up person in the family,

I'm going to tell my truth. I've been fucking Kameron just as long as Camille have, probably even longer."

"Oh, shit," Matthew and Leon, both, said at the same time. Without hesitation, Camille picked up the carving knife and threw it right at Candace face only missing her by the skin of her teeth. The knife flew by her face and landed in the wall.

"Ahhhhhhh!" Candace jumped down out of her chair and under the table. She knew Camille was mad, but to try and kill her in front of everybody made her literally piss her pants.

"Fuck!" DJ said, jumping up. "Kyron and Charlie, get the kids out of here."

Kyron quickly and quietly got the kids out of the room.

"Millie," Caddie whispered her name but Camille ignored her. She had one thing on her mind, and that was beating Candace's ass. This was the ultimate betrayal. Scooting her chair back, she reached under the table and pulled a screaming Candace by her foot. She pulled her from underneath the table and started punching her in the face, not showing her any mercy. All Camille was seeing was red. Blinded my rage, she didn't know she was literally breaking damn near every bone in her sister's face.

"Pleassssse, stop!" Candace screamed at the top of her lungs. She felt like everybody was sitting around watching her get her ass beat and no one was attempting to help, but that was furthest from the truth.

DJ and Matthew were both trying to pull Camille off of her, but she was like the female version of the hulk.

"Millie, please. You going to kill her and the baby," Caddie yelled, crying as she watched in horror, but hearing the word, baby, only made Camille go in even harder.

"Camille," DJ barked, finally getting a good enough grip on her and pulling her off into the kitchen. "Calm down!"

"Fuck that! I'm about to kill that bitch! Ya'll got me the fuck chopped if you think I'm going to allow this to fucking slide. After all the shit I did for the both of them, they been fucking behind my back!" Camille snapped, trying to get around DJ to go back into the dining room to continue to beat Candace's ass. She wasn't satisfied with the bodily harm she had already caused. She wanted Candace barely breathing and her unborn child dead.

"Yo, chill the fuck out!" DJ was beyond pissed with the way Camille was acting. "Look at yourself, you're covered in that bitch's blood. Trust me, you caused enough damage. What are you trying to do? Lose everything you build behind your ex-husband. Fuck him, and that hoe in there! You are above this shit."

"You don't understand! I'm heartbroken over this. My sister and my husband had an affair for years behind my back. While I was doing everything to make sure that man reached his goals. I love him and gave him my all. Why wasn't I enough! Like, nigga, really? Fuck my twin, and this bitch hated me since birth, but I never thought she would stoop this low," Camille cried, trying to lean into DJ's arms but he gently pushed her aside, declining her call for comfort.

DJ refused to comfort her while she was crying over another man. Not only did she call Kameron her husband, like they were still married, she confessed her love for him. He understood why she might have been hurt over the deceitful act Kameron had committed with Candace but, the jealous side of him felt like this was small shit to a giant. She was with a better man that treated her like the queen, who showed her a love no man had ever shown her.

"Yo, I'm out," DJ said, turning around to leave her in the kitchen crying her eyes out. "I'm over this shit. You sitting her crying over the next nigga. You obviously still have feelings for him."

"DJ! I don't have feelings for him!" She called out to him only for her to hear him say goodbye to her family. Cynthia quickly took that as her time to leave, too.

"Millie…" Kelly called out, walking into the kitchen.

"Kelly, get everybody the fuck out of my house!" Camille's heart literally felt like it was breaking. Not for what Candace and Kameron had done, but she knew she had just fucked up big time with DJ. Even though their little argument were never as explosive as this one, he never left her angry. He always made it a point to make sure they were on good terms, but for some reason, she felt like he had just broken up with her.

"Okay. I'm going to take my god kids with me," Kelly

said before doing what her best friend told her to. Caddie was already taking Candace to the hospital.

"This is some ghetto shit." Cassie said as everybody was walking out the door. Camille stayed in the kitchen until she heard her alarm say front door had been close. She was too embarrassed to face her family, and her kids.

25

HAIL MARY

Tupac Shakur: *I ain't a killer but don't push me!*

"Kyron, please come straight to my house after you drop Charlie off. Charlie, it was very nice meeting you. I'm sorry that this was the first impression you got of the family." Kelly said.

"Nice, to meet you, too." Charlie said with a smile. This little craziness didn't faze her one bit. The family dinner at the Blacks can get crazy as well.

"Okay, Aunt Kelly," Kyron said before pulling off.

"Are you okay?" Charlie asked. She knew Kyron was embarrassed and upset about what'd happened at his family dinner.

"Naw. I'm fucking tired of this nigga taking my mom through this bullshit."

"Babe, you have to stay out of this," Charlie told him, trying to make him understand that his parents drama had nothing to do with him.

"Naw, somebody need to put this nigga in his place. I'm about to take you home," Kyron said. He already knew he wasn't going straight to his god mom's house. He was about to confront his father face to face, man to man.

"No, just take me to where you going." Charlie knew Kyron wasn't going straight to his aunt's house, and she refused to let him go alone to confront his dad.

"Charlie…."

"Waste your time if you want, driving me to my uncle's house, but I'm not getting out of the car." Charlie said. Kyron knew there was no sense in arguing with her because Charlie was extra as hell, and he would have to literally drag her out of his car. Kyron changed his direction and headed to his father's house. The closer he got, the more rage he felt.

He pulled up to the new house that Kameron had bought for him and Olive to share. Kyron had only been there a few times. He and his father had been on bad terms ever since his homecoming game, and as of now, he wasn't sure if he would ever want a relationship with Kameron again. As soon as he parked the car, Kyron hopped out with Charlie on his heels. He walked up to the front door and started banging it.

"Kyron…." Olive said his name as soon as she snatched open the door. She was utterly upset by the way he was banging on her door. She had just put her son to sleep and didn't want him waking back up. "Why are you banging on the door like you've lost your mind?"

Kyron didn't even bother to speak. Instead, he brushed passed her, in search of his father.

"Kameron!" Kyron barked, calling his father's name.

"Kyron, I just put your brother to sleep. Stop yelling in my house!" Olive said, looking like she was about to cry. Being a mother was serious taking a toll on her, especially since baby Kam was a fussy baby. So she appreciated the time she had when he was asleep.

"What the hell is going on here?" Kameron asked, walking down the steps in his silk pajamas and slipper. Looking at his son who looked like a raging bull. Kameron knew something was wrong.

"Nigga you been fucking my mom's twin sister? You really got Aunt Candace pregnant?"

"What!" Olive yelled, knowing she didn't hear Kyron correctly. She knew the man she loved did not cheat on her. "What is he talking about, Kameron?"

"I don't know. Son, why would you come in here spreading lies?" Kameron's heart was beating out of his chest, not understanding how Kyron would know he was sleeping with Candace.

"I'm lying? What the fuck I have to lie for?" Kyron said, looking at his dad like he'd lost his mind.

"Maybe because you don't want to see your father happy," Olive butted in, adding her two cent to the faceoff between the father and son. She refused to accept that she was now on the opposite end of Kameron's cheating.

"Kyron, come on," Charlie spoke up. She could tell Kyron was getting madder and madder. A blind person could see his father was shocked that he knew the truth, but was trying to save faces in front of his fiancée.

"Olive, you dumber than I thought. I have nothing to lie about. You're not as special as you think. He's been fucking my aunt while my mother was married to him and still fucking her. I don't have to lie, and neither do my little cousin who saw him at their house. All I have to say to you is that your fucking dead to me, and stay the fuck out of mine and my mom's life. All you do is bring heartache to her. I swear to God, if my mom go back down that depression path, I'm going to beat you the fuck up."

"Kyron, who the fuck you think you pumping your chest out at?" Kameron snapped. He had dealt with Kyron's attitude for the longest, and now he needed to show him who the fuck the boss was. "You smelling yourself because ya little fucking fast ass girlfriend here…"

Kameron couldn't finish his statement because Kyron hauled back and punched him in the face. The punch took Kameron by surprise and before he could recover from it, Kyron was throwing another haymaker to the jaw. Kameron started to throw some punches of his own, but he was too upset that he'd underestimated his son. They were the same height and frame, and as sad as it was, Kyron was definitely giving his father a run for his money.

"Get off of him!" Olive yelled, getting ready to jump in only for Charlie to step in front of her.

"Try me if you want!" Charlie snapped, not liking how Olive looked like she was about to jump in the fight between Kyron and his father.

"I'm calling the cops!" Olive yelled before running to get the house phone. Kameron and Kyron were tearing her house up, and they had to be stopped.

"You thought you could fucking beat me, Kyron?" Kameron yelled, feeling vindicated when one of his punches knocked Kyron off his square. Wiping the blood from his lip, Kyron let out a chuckle before he tackled his father through the glass living room coffee table.

"Fuck!" Kameron groaned before Kyron jumped up and started to stomp his father. Kameron never thought him and Kyron would actually come to blows. Now he was trying to shield himself from his own son's vicious kicks. Kameron knew there was no coming back from this, and he had lost any and all respect from his son.

Kyron didn't even fear him, so there was nothing he could do or say to ever keep him in his place. The rage Kyron felt inside him was at an all-time high. Right now, Kyron was not thinking rationally, and all he wanted was for his father to feel all of the pain that he'd caused his mother.

"Stop!" The police screamed as soon as Olive opened the door for them. " Back away from your dad!"

"You really called the fucking cops?" Charlie said, pulling out her phone to call her Uncle Kelz's fiancé,

Queen. She didn't know what was about to happen, but she had a feeling that she needed Queen to meet her at the police station to bail her boyfriend out of jail.

Kyron was in such a blinding rage that he didn't even noticed the cops were in the room until it was too late and they were tackling him, screaming, *Stop resisting!*

"Charlie, take my car and go home!" Kyron yelled as he was being escorted off his father's property. He couldn't believe his soon to be stepmother had call the cops on him. The last thing he wanted was to call his mother from jail.

"Babe, are you okay?" Olive rushed to Kameron's side, trying to help him up. "Let me get my medical bag," She said as she inspected the deep gash he had on his head.

"Where's Kyron?" Kameron asked. He had blacked out a little while, while Kyron was stomping him and he needed to have a civil conversation so he could lie in his face. As far as he was concerned, it was his word against everybody until the baby came out, and he knew if Camille had found out about the baby Candace was carrying, it was a high chance that the baby wouldn't have survived.

"I...I... I got him arrested," Olive stuttered. She knew she may have taken things too far, but she didn't know what else to do. She was honestly afraid for her and Kameron's life.

"You did what!" Kameron barked, and on cue, baby Kam started screaming his lungs out. "You called the cops on my son?"

"I didn't know what else to do!" Olive screamed back,

hating that he was making her feel like shit for protecting him.

"Fuck!"

Little did Olive know, she had made things go from bad to worse. He didn't know how to even fix this. All he knew was that he needed to get his son out of jail before his mother find out.

&

"Urghhhhhh!" Camille groaned as the notification of her phone kept going off. She'd been trying to get some sleep without tossing and turning. She had been up all night trying to process all of the drama, but the main thing that was on her mind was DJ. He hadn't been answering her phone calls. She even drove pass his house only to find his car was not in the driveway. Finally, at three in the morning, she decided to call it a night and try to get some sleep.

Camille hated the space that she and DJ was currently in. She never wanted to offend him by snapping out. There was no misunderstanding. DJ had her heart. However, Camille couldn't understand why he couldn't see where she was coming from in this situation. Anybody in there right frame of mind would have agreed that Candace deserved that ass whooping, and when she caught up with Kameron, he deserved the one she was going to give him.

Camille just needed DJ to understand her actions weren't because she still had feelings for Kameron. Those feelings of love died a long time ago. She was just tired of people screwing her over.

"Hello?" Camille answered her phone, grouchily.

"Millie, are you okay? Why haven't you answered your phone?" Cassie asked questions after questions, not evening allowing Camille to answer.

"I'm okay. Did I kill her?

"No. That bitch still alive and breathing unfortunately, but fuck her. I'm going over mommy and daddy's house and kick her out. Fuck that bitch! She won't be living off our hard earned money. We all know mommy didn't leave her anything in the will," Cassie was really done with her sister. She felt like if she disrespected Camille that way, none of them were safe. Candace was selfish and jealous, and now her ways had made her lose her family and any type of stability that they were providing for her.

"What about Leon Jr. and Aleah?" Camille was mad, but at the end of the day, her niece and nephew was innocent in all of this nonsense.

"They have a father that is very capable of taking care of them full time. As a matter of fact, I told Leon last night what it was. I'm over Candace."

" Damn, why my phone been going crazy?"

"Yeah that's what I was calling you about. Sis, don't believe everything you see on social media."

"What did you see?" Camille asked, not waiting for an answer. There were multiple links that everybody had been tagging her in. The first link led her to an article titled *DJ and Yazmine rekindling the fire.* There was a picture of DJ and Yazmine kissing one another. It looked very recent, too. As a matter of fact, he was carrying her baby's car seat.

"What the fuck?" Camille muttered, going to the next link. What she saw made her heart drop to the pit of her stomach. *Must see, NFL star quarterback, DJ Roberts, and ex, Yazmine, uncensored sex tape!!!!!!!*

Camille stomach turned as she watched her man making love to his ex. The way he handled Yazmine's body was just the way he handled hers. Listening to her man moan at another woman satisfying him was killing her softly.

"Sis, I know this looked bad right now, but…."

"How could he do this to me?" Camille said, cutting Cassie off. Her mind was racing with crazy thoughts.

"Camille, don't look at anything else," Cassie said, Camille was tagged in another link.

2004 Arrest Record of Eagles Quarterback, DJ Roberts, current girlfriend, Camille Davidson, for Involuntarily Vehicular Manslaughter. A close source states this accident was no accident and she purposely ran her ex-husband, Kameron Davison, and an unknown woman off the road…..

Camille literally felt like her world was crashing around her as she looked at her mugshot she'd taken, the night she was arrested…

To Be Continued…

CPSIA information can be obtained
at www.ICGtesting.com
Printed in the USA
LVHW081936061120
670969LV00004B/72